WAITING FOR THE STORM

A GREEN NEW DEAL NOVEL

JANE G. HAIGH

www.waiting4thestorm.com

ISBN: 978-0-9627530-9-1

Printed in the United States of America

WAITING FOR THE STORM: A GREEN NEW DEAL NOVEL

MONDAY

SEPTEMBER 17, 2040

1 | A STORM IS COMING

When Jazz walked into Barney's Brew Pub, in the old downtown of Dover, New Hampshire, that Monday morning, she already knew that a storm was coming. Everyone knew that a storm was coming. Most everyone had seen the report on the evening news, or heard it on the morning news, or from Twitter, or Spin, or chat-rooms, or Instagram, or from 3F, Friends-For-Friends.

Waking up in her flat in the new Station Square, with the Monday-morning light shining in through the windows overlooking woods and the river, Jazz took her emotional temperature and found that she was actually feeling rather content. A feeling she wasn't used to. She had only been living in her own place for a few weeks, since her return from Alaska, but it felt right. She had grown so used to Alaska—the wide-open spaces, the single-family houses on five-acre lots. Everyone she knew said it would be impossible to live cooped up in an apartment. But this wasn't bad at all.

Living next to the DART light rail station in downtown Dover was easy, it was convenient, and it was companionable. She had no utility bills; electricity was provided by the solar panels on the roof, and there was so much insulation that the building used hardly any heat or cooling, and what was required was provided by efficient heat-pumps.

Most important, there was a sense of community. Back in Alaska, the isolation—the "every man for himself" ideology—was out of control, and face it, it just wasn't fun. Of course, "Live Free or Die" New Hampshire had many of the same types, but Dover, and The Corridor of apartments and condos along the new DART light-rail, attracted the more community-minded folks. All of it was new since she'd left nearby Durham after college ten years before.

It was a beautiful fall day, sunny and warm with just a hint of a breeze, as Jazz left her flat and headed out on the short trail along the river, then across the bridge over the river and past the solid, four-story, blocks-long old brick textile factories that made up the center of town.

Jazz wasn't particularly worried about a storm; Dover was a good fifteen miles from the coast. Still, the Cocheco River running through Dover emptied into the Great Bay, close enough to actually have a tide station right in town. Hurricanes brought rain, and if the tide was high, and the rain couldn't drain into the bay, then what? She would be fine; her friends, for the most part, would be fine. But no one could say what would happen on the coast, or to farther-flung rural towns that had not been as proactive as Dover.

Sometimes it helped to just talk to people. And if you wanted to talk to people, Barney's was the place. Barney had started it as a brewpub, but by now it was so much more; right now, it was the breakfast place in town where the old guys had their table in the corner. Barney himself, who had just turned sixty, was a bit paunchy; in his usual overalls and plaid flannel shirt, with the remains of his red hair in a ponytail, he presided behind the breakfast bar, wiping down the huge pine-slab counter that had been a feature of the place since the very beginning. Truth be told, Barney no longer had to come in himself and make espressos in the morning, but it was where he wanted to be, his command post. This morning, the TV was tuned to the Climate Channel, and all eyes were on it. As usual, Maya was holding down the morning desk.

The storm now had a name: Hurricane Mitch. It had first been announced just a few days earlier when it was east of the Bahamas.

Now the prognosticators, the meteorologists, were all over it with their different projected storm tracks. And the previous night, they had drawn a track that might take it all the way north to Cape Cod, Boston, and right here in New Hampshire.

"This storm is going to hit New England," Maya said, "so we are bringing in Eric from the National Weather Service in Gray, Maine, to analyze this for us."

She cut to Eric, at the National Weather Service office, just over the border in Maine. Now Eric was explaining the highs and the lows and the winds with maps and charts. "If you think this can't happen here, folks, let me review for you," Eric said. "The projections are pretty close to the track of Hurricane Bob, back in 1991. In North Carolina, 100,000 people evacuated to escape Bob. In Massachusetts, 50,000 evacuated from Cape Cod and Bob did a billion dollars' worth of damage.

"But keep in mind, that was almost fifty years ago. The population on the coast has almost doubled since then. And storms have been intensifying. So, picture Bob at twice the intensity and with twice the number of people impacted.

"And let me remind you," Eric went on, "of the famous Hurricane of 1938. Before they could even warn people, it had made a direct hit on Long Island, crossed the Sound, devastated Connecticut, and then made a direct hit on Rhode Island, pushing a 25-foot storm surge into the harbor and devastating Providence."

When Eric put up the photo of a devastated Providence, Jazz remembered that her great-grandmother talked about a two-story house floating into the Providence harbor and out to sea. Hundreds drowned in their homes or cars, and many were simply lost in the tides and the seas.

Modern reanalysis, Eric was saying, showed that the 1938 hurricane had deteriorated to a Category 1 by the time it hit New Hampshire. But, still, hundreds of thousands of trees were blown down by ferocious winds—more than 160,000 acres of forest. There on TV were the black-and-white photos of apocalyptic forests, acres of downed trees criss-crossed like matchsticks, as if some kind of infernal tornado had blown through.

Harrison, the retired lineman at the end of the bar, chimed in: "I remember Dad and Grandpa worked in the forest for years cleaning up that one, hundreds of thousands of feet of lumber."

Then all of the old guys chimed in:

"Yeah, Grandma remembered that they sent in the CCC to help with processing the timber."

"People thought it was a powder keg, all those dead trees."

"You know, so many miles of forest roads are left from that one blow-down; someone told me it was 10,000 miles of roads and trails."

"So, folks," Eric was saying on the TV, "get ready. I mean, tie everything down. This thing could be here before we know it."

"Wow," said Jazz. Everyone was just staring at the screen.

"We're already hearing warnings from Florida," said Eric, "and North and South Carolina, and... hold on a minute ..." Eric listened intently to his earpiece. "There will be an announcement shortly from the Governor of Massachusetts. Stay tuned here, folks."

2 | BARNEY'S BREWPUB, SOLAR NH, AND THE RUMP CAUCUS

Barney had started his brewpub in the vast basement of one of the huge, abandoned one-hundred-and-fifty-year-old mill buildings in Dover. By the mid-twentieth century the mill owners closed up and moved jobs to the south, where labor was cheaper. The old mills stood empty for years. When Barney started back right after college, downtown Dover was a dead space, and the mill scene was far from trendy. Barney was one of the first of the young entrepreneurs to begin to revive the area by converting them to businesses, and then trendy lofts and offices for tech companies.

Barney, Katrina, and Chip had all met as students at UNH, majoring in sustainability in the mid-2000s. When they graduated in 2006, Chip and Katrina started their solar installation business, Solar NH, and Barney had his brew pub up and going, at least the beginnings of it, with the live edge bar with taps behind, an assortment of antique tables and chairs, a few snacks, but not much more.

Still, they wanted to continue their work as activists focused on the livability and sustainability of the Dover-Durham region as they faced radical climate change. So they gathered a few of their college friends and began meeting on Monday nights to try to figure out how they could influence progress in their local region.

Planning would have to link efforts in housing, transportation, and energy so that, locally and regionally, people did not have to drive polluting, gas-guzzling cars from their rural and suburban homes to work, school, and strip shopping malls. Electricity production would have to rely more on renewables, and grid transmission had to be modernized. And they would have to address housing; affordable housing was scarce in the entire region, and what housing there was had been built in areas nearly inaccessible without a car. There would be an opportunity to build new housing along rapid transportation corridors.

It seemed an unlikely group. Spencer, a freewheeling New Hampshire surfer, was working at a sports shop. Alex had grown up in the North Woods and became a civil engineer. Nic got a job in the planning department at UNH. Avery went to MIT for a master's degree in planning.

At first, they worked with groups in New Hampshire, and throughout New England, and through existing channels like the planning commissions, and the legislatures, but they found it frustratingly difficult to make any real impact. That's when they decided on their radical go-local plan. The whole region might not adopt radical change—there were too many holdouts in New Hampshire who would never give up their waterfront property or their rural lifestyles or their SUVs and pickup trucks—but at least they could institute change in their small part of the world.

Katrina, always the planner, devised a three-pronged plan. First, they would have to understand how local decisions were made. Who made the decisions, and where did they get their information? How could they intervene? Then, they could reach out for expertise, make their own plan, and finally, they could get their members onto the boards and commissions that made decisions.

From the very beginning, they dreamed of a light-rail connection between Durham, the home of UNH, and the larger city of Dover. They referred to it as "The Connector" or DART—the Dover-

Durham Area Transit. They had always envisioned it as the driver of the new economy connecting the two towns, only six miles apart—but more importantly, it would anchor what they were calling "The Corridor." Gradually, they began to realize that they would have to do an end run around the official county and town planning groups if they wanted to get anything done, and they began calling themselves the Rump Caucus.

The Rump Caucus adopted the long game, each working their way up in various administrations. Nic got a job in the planning department at UNH. Avery got a job in the planning department for the City of Dover. Others got themselves elected to local commissions and planning boards. Chip and Spencer won election to the New Hampshire State House.

Together they were planning the entire time, and the game was to be ready with detailed plans when the time was right. When the Green New Deal money finally began to flow, they were ready to make their small part of the world more sustainable for their community, for generations to come. All the while they had their eyes on the prize—they envisioned a light rail connection between Dover and Durham becoming the spine of all new sustainable developments.

Right from the beginning, Barney and friends worked with UNH faculty in Durham, many of whom they had conveniently gone to school with. UNH planners created a strategic growth plan that recognized the challenges of climate change. They started by adopting a 100% renewable energy goal which they achieved by 2020. That turned out to be the easiest part.

While Chip and Katrina themselves had focused on solar energy for individual homes, the entire electric grid was a bigger problem—an artifact of the mid-twentieth century which, at the time, had not been modernized for decades. New Hampshire's utilities commission had entirely failed to upgrade to a smart grid, which might have provided incentives for consumers to alter usage during different times of day based on pricing signals.

Transportation and housing were the next issues. But it was a chicken-and-egg problem. People did not see the point of living clustered along the train tracks if there were only one or two trains running each day. Detractors complained that it wasn't practical to increase train service or build light rail, because everyone already had cars and wouldn't give them up. Year after year, all through the 2000s and 2010s, New Hampshire (like all the other states) spent billions on expanding interstates from two lanes to three, and then four—and still the traffic got worse.

And they had been successful! The University in Durham had worked with the community activists on the plan right from the beginning, even before they had managed to pack the planning boards in both Durham and Dover. With some prodding from activists the university resolved to build all its new buildings in The Corridor: every new dorm, all new faculty housing, and most of the new research facilities and classroom buildings. The rest of the campus— the legacy dorms, administration, classroom and office buildings, and labs—would be accessible with the electric, self-driving "last-mile autonomous vehicles" (LaMAs) and UNH's electric trams, which ran every five minutes. The Transportation Project Lab had designed those too.

By the time Jazz had returned to Dover, sustainable, affordable condos, apartments, and retail establishments had grown up on the Dover end of the DART, including the townhouse and apartment project where Jazz now lived, once a barren parking lot for the Amtrak rail station that carried commuters to Boston, now no longer needed, thanks to DART. Beyond Dover, more apartments and condos, as well as workshops, light industry, and business, had grown up along The Corridor.

For those who lived and worked in The Corridor, the LaMAs and trams weren't even necessary; no buildings on The Corridor were more than a five-minute walk from the DART.

Jazz remembered living in one of the older-style apartment housing complexes, built out beyond the city centers, because that was what was available—and because they provided parking, which was essential in the old economy. She and her roommates had had to drive everywhere. All of them had been raised in the old economy, relying on cars. Many needed cars to get to a job, or to get home to visit their parents in rural or suburban New Hampshire or Massachusetts. It was a self-reinforcing circle. But the new dorms and apartments on The Corridor broke the circle for new students. There were many jobs available at UNH, or in Dover or Durham— no car necessary.

* * * *

Jazz enjoyed the expanded sense of community she found in Dover. She loved the solemn old brick mills and the vibrant feel of downtown Dover, now enlivened with the new development along The Corridor. She loved how easy it was to get around on the new DART and the LaMAs. She didn't even need a car. Things had changed a lot in the ten years since she'd left the area.

Jazz now worked for Chip and Katrina at Solar New Hampshire after finally leaving behind a failed marriage in the far-flung oil town in Alaska where she grew up. Thankfully, she had used her time there to become a certified electrician, making it easy for Chip and Katrina to hire her. In the middle of the Climate Channel's discussion about storm paths, Jazz got a text from her work partner, Jeff; he would pick her up at the DART station in Durham to begin their workday. Time to go. As she walked the four blocks from Barney's in the Mill District up to Station Square to catch the DART, she thought about how much she appreciated just being able to walk—not having to hop into a car—and the sense of community she had here. That was one reason she had had to leave Kenai, where she and her husband had lived in a single-family rural home, in a community of oilfield workers, surrounded by actual oil and gas fields, with strip malls strung out along fifteen miles of highway. She had to drive everywhere, and then drive the kids everywhere. It was tough leaving the kids, but it was all just too much.

At the DART station, Jazz stopped at the Nature/Nurture takeout café to get a sandwich, a granola bar, and an apple for lunch and a quick check in with Joon, behind the counter.

"You heard about the storm, right?" Joon asked. She had the TV on behind the counter. "Do you think we should worry?"

"I think it's going to be the big one, and it's going to hit the coast," said Jazz. "At least that's what Eric at the weather service station in Maine is saying. And Barney is concerned."

"But will it affect us here, fifteen miles from the Seacoast?"

"I don't know. Nobody knows," said Jazz. "Remember how much rain North Carolina got a few years ago? Eric on the TV was just starting to explain about extratropical storms and rain bands when I left. We could get a lot of flooding. And the Massachusetts Governor is about to have a press conference announcing evacuations on the Cape. Starting now. Sounds pretty real."

"What are the guys at Barney's saying?" asked Joon.

"Barney is talking about laying in extra supplies. I guess I would too if I were you."

"But the storm isn't supposed to hit until Wednesday, right?" asked Joon. Two days off could seem like a comfortable amount of time to someone who didn't want to get anxious or begin planning, or getting upset, or anxious. Wanting to at least put it off for some less definite future.

"Yeah, but it's going to hit Connecticut and Rhode Island Tuesday night," said Jazz. "Things will start to get really chaotic. I mean, suppose they decide to evacuate part of Boston?"

They both fell silent. Evacuating Boston was too big to think about. How many people would that be? Where would they go? Certainly, Bostonians couldn't wait until Tuesday night to start packing—and Tuesday was tomorrow. They would have to start evacuating today. Too hard to imagine. Jazz said her goodbyes to Joon, picked up her lunch, and headed for the train.

Of all the things that had improved since she had graduated from UNH, Jazz thought that this whole new transportation network was the best, including trains that actually ran on time, and frequently, every ten minutes or so, and were free. No more checking watches or schedules like she had when she first got to the campus in Durham, or timing trips to coincide with buses on the hour or half-hour.

One thing Jazz especially liked about the new light rail was that it forced everyone out of their cars. Getting to and from the DART, everyone was a pedestrian. It made dropping in on a small shop easy, enticing, convenient. In the old days, and even now back in Alaska you jumped into your car in front of the house, drove to a big parking lot, and went into an office or shopped in a warehouse store with few people even around to help. In fact, they had already replaced most of the checkout clerks with machines. It seemed like human contact was over, and it was depressing.

Bringing back human interaction in daily life had been another goal of The Corridor's planners. The streets and walkways were now full of small shops and cafes, and every dorm and apartment or condo building had plenty of public space on the ground floor that was designed to be used: cafés, co-working spaces, small shops, game rooms, gyms. And the plan was working well.

Back in 2020, workers in trendy Portsmouth had already been moving to Dover and other towns in Strafford County, drawn by the more affordable housing. The trend only accelerated during the pandemic, as those who worked at home and could afford the price tag began to flee Boston and New York City, pushing housing prices even higher in Portsmouth. But transportation was horrible back then. There were busses, but the busses didn't run after 10:00 PM, completely ignoring all the restaurant and bar workers who got off work at 1:00 or 2:00 AM. Back then, almost everyone just drove, one person to a powerful gasoline-powered car, and then spent ten minutes trying to find a parking space, and ten more minutes walking to wherever they needed to be. It was all such a colossal waste of time and energy, not to mention all of the land taken up by parking lots, where those expensive cars sat parked all day.

Waiting on the station platform, Jazz greeted people she

recognized. Some were being dropped off by LaMAs — the Last Mile Autonomous vehicles that provided that last-mile transport from home to station. Some people still drove cars, but the old park-and-ride lot was much smaller than it had once been. And new housing had been built on the excess parking area, including the mixed townhouse and apartment development Jazz now lived in. Jazz pondered all of this as she hopped on the sleek electric DART train. As the last of Dover slipped by, she began to see the small workshops, IT businesses, and small manufacturing facilities, interspersed with small farms. In less than five minutes, the UNH Corridor began.

After passing some of the new condos and university offices, Jazz got off the DART at the Durham Station. Jeff was waiting in a yellow e-truck with the yellow-and-red Solar NH logo on the doors. He already had his computer out, going over the client notes for the day.

3 | PLANNING AN AGRIHOOD

By the time Jazz climbed into the cab of the company truck, Jeff had their route for the day plotted out. The Climate Channel was streaming on his tablet, but he was paying scant attention to the news about the storm's arrival. "Do you know about the storm?" Jazz asked.

"Oh yeah. Mitch bitch, Jazz. It's a beautiful fall day. Leaves are turning, the sun is bright, forget about it." Typical laid-back Jeff, who didn't worry about much of anything.

Their first site visit was at Goat Hill, a farm outside of town. Jazz drove while Jeff navigated the winding roads through the woods, passing the farmhouses and steepled white community churches that had defined New Hampshire to itself for centuries. What lay beyond, off the main roads, was changing though. After about ten miles, they turned onto a smaller paved road, and then a gravel road that was even narrower.

Finally, they got to the drive with the sign they were looking for: Goat Hill Farm. The farmhouse did look ancient, maybe Victorian, maybe colonial. Its classic form had all been covered with aluminum siding long ago.

Tammie and Sidney had just bought it from the estate of someone whose grandchildren couldn't agree on whether to sell it until the previous year, so it hadn't been renovated in decades. They had big plans for the property, and they'd already begun to work on the house. At this point, they were ready to put solar panels on the house and the barn.

Sidney—sturdy, short hair, maybe early forties—met them at the door. The inside of the house was rough, with peeling plaster and wallpaper in the front room. The kitchen looked like somebody's great-grandmother had just stepped out to feed the chickens, with an ancient propane stove from the 1950s and an old, vinyl brick-look floor.

"This place was just what we were looking for," said Tammie, tall, in shorts and a trim t-shirt and with a ponytail and glasses. "It's not so easy to find an unrenovated house. Mostly they were all redone in the 1990s or 2000s, stripped to the studs, walls ripped out, open floor plan, with Home Depot cabinets, and granite countertops. Yuck. We just wanted to do it ourselves, preserve the farmhouse look."

"We've gotten started on the exterior with GreenHomes, you know, the sustainable homes architects in Dover. We have new windows, insulation, and roof."

"Now we're on to the heating system and energy upgrades," said Sidney. "We'd like to get the solar going and install an efficient heat pump for space heating and cooling."

"Yeah," added Tammie. "Every morning I wake up with the rumble of that old oil boiler in the basement. It must be more than fifty years old. And there is actually an oil tank in the basement. Never replaced. An oil tank, in the basement! Can you imagine? Guess there are enough of these out there that we can still get oil delivered, thank God. I don't know for how much longer, though. I think maybe no one really lived in this place for the last ten years after the old folks died; the next generation just rented out the land for hay."

"And," Sidney continued, "we've been working with Renew Planners for the last year on our Agrihood plan. Meanwhile, Tammie works remotely in IT operations, and I'm a nurse at the local hospital."

"Agrihood" was the new term for what Chip and Katrina had inadvertently started thirty-five years before. The concept was that small farms could not really sustain themselves, so the farm was expanded into a community. Instead of forty houses, each on a two- or three-acre lot, with looping roads and cul-de-sacs that paved over even more land, the Agrihood featured fewer houses, all grouped together, around farmland where previous eras might have surrounded a golf course. This way, the farmland was preserved from future development. In some cases, all residents owned the farmland cooperatively, while in others, residents own just their house, as in a condo development. With some residents farming, some working off-site like Sidney, and some working from home like Tammie, everyone could afford the rural life, with all the amenities like fast Internet and reliable renewable energy systems. Another advantage was that young people could lease farmland, even if they just needed six or ten acres.

"An Agrihood is kind of like the old golf-course retirement communities, but with a farm instead of a golf course," explained Sidney.

"Here's the basic plan," said Tammie, unrolling a set of drawings. "Here's our farmhouse," she said pointing to the drawing, "with the old outbuildings and the barn." It was one of those classic New Hampshire farmsteads with the big barn attached to the house through a series of connecting small buildings. "We have eight lots plotted down along the road you came up for larger homes. And there are eight more lots in a group down by the woods at the edge of the field for smaller cottages. Attached to the barn, we'll have a community space for a co-working space, with a coffee shop and small market, too, for the whole neighborhood."

"And there will be a commercially certified kitchen for folks on the farm to produce things like breads or jam. We'll be able to lease it out to others in the area, too."

"So, we already have Lynn, who wants to come in and start a greenhouse and nursery," Tammie continued. "And Ken, who wants to put up a few greenhouses and expand his hot pepper and hot sauce business. He'll be helping to get the kitchen going, too. They'll both be leasing land and bringing in tiny houses to get started."

"We're working on a water system," said Sidney, "and we're hoping to get the latest composting toilets so we can avoid having to install a giant septic system. Now we'd like you to help us plan a centralized solar-panel and battery storage system for the whole neighborhood. We're hopeful we can get started here with just our farmhouse, and then expand incrementally."

"OK, then," said Jeff, "electrical panel in the basement?"

"Oh, sure, the stairs go down from the kitchen here," said Tammie, opening a door to an old staircase. Jazz headed down to the ancient basement—200 years old! The basement walls were made of granite blocks two or three feet thick, and the place had the usual musty smell and plenty of spiderwebs. Luckily, the basement floor was concrete, not earth. As Tammie had mentioned, there was the old oil-fired boiler and, as usual, an oil tank—1950s technology. Scary. As everyone converted to solar and electric heat pumps, it was getting harder and more expensive to get oil delivered.

Jazz inspected the electrical panel, which hadn't been upgraded in the last twenty years. She made notes on the connections and drew on her tablet the space required for the new inverter and storage battery. It was hard to believe that twenty years ago, batteries for solar-electric systems were prohibitively expensive, but they were standard, affordable features now.

Jazz emerged from the basement to join Tammie, Sidney, and Jeff for coffee and further discussion. "We can certainly design a modest solar system for the house that you can get started with," she said, "and later it can be connected to a microgrid for the whole community."

"Great," said Tammie. "I have a tech background, too, so we'll have our own server farm, ISP, high-speed connections, and network. If we get enough residents, we can get on the e-tram system and get 10-minute service."

"Great idea, great idea," said Jazz, full of admiration. Jazz had always admired women with a plan and determination. Wow. She wanted to be part of it. Not that she really wanted to live outside of town, whether it was a farm or an Agrihood. She really just wanted to be like Tammie and Sidney: mature women, sure of themselves, unconcerned about how others saw them.

"We'll have net-zero-energy, super-insulated homes—some multifamily, some cottages, some duplexes," Tammie continued. "We might even develop a small, tiny-house village. If we are on the e-tram, folks won't need cars at all. We're leasing out the farmland now, but we hope to attract someone to run a CSA—you know, Community Supported Agriculture. There are a lot of them now, I know, but not so many in this area. And there will be an almost guaranteed customer base here on Goat Hill and a couple of the older subdivisions nearby."

"Yeah, and with a good amount of farmland," added Sidney, "we can take advantage of carbon credits for sustainable ag. We haven't figured out yet whether everyone will get a share of the credits, or whether the credits will be used to support infrastructure."

"It's really true that the land can support more than the one farmhouse," Tammie said. "But the old model of dividing it all up into two- or five-acre lots was ridiculous. Yeah, one family, a 2,500-square-foot house, two cars parked in the driveway all night and at work all day, half an acre of pavement for the long driveway, and oil heat. Hard to believe anyone thought that was a good idea."

"And it was so normalized," said Sidney. "Even the staid old Town of Lee finally refused to permit any more of those subdivisions fifteen years ago. I mean, sure some people like that lifestyle, but we sure as hell don't need to build any more of those subdivisions."

"I'm sure you know what Chip and Katrina have done with their farm, Everlee," said Jeff.

"Oh, of course, we've visited their place," said Tammie. "They really blazed a trail. But, you know, they developed Everlee more than twenty years ago. Incentives, possibilities—it was all different then. They had a CSA, but no ag carbon credits. There was no planning or zoning format for a multifamily development that wasn't just a subdivision or four apartment buildings."

"True," said Jazz. "And I remember they were mostly focused on getting their Solar New Hampshire business going, not on developing the farm. They had a farm, but they hired a farm manager to run the CSA."

"Yeah," Tammie said. "They showed us the part of the barn they had converted into small dorm rooms for the interns and farmworkers. Probably not what they would do now, but the county wouldn't have approved a tiny house village at the time." They all gazed, musing into their coffee mugs for a few moments, envisioning what Goat Hill might become.

"You know, I actually lived there at Everlee for a few months, when I first came back to New Hampshire," said Jazz, almost to herself. "I left New Hampshire after UNH. Then ten years in Alaska, failed marriage. I'll tell you about it sometime." That was what she said. She was really thinking, always thinking, about Kisala. Kisala, the real love of her life. Kisala, whom she had met in college. Kisala who was now an architect and developer, sometimes on projects where Chip and Katrina supplied the solar energy expertise.

She had left Kisala, she now knew, because she didn't want to move to Boston where Kisala was pursuing a master's degree, and because she couldn't admit her identity as Bi. Left to prove it wasn't true by marrying the hapless Kirk, her boyfriend from high school in Alaska who had followed his father into the gas and oilfields as a pipefitter. Trying to make it in a world of retrograde fossil-fuel supporters. What had she been thinking? It somehow made total sense at the time. It seemed like the only thing that made sense. But it still didn't really make any sense. So, when she had two sons, and then decided to leave Kirk, and leave Kenai … It was hard to remember exactly how this had all happened, but she left the boys with Kirk, and with his parents, and with the soon-to-be new wife who was so eager to be part of that community. That's what Jazz was thinking about as Jeff and Sidney and Tammie discussed the Agrihood.

When she was finally ready to leave Kenai, the job offer from Chip and Katrina had certainly been a lifesaver tossed out to a sinking ship that saved her from herself and drew her into a sane world. Chip and Katrina had offered her a job, a place to stay for a while, and a life among people who were planning for a life she could believe in. They even let her move in with her kids for the summer.

"OK," said Jeff to Sidney and Tammie, "we'll get back to you with some options. Of course, the state renewable energy fund will cover costs for the solar array for the house and the first phase of the farm. Planning and financing for the Agrihood and other stuff might be a bit more complex, so we'll work with your planners to structure that. Katrina is our expert on financing. And of course, with this possible hurricane on the horizon, we're all thinking about resilience, too."

"Yup, all of it," said Sidney as she showed them to the door.

As they drove away, Jazz was still thinking about Kisala.

4 | BACK AT BARNEY'S

Monday morning, 11:00 AM,
Hurricane Mitch off of Florida

While Jazz and Jeff were visiting Goat Hill, the crew and regular mid-morning crowd at Barney's were still tuned into the Climate Channel. Experts had been warning for years that a hurricane could hit Boston someday. But for the thirty years Barney had been behind his bar, none had come close. Of course, there had been Emma in 2020, which was much like Hurricane Irene twenty years before that. Emma had tracked into the Connecticut River Valley, bringing so much rain that roads and bridges were wiped out. Then there had been Andy, in 2027. Everyone thought Andy might be the big one, projected to track directly over Cape Cod. But at the last minute it veered just far enough east that the terrifying Northeasterly winds never hit Boston Harbor with their full potential; Andy had fortuitously swiped by at low tide, too. In 2031, Cecile had wiped out Amtrak train tracks in many low-lying areas, but that damage had been kind of fortuitous and well timed, too, as Green New Deal funding had ramped up by then; Amtrak had been able to replace miles of the old, uneven track and older bridges with new bridges and more stable track, making for a smother and faster ride. But now it was September, famous for its King Tides the highest tides of the year which already regularly flooded low lying areas. And Mitch was headed for New England.

The Massachusetts Governor, Jocelyn Garcia, was just beginning her press conference. She stepped up to the microphone.

"As you know," she began, "we have made a concerted effort over the last fifteen years to transition to a low-carbon economy, which has meant persuading people to give up their cars and use public transportation. When people had their own cars, they could self-evacuate—but they faced tremendous traffic jams. This time around, we face tremendous logistical challenge to get everyone out who needs to get out."

Then she introduced her Emergency Services Manager, Mordechai "Morty" Levinson, who had news about evacuations. Levinson stepped up to the mic, with the map of evacuation zones behind him. "Ok, folks, Hurricane Mitch is moving much faster than first predicted. We are calling for evacuations for all of Cape Cod and the South Shore, starting immediately. That's our Evacuation A zones."

Everyone knew that coastal towns like Sandwich and Scituate, south of Boston, flooded every time there was a high tide now.

"*Le cou de pied*," said Ashley, one of Barney's brewery operators to no one in particular as she looked at the map of the Cape.

"What?"

"The *cou de pied*. That's the ballet term from French for "the neck of the foot," the ankle. Sandwich is like the neck of the foot of Cape Cod. The elbow. And it faces directly northeast, so winds race into the bay and the water piles up whenever there is a Northeast storm. It's amazing that Sandwich is still there at all." It was true; Sandwich, facing northeast on Cape Cod Bay nearly always sustained damage in the face of the wicked Northeaster storms that plagued New England. Scituate on the other hand faced the open ocean directly and was famous for the pounding twenty-foot waves against its seawall whenever there was a big storm.

"Those are definitely the places to watch," Barney agreed.

On Sunday night, few people—even people on the South Shore—

had been convinced that the hurricane posed a threat to them. Those who thought about leaving were getting ready to go at a leisurely pace, maybe to a friend's house farther from the water. But now Levinson's tone was urgent.

"We can't emphasize this enough, folks. This hurricane is definitely coming for us. If you're on Cape Cod, prepare to evacuate. We'll be going door to door on the Outer Cape, which we expect to be cut off completely. And now I am going to turn this over to our emergency transportation manager, Loretta McKay. Loretta?"

Everyone knew Loretta McKay. She had been one of the feisty voices on the Boston City Council, agitating for more robust public transportation—a position she continued to champion after she was elected to the State Legislature. From there, she was appointed to a leadership position by the governor.

Loretta stepped up to the mic, in front of an electronic map, with her afro pulled back on top of her head. "The governor is correct. Since beginning our transition to a low-carbon economy, many people have indeed been able to give up their cars and use public transportation. Now we have hundreds of thousands of people on the Cape and the South Shore who will not be able to self-evacuate. But I want to emphasize we have planned for this. We have done a lot of planning around this eventuality. Those of you who are in the primary evacuation zones should have already gotten this information in the mail, and it is also available at our Massachusetts Emergency Services website.

"Even if you have a car," she continued, "you might want to take a bus off the Cape. Starting tomorrow at noon, all lanes on both bridges will be off-Cape only, and we will have bus-only lanes. If you are on the bus, you won't have to wait in those traffic jams. You can get on an off-Cape bus at any of our shelters. And don't even think of calling a ride service to get off the Cape. We will be working with our ride services to get folks to emergency shelters on the Cape, but there will be no ride services to get off the Cape. Let me repeat that: there will be no ride services to get off the Cape."

"But for those of you who do decide to drive your own cars, please remember: there will be a bus-only lane, and when you get off the Cape, do not attempt to drive north or south. You must, I repeat, *must* head west out of the coastal zone.

"Now, this applies also for those of you on the South Shore. Folks on the Cape and south of Plymouth, you will have to get to I-495 North. Folks in Plymouth, take Rt. 44 West. We will have troopers directing traffic. Now, it's going to be more difficult for folks in Scituate, Cohasset, and Hingham. We are going to restrict traffic on Rt. 123 to allow traffic to flow west only. Don't even think about using Rt. 123 if you are going out for groceries to hunker down.

"Every town from Rt. 3 west will be opening shelters for folks from the coast. Including South Shore Regional and Hanover High School. Check your Mass Emergency App, which will show you available shelters in real time."

The crowd at Barney's stared at the Massachusetts map, dumbfounded. So much of the Massachusetts coast south of Boston— the South Shore—was totally exposed, directly facing the Atlantic, with very few routes west. They could only imagine the traffic scene.

The emergency crew members at Barney's were especially skeptical.

"Real time?" said Avery. "They think they are going to be able to update availability in real time? This is going to be a nightmare."

They could all see how this same nightmare would soon be playing out on the North Shore, north of Boston and closer to New Hampshire. Older folks still remembered seeing the nightmare evacuations from Houston during Rita in 2005, and from New Orleans, and the North and South Carolina coasts. For everyone else, the Climate Channel had been replaying those historical scenes on an endless loop, every thirty minutes since Sunday night. As Hurricane Rita threatened in 2005, Texas officials had tried to evacuate 2.5 million people, but they'd waited too long to change traffic patterns to allow people to use both sides of the highway to leave the city. Hundreds of thousands of people had been stranded on the highways for hours. And, unbelievably, it had happened over and over again since then.

"Hell, so many people in Massachusetts and New Hampshire have refused to give up private cars. The intersection of I-93 North and I-495 is backed up all the time under normal conditions. You can imagine what it will be like tomorrow," said Avery.

"Turning to Boston and northward," said McKay, as if in response, "beginning tomorrow at 9:00 AM, we are directing the State Troopers to change I-93 and I-95 to all northbound lanes, for the evacuation of those on the North Shore, Revere, Peabody, Salem, and adjacent areas. But I-95 North will be cut off from Boston, except for buses, and will not be available as an evacuation route for those from Boston. As of 2:00 PM Tuesday," she continued, "we will be limiting access to Boston from the western suburbs. All lanes of the Mass Pike will be for traffic heading west, out of the city."

The crowd at Barney's was quiet, pondering the implications. Not everyone could justify taking Monday and Tuesday off work, and—in apparent contradiction to the evacuation effort—Tuesday was still a workday for many state workers in Boston. Many businesses and schools followed suit. While the state authorities had acknowledged that there might be a storm coming, they apparently hadn't thought about how long it might take for folks to evacuate.

"Again, I repeat, we are closing entrances to I-95 North from I-93," said McKay. "Too many people from Salem, Revere, Essex, and Ipswich will have to use that route to evacuate. And," she continued, "we will have buses running from all neighborhoods, out to western towns and to evacuation centers. Stay tuned here for more details. If you still have questions, call 611."

"Is this a joke?" asked Ben, one of the regulars, rhetorically to the TV. "Who could manage an evacuation like that, with phone inquiries?"

Regional transportation and rapid transit initiatives had finally been funded only after the Great Gridlock of 2023, one of the events that spurred the agreements that solidified the New New England

Regional Compact. Finally realizing that more rail service, rapid transit, and transit options of all kinds was the only way out of the traffic problems, the state governments had come together and agreed to fund trains, trams, light rail, and electric bus lines all over the region. And it had worked. Many people found it was easier not to have a car. But how would they evacuate? Now McKay was charged with making the system work for the tens of thousands of evacuees without individual cars and trucks. But those who had followed her career had utmost confidence in her as one of the great analytic minds working in the area.

"So here is the plan," said McKay. stepping up again, this time she was in front of a detailed map of "A" zones, divided into districts, each with a bus route. "We'll have pickup times every hour, starting at noon today; you can see the stops marked with stars on the map here. You can find the map online, and find your pickup time, and we will post the maps electronically at all of the regular bus stops."

5 | BARNEY'S BREWS

Barney had started the brewpub not long after college, in the mid-2000s. While he was at UNH he had always been the source for homebrew, crafted in his garage. Once out of college, he got serious. First, he went to work for some of the breweries close to home in New England, and then he made the traditional tour of breweries in Colorado, California, Germany, and Belgium, and as far away as Alaska gathering ideas for his processes and his brews. With his degree in ecology and sustainability, he focused everything on sustainability, renewable energy, and local products as much as possible.

Barney knew that he wanted to locate his brewpub in one of the huge brick textile-mill buildings in downtown Dover. By the mid-twentieth century, the mills had closed up and moved to the south, where labor was cheaper. The abandoned mills stood empty for years. When Barney took over the basement of an old mill building after college, downtown Dover was a dead space and not yet trendy. Barney was one of the first young entrepreneurs to revive the area by converting the old mill buildings into businesses, and others eventually remodeled them into trendy lofts and offices for tech companies.

At UNH, Barney had become friendly with Katrina and Chip, who started a solar-electric company soon after graduation. Katrina had majored in business, then gone on to get an MBA, so he enlisted her to help him with a business plan.

Katrina outlined a path for Barney's Brewpub, starting relatively small: fixing up a basement space with a few brewing tanks, a few brews, and a simple brewpub setup without food. With Katrina's plan in hand, Barney was able to get solid funding. That had set him up for profitability, and then he was able to get an option to lease more space when he was ready. After a few years, he was able to go back to the bank for money to expand. Mindful of the growing number of breweries, he was careful not to expand too fast.

Barney started with the most sustainable, most energy-efficient brewing system he could find. Early on, he had talked the building owner into letting him put his own solar collectors on the roof, which covered at least half of his electricity needs. Then he installed a carbon dioxide (CO_2) reclamation system, a process first used in a brewery he'd visited in Alaska. Barney had actually traveled to Juneau to see what they were up to. He had since improved on the CO_2 processes with the help of some UNH chemistry grad students. He adopted the Alaskan's "mash filter press process," drastically reducing the amount of water, malt, and hops used to make the beer. He also used their spent-grain boiler system, which converted the spent grains into fuel to make steam. Any leftover grain he sent to a local farmer to feed her pigs. To complete the cycle, the pork from that farm was processed by Tom, a local butcher and sausage-maker, who made a custom sausage for Barney's—a favorite at the bar when he began to serve food.

Barney had always wanted to expand into farm-to-table food service. So, when the brewery and tasting room were up and running profitably, he started his restaurant. The mill building offered almost unlimited room for expansion, and Barney carved out an atmospheric space that highlighted the original rough brick walls and wooden floors. Tables in the front window, where the basement emerged on the slope of a hill going down to the river were especially popular for breakfast and lunch, and there was a larger dining room, meeting spaces, an informal co-working space with a few tables and couches, and even a table.

Barney teamed up with a local chef, Patrick, with the goal of using as many local ingredients as possible. Patrick and his friend Dix scoured the local area to find sources for greens, grains, baked goods, and more. They visited oyster farms and went down to Portsmouth, York, Kittery, and Hampton Harbor on the coast to make deals at the fishing and lobster boats. Then they went out to farms in the nearby area to find grass-fed beef, and lamb, forest raised pork, and free-range eggs, and chickens. Dix was a specialist in wild foods, and brought in mushrooms, seaweed, and greens in season.

Now Barney's was a popular brewpub, and Barney's Farm-to-Table Restaurant a popular meeting place and hangout that served three meals a day.

6 | MEETING KISALA

Jeff and Jazz left Goat Hill and headed to their next survey site. But Jazz was still thinking about Kisala.

Jazz had met Kisala in her freshman year at UNH. Jazz had come from Alaska to UNH because of family connections. Chip wasn't really a cousin, more like a family uncle, the son of family friends. He had frequently visited his grandparents in New Hampshire, so it was no surprise that he decided to go to UNH. That was back in 1999. Then, he had met Katrina and stayed. And Jazz had followed.

What had they seen in each other? There was no question what Jazz had seen in Kisala. She was so definitively herself, willowy, with her long, tight braids., and a lilting musical laugh that told Jazz not to take everything so seriously. She was interested in everything. And, just like Jazz, she wore overalls. From a family of Somali refugees who had resettled in Nashua, New Hampshire, Kisala was smart enough that she could have gone to college anywhere. But she considered Harvard snobbish and felt more comfortable in New Hampshire. Jazz was drawn into Kisala's magnetic orbit. The real question was what Kisala had seen in Jazz. Truth was, Jazz was the exotic one. Being from Alaska had that effect on people—made them want to hang out and ask questions: "Did you really hike on glaciers? Did you really catch twenty big salmon in one day?" Kisala also loved to hang out with Jazz's impossibly smart Indigenous Alaskan friends when they came to visit from Dartmouth and BU and Harvard.

Chip and Katrina's son, Cody, was the same age as Jazz; he'd started at UNH the same year. Jazz and Kisala majored in sustainability, specializing in renewable energy, environmental studies, and eco-planning, while Cody went right into electrical engineering. Then Kisala switched to community planning. Jazz just wanted to finish with enough credits to graduate.

Chip had told Jazz that she would like New Hampshire because it was comfortable—easy to keep wearing jeans and flannel, not too crowded—"Alaska lite." At first, she didn't really like New Hampshire. UNH itself, with its 30,000 students, was bigger than her entire hometown. She didn't know how to make new friends, and she was so used to the pressure from high school to find a boyfriend, to attach herself to some macho guy, that that's what she'd tried to do—with disastrous results. Chip, Katrina, and Cody had all tried to warn her about the frats and frat parties, but she didn't get it. Drunk frat guys hitting on girls was the only thing familiar to her, the only world she thought she understood. She really was not prepared for the feelings she had for Kisala.

Everyone called Jazz petite, and though it was true that she was small and thin, she didn't see it as a compliment. She was a bundle of energy, with mussy brown hair that she always wanted to keep short. Out of place in high school, she never wanted to dress up, always wanted to wear jeans, or overalls, and flannel. Luckily, for a while, that itself was in style. But being a math geek was never in style—and she loved math. Still, she got through high school with minimal emotional damage, probably because, despite everything, she had a boyfriend, that essential high school accoutrement. What did laid-back Kirk see in her? He was a bit off-the-wall himself, he wasn't particular, and for whatever reason, he liked the fact that she was a math geek.

And then she met Kisala in the freshman dorm. Kisala was radiant: The light of her day when she saw her on campus, and got to know her, black and radiant. Hair tied up in short squiggly braids. Soon they were friends. Then Kisala wanted it to be more. And for a while it was more—much more. But Jazz was never entirely comfortable with it all.

After graduation, Kisala had moved on to Boston to earn an MA in the architecture and planning department at MIT. She was indeed a rising star. She had actually asked Jazz to move with her. But at the time, Jazz had only been to Boston a few times, it was too big, too busy, too intimidating. So, Jazz had moved back to Alaska to marry the hapless Kirk. Why? Because it was what she had dreamed of in high school. Two steps back. Then two steps forward: Hal and Joey. Yes, she missed them. But she would not be responsible for removing them from their element, their family, their life. At least she'd had them for a month in the summer.

* * * *

Jazz's and Jeff's day continued, with more visits to potential solar sites, more data entered into their laptop, finishing with one of the older apartment complexes, built in the late-twentieth century when solar was not required and building codes had been lax. There was nothing at all complicated about the job: big roof, simple calcs. The building used a lot of natural gas for heat. But what incentive did the owners have to convert to solar or heat pumps, when the tenants paid for heat?

"I wonder why it doesn't have solar panels yet," Jazz mused out loud.

"I was looking at the paperwork while you were doing the calculations at the last job," said Jeff. "Seems like it was just sold. The previous owner opted out. Out of all the last twenty years of programs that would have subsidized the transition to renewable energy. A lot of political conservatives didn't believe in climate change and didn't want anything to do with government subsidies."

Now the new owners were ready to take advantage of New New England subsidies. This was the new system that had been in place since the New England states had formed the New New England Compact to move forward on renewables, and the Green New Deal had finally been passed to fund the changes. The power agency identified houses, businesses, warehouses, and roofs of all kinds that were suitable for solar panels and made the lists available to all solar contractors. Contractors could solicit the customers, knowing the math would work, because the NNE power agency provided a no-interest loan, payable on their power bill. It was a no-brainer, really. Except for those conservatives who simply did not believe in displacing fossil fuels.

"This should have been done years ago," said Jazz, in disbelief.

"That old owner— sheer stubbornness, I guess," opined Jeff. "Must have been an asshole."

"Yeah, imagine paying more for fuel, and to the electric company just to preserve your conservative credentials."

"But it wasn't him paying the bills, it was his tenants. Just screw the tenants."

They both sighed. They'd had this conversation before, every time they came to one of these older apartment buildings that had not been converted to solar and heat pumps.

7 | SOLAR NEW HAMPSHIRE

Monday afternoon, September 17, 2040, 4:00 PM:
Hurricane Mitch off the coast of Florida, moving NE at 40 mph

When Jazz and Jeff arrived back at Solar NH headquarters, Jazz drove around to the back of the old colonial house. where the office was in the ell between the house and the huge, attached barn on Chip and Katrina's farm, Everlee. The house and barn were set back off one of the main roads into Durham behind a few huge old oak trees.

Jazz and Jeff went in through the ell to the office; there were Chip and Katrina, discussing what the storm meant for the business, and what they should do first. One of those young/old hippies now, Chip, tall, medium build, still with a full head of hair, was still the charismatic salesman, always busy, always planning something, his mind going a mile a minute—always. If he hadn't found Katrina—in some ways his opposite, everyone said—he would have burned through two or three wives by now.

Katrina and Chip had met at UNH, both already into sustainability. Chip, fresh from Alaska, had been a relatively naïve UNH freshman interested in mechanical engineering. He loved how close Durham was to the mountains and the beach, and he loved skiing. He met Katrina almost immediately, and both of them hung out in the sustainability committee with Barney and others. By their sophomore year, Chip and Katrina were a constant pair, and visited with Katrina's parents at Everlee frequently. They knew they were going to get married but were in no hurry. After college, some of their friends went straight into jobs in environmental organizations, and some went into local and state politics.

Katrina, tall and willowy, with dark hair that she wore pulled back messily with a large clip, had grown up on Everlee, inherited by her parents from her grandparents. They still lived in a cottage there, part of their own small Agrihood, but built before there was even that name for it.

Everyone who knew Katrina said that she was the innately smartest person they knew. Katrina had realized early on that just understanding the technology of sustainability was not going to be enough, no matter how logical and appealing it was. She realized that one of the keys was going to be business management, and particularly financing. So she followed her BS with an MBA, with a concentration in finance. After that, she worked at a financial services firm in Boston for a few years.

With her MBA and experience in finance, she could easily have had a conventional career in a fancy executive suite in downtown Boston. Instead, she chose to be an executive of their own solar energy business, while also being a business consultant in Dover, focusing on financing small sustainability-oriented businesses. In Dover, she didn't have to wear suits and pumps; she could dress comfortably in what she liked to wear: jeans and a long-sleeved T-shirt with a flannel shirt for a jacket, and her L.L.Bean rubber-bottom shoes.

She and Chip had agreed that they didn't want to grow the Solar NH business too fast or too big. Early on, she had assembled a crack team: IT, data analysis, web design, management strategy, and planning. Once Solar New Hampshire was data-driven and running smoothly Katrina and her team also contracted themselves out as management consultants for start-ups and novice entrepreneurs in the sustainability sector. Katrina was working on building the sustainable renewable future with her own expertise.

Chip and Katrina had gotten married and moved in at Everlee right out of college before they started their business. They immediately set up their office in the barn and began renovating it for their warehouse. When they were first married, they lived in a cottage on the farm while Katrina's parents stayed in the house. Then, when Chip and Katrina had kids, they moved into the farmhouse and her parents moved to the cottage.

Then, when Katrina went off to work at a financial services firm in Boston for a few years, Chip stayed in Durham and actually lived with her parents at Everlee, being by then pretty much a member of the family. He apprenticed himself to a small solar installer, read up on the solar energy business, and tinkered in the barn while watching the cost of photovoltaic panels continue to drop. Katrina had created a business plan for Solar NH as part of her MBA work, and on weekends they continued to expand and refine that plan over the next few years.

With their solid business plan in hand, and Katrina's connections in finance, they were able to launch the company at a scale that was profitable in short order. But before they incorporated, they decided that they had to get married. They cleaned out the barn for the big wedding.

Their next business move was to fix up the ell between the house and the barn, turning it into an office. They filled the barn with solar panels and materials. At first, Chip designed all of the solar systems for their clients; as the business grew, he trained their first employees; there was always a steady stream of eager candidates coming out of UNH. The company quickly grew to twenty or thirty people. By now, they had teams of system designers, site evaluators, and installers. Katrina and Chip weren't interested in growing the business much larger, as some of their competitors had. Katrina continued with her focus on the business, as Chip got more and more involved with local government and planning efforts.

Solar New Hampshire was mainly focused on individual home

solar installations. In the beginning, solar energy hardly offered a decent payback. Only the environmentally self-righteous who could afford it were their customers. Now those older systems all needed upgrading, and with state and federal incentives to promote renewables, there were always customers. With advances in battery energy storage for homes, home solar-electricity systems became more affordable. Then, with the Green New Deal, anyone could get a loan from their power company and pay it off as part of their electric bill. That was a game-changer for Solar New Hampshire, and they'd been upgrading and installing new systems at a record pace ever since. There was never any shortage of jobs for installers, or for systems-configuration experts like Jazz.

* * * *

As Jazz and Jeff walked into the office, the sun-filled fall day immediately faded into the background; all was chaos. Chip had moved the household TV into the office, where they'd never had a TV before. Now the TV was tuned to the Climate Channel. Everyone was focused on the blob that was Hurricane Mitch.

Chip, long a member of the town and the county disaster preparation boards, was now on the All-New England Board. His sources had told him that this was one to take seriously. Really seriously.

"Stick around," he said to Jazz and Jeff. "We're going to tie down everything in sight here, on the rest of the property, and in our other equipment yards this afternoon and tomorrow. We'll make our people and our trucks available for the rest of the county all week. We're canceling all your appointments for the rest of this week. We're also turning this office into a remote backup branch of the county disaster prep center, linked into the New England network. We already have the capability set up. Carl here," he indicated a curly-haired fellow under the desks at that moment, "is working on the linkups. We'll be testing tonight.

"We don't know where this thing will land—might be Cape Cod, might be the Boston airport, could be right over Pease," said Chip, referring to the Pease International Airport, only ten miles away. Pease had been abandoned as a military airbase during a cutback in the 1990s, and there was a regional effort to capitalize on the property. It had long been identified as one of the logical places to take up the slack if anything happened to the Boston airport. And something happening to the low-lying Boston airport was the inevitability that everyone in New England had been dreading.

Jazz and Jeff headed back to the office and got to work on the last of their calculations for Goat Hill Farm. Katrina handled all of the business deals, now put on hold, but also supervised the business staff. Of course, Katrina was her usual calm self in the face of a storm, but she was all business.

"Well, for sure no one is interested in long-term planning this week," she said. "Every meeting I had has been canceled."

Katrina always had a global view of what needed to happen. The first thing she landed on was what Chip had thought of the night before: If any of the systems they had installed failed in Hurricane Mitch, their business reputation would take a hit.

"Go through all of your past accounts," Katrina directed the office staff, "and ferret out installations that might be vulnerable to a wind event—especially the ground-mounted tracking systems.

"First communicate to them the seriousness of the threat," she added. "Let them know that we will be available to come out and evaluate the risks. Fast, too, so they can get a tree service out to cut or trim trees, now."

They had an idea about which systems were most vulnerable, but even so, Katrina directed all their office staff to call every client they'd ever had. Solar NH had been in business for over twenty-five years, installing ten or twelve systems for the first four or five years. But they'd ramped up every year, until they now did four or five installations a month. That was sixty a year for the last seven or eight years; there were more than five hundred customers to contact.

"Send all the customers emails, then follow up with phone calls," said Katrina. "If anyone reports any concerns at all, we'll send out techs to make sure everything is working properly."

That would be the job for Jeff and Jazz, the installers, the fabricators, and a dozen others who had worked for the company at any time in the last few years. They all put their current company assignments on hold, begged and borrowed cars, and brought their infants along, if they had them. If there were any issues at all, they would call in to the office, where the onsite diagnostic technicians would direct repairs. If the temporary techs couldn't handle the problem, it went on Jeff and Jazz's list.

"So where is Cody?" asked Jazz.

"Cody is evaluating our large projects on The Corridor," said Chip as he came into the office. "He's helping the contractors tie down everything that might be exposed."

"So, Jeff and Jazz, take the truck and go help Cody; he's at the newest building on The Corridor at the end of Gallagher Street. And then, meet us afterward at Barney's."

8 | CODY, ALYSSA: MICROGRIDS AND FARMING

Monday evening, September 17, 2040, 5:00 PM:
Hurricane Mitch off the coast of Florida, moving NE at 40 mph

Jeff and Jazz found Cody out in back of the construction site for the University's new lab building. Cody's regular job was with an electrical engineering company, and he was supervising this solar installation as a second job to help out his folks. Now he was trying to organize and tie down piles of aluminum collector frames and supports and lumber, Luckily the collectors and insulation were still in the containers. But they were tying those down too, with cables and ground anchors. Ten years after college, Cody was still tall and lanky, but he'd filled out some. He had the wild, wavy, out-of-control, dark head of hair he'd inherited from his mother, and he'd learned some social skills to balance out his obsession with math and electronics. Jeff and Jazz jumped in to help Cody and the construction workers tie inch-thick polymer cables to hold down the materials. While they worked, Cody told them about the project.

"We're adding new resiliency features to the microgrid here, while we're at it," he said. Cody had been working on microgrids since he'd been an electrical engineering student at the university. Microgrids were developed to integrate solar or other renewable-energy sources with battery storage, or maybe even a generator into a small localized electrical system that could be "islanded" off the electrical grid so that it continued to function if the grid went down. When Cody started at UNH in 2025, microgrids were already in use, but new control systems were constantly being developed and upgraded. Not many people knew that UNH had managed to move to 100% renewable energy by 2017. At that time, most of their renewable energy was generated from recycled landfill gas; they hadn't even needed to move seriously into solar photovoltaics. And that was before battery storage became widely available and affordable. Of course, since then the university materials science department had been working on new forms of energy storage, along with perhaps every other materials science program in the world, and advances had been made.

When Cody started there, UNH had just signed an agreement with the major local power company to begin installation of a microgrid for the campus. After the demise of Northern Pass, the big long-distance power line the utilities had been championing, it had seemed that the utility companies might have learned their lesson and would pursue (or at least stop fighting) distributed energy like rooftop solar. But nope, the private utilities were set up to protect their own interests and their own profits, and thus were destined to forever be champions of centralized power production, distributed on a fragile grid of above-ground wires. Because the UNH project was an experimental demonstration microgrid, it didn't need legislative or utility commission approval, and the utilities did not have to give up any of the regulatory ground they continued to fight for every time they resisted new renewable energy projects.

At the same time, photovoltaic solar panels and batteries were constantly getting more affordable. Cody spent his whole college career in the electrical engineering lab run by Ahmed Fahmy, working on new innovations and applications. For his Electrical Engineering Master's Degree, he designed an advanced microgrid with battery storage for the Dover Emergency Services Center which also connected the High School and a senior housing facility as well. If anything happened to the grid the emergency services would still be up and running and the High School could be used as an emergency shelter. With his newly minted degree, Cody went to work for one of the large engineering firms, still focusing on microgrids.

Jazz really was interested in what Chip was saying, but she could see that Jeff's interest was fading. Jeff liked the job they did because he liked driving around the countryside and talking to the homeowners, and the calculations came easy to him. But when it came to the greater good of microgrids and renewables, he was apt to drift off into a cloud of pot smoke—especially when Cody was explaining things, because Cody tended to get off caught up in the details and might never stop.

Just then, Cody's ex-wife Alyssa drove up. Cody waved to their boys, who were crammed into her truck's cab. The kids usually stayed in town with Cody for the week, but with but with the storm coming, Alyssa wanted the kids to stay with her.

Alyssa and Cody had been an item ever since she'd moved into Everlee as a farmworker, just when he'd graduated from UNH and moved back home. They seemed an unlikely match, except for their mutual interests in sustainability and renewable energy. She was a few years older—maybe that was part of the attraction—but more into the organic farming side of sustainability. Cody, frankly, had a limited ability to socialize, and was flattered by Alyssa's attention. It was proximity that threw them together, and Alyssa's fantasy that, because Cody was living on the farm, he really wanted a farm lifestyle. Or maybe she just wanted to be part of the family. But Cody was one of those guys who never really thought about what kind of lifestyle he wanted. He had just moved back to Everlee because it was convenient, and he didn't really care where he lived. Maybe their hookup was inevitable, given the proximity. A few years later, they got married. Then they had two kids, Ethan and Jody, who were now twelve and eight years old. Maybe Cody had been too young for fatherhood back when they were born. They were great kids, though. Hockey kids. Jazz could still clearly picture Alyssa in those days: tall, slim and muscular, with kinky reddish hair that had been in dreads usually tied up in a bandana for as long as anyone could remember. From where Jazz and Jeff were standing, it looked like things were getting kind of heated, which was odd because Cody and Alyssa still got along well—and not just for the sake of the kids. They were genuinely friends who had gone their separate ways. Their split had started when Cody was working on the first of the market-rate condo buildings on The Corridor and he was on a final inspection tour with the rest of the construction team. The condos appealed to him, with their white tile, new bamboo floors, new appliances, and slick quartz countertops. It was a world of difference from the farm, and a world he wanted to be part of. He liked the whole idea of living on The Corridor, where the kids could get to school and to hockey practice by themselves. He liked the idea that he could run downstairs and just a few blocks over to a store if he ran out of coffee, instead of driving to the store or calling for a grocery delivery, which still seemed like a big deal for a small item. Living along The Corridor would be so much more sustainable. It would lower his carbon footprint, even though he already drove a solar power charged electric truck. He decided that he didn't want to live on the farm; he really wanted to move into the condos.

Cody truly believed in The Corridor and the DART connector. He had grown up on his parents' farm, being shuttled in the minivan or SUV to his hockey practices and games, and even to his friends' houses. He had sometimes gone with his dad, Chip, when he attended endless meetings to get The Corridor idea going. And by the time he started college at UNH, they had finally gotten commuter service going between Dover and Durham. His desire to live on The Corridor was a revelation.

But Alyssa had watched the developments on The Corridor with exactly the opposite feelings. Alyssa didn't like the creeping metropolization of The Corridor; she didn't like crowds, or trains, or schedules. She never wanted to live in an environment that was so planned, so orderly. To her, sustainable still meant back-to- the-land. She wanted to move farther away from it all. Farming was all she had ever wanted.

Alyssa had started at Everlee as a farmworker and worked her way up to managing the farm. After she'd married Cody, Chip and Katrina had built them their own cottage at Everlee. Her future seemed assured. But when Cody decided to move to The Corridor, it finally occurred to her that, though she had learned a lot from Katrina, she was ready to move on to her own place. Alyssa never veered from her path of sustainable agriculture, only developing her interests more deeply in growing, processing, storing, and using the products of the farm. So Alyssa and Cody amicably decided to separate, and Alyssa looked for a new place.

And that's where Barney's farm, Little River, in Maine came in. It was just over the border, close to Dover, but out of The Corridor altogether. Barney had had a series of farm managers since he'd bought the place, but he was never happy with any of them. He just happened to be looking for a new farm manager when Alyssa was looking for a new farm to manage. When he heard Alyssa was available, it was just logical that he would hire her. It seemed like a piece of great good fortune for them both. So, Alyssa had moved to Little River.

While Alyssa got more into farming, Cody kept picking up and developing larger ideas about structural sustainability—a world in which people lived closer together, used less land, drove less, and lived in buildings that used less energy.

Now Cody and Alyssa were standing by their vehicles amid the construction materials, discussing the hurricane. Cody looked worried, telling Alyssa that he had so much to inspect and tie down—not just on this project, millions of dollars' worth of materials.

Alyssa looked pale, panicked. Jazz had never seen her so upset. She was saying, "What about the animals?"

She had only one more day to make sure she had stocked enough to feed both the animals and the crew at the farm. And she was stocking up more than they needed, in case refugees came from the coast, or even Boston. But what she really wanted was to take the boys back to her place, where she could see them and know they were safe. Cody thought they'd be safer on The Corridor. All of the buildings on the corridor were built to the latest codes, and the electricity wouldn't go out because they were all connected with a power storing microgrid that would disconnect from the larger grid if that went down.

"And the boys," he asked, "how do they feel?"

And then they both came down from their panicked thinking and actually started talking to the boys.

Cody poked his head into Alyssa's truck. "Gramps says this is going to be the big one," he told the boys.

"We know," said Ethan, "named Mitch." He showed Cody his tablet and flicked to the screen with the Climate Channel.

"We're using Mitch for our math and physics examples this week. I know all about it."

"Well then," said Cody, who had not had time to closely follow the path of the storm, "you tell me."

"Right now, it's, let's see, twenty miles east of Cuba and traveling north at twenty miles per hour," said Ethan. "There is a high coming across Canada that will push it to the east. Let me check the figures again and refine the path."

"So, Dad," Ethan said, looking up from the tablet, "I want to stay with you and go to school tomorrow and maybe hockey practice. My teacher, Ms. Simmons says we'll have school tomorrow. We can take care of ourselves when you're working. We always do anyway. Yeah, the good thing about your place: it's on The Corridor, so we can take the DART to hockey practice, and we can walk to the corner store. We'll be OK. Please, Dad?"

"Let's get real, Alyssa," said Cody, "you're going to be busy as hell on the farm; they'll just be playing on their tablets or watching TV no matter where they are. They might have school tomorrow, but it will surely be cancelled on Wednesday, probably for the rest of the week. And they probably won't have hockey practice either."

"Well, OK," said Alyssa. "you're right — I have a lot to do on the farm. And I wouldn't be surprised if the power goes out either. We could even be stranded if the road washes out.

Jody, only 8, was definitely more attached to Alyssa. Facing a storm that he didn't know much about, he would rather have gone back to the farm, but he also liked to follow his older brother. He hated getting in the middle of these arguments. But he put on a good face and focused on being as brave as Ethan.

"Ok, then," said Cody. He was so proud of those kids and how independent they could be when necessary. They really could take care of themselves, mostly, if they had to. Being able to get to hockey practice and to school by themselves on the DART made such a huge difference; they could now truly be independent. Mostly, they spent the weekends with their mom on the farm and the weekdays in town with their dad, where they could get around by themselves and play with other kids.

9 | KISALA'S PROJECTS

Monday, 5:00 PM:
Hurricane Mitch off the coast of Florida, moving NE at 40 mph

They had just about gotten things tied up at the lab building when Cody started texting with Kisala. Kisala herself was nowhere to be seen. The apartment building at the end of the block on Hudson Street on The Corridor was one of her projects he told Jazz and Jeff, and knowing they were out there, she wanted them to check on materials there too. So, they all drove the few blocks over and Jazz and Jeff pulled some rope out of Cody's pickup and began tying down stacks of lumber, sheeting panels, and rolls—anything that might blow away. Jazz wasn't sure why Cody was doing this for Kisala; he didn't work for her.

"Where's Kisala?" asked Jazz.

"Where is Kisala?" Cody asked somewhat sarcastically. "Down on the Seacoast, with Dan," he said shaking his head. "Yeah," said Cody again. "Kisala's down on the Seacoast, on her project down there."

Maybe there was something going on between Cody and Kisala now, Jazz thought. Or maybe there had been? Jazz knew about the project on the Seacoast, for the mysterious Dan—a multi-million-dollar house across from the harbor in the tony seacoast town of Rye. Just once over the past summer, Kisala had taken Jazz down there for a tour and she had even met Dan briefly. A young tech bro, it seemed, but both Jazz and Kisala had been busy with work and Jazz hadn't paid that much attention. Also, Jazz's kids were there with her for the summer, Kisala got to meet them, but it was something of a shock. Kisala and Jazz hadn't seen each other for 10 years. At first, they wrote each other, but then as Jazz got more wrapped up in the family, and Kisala in work, communication tailed off. Kisala never mentioned whether she had had other relationships.

Dan had actually torn down an old cottage to build his mansion—exactly the kind of project Jazz and Kisala had always made fun of. She couldn't quite believe that Kisala had gone over to the dark side, after all their discussions about affordable housing, housing for the people. But, as Kisala had tried to explain to Jazz, Dan wanted all the latest in energy-efficiency and solar technology—all the gadgets and sensors, all the bells and whistles. She had rarely had clients who really wanted to or could afford the latest technology. It was a project that could really make Kisala's career.

"You think we have problems," continued Cody. "It might get windy and rainy here, but the storm might actually make landfall at Rye Harbor."

"That's what Eric from the weather service says," chimed in Ethan. He and Jody had been hanging out in the cab of Cody's truck. "That's if it doesn't blow out into an extratropical storm after crossing the Cape."

"Is that right, Ethan? What's the latest?" asked Cody leaning his head into the truck.

"Man, Dad. Did you know the storm in 1938 was traveling at forty miles per hour? Let me do some quick calculations."

"Yup," Ethan added in a few minutes, "even if it's only going twenty-five miles per hour, it could make landfall on Cape Cod at noon on Wednesday.

"Wednesday at noon," he repeated. "That's forty-three hours. And then Boston at 3:00 PM, and Rye Harbor say about 6:00 PM Wednesday."

"Wow," said Cody. Jeff and Jazz were silent; it was almost unimaginable.

When Jazz had been down on the Seacoast at Dan's house, the place was framed up, but not yet closed in. Kisala had shown her all the special features that were going to go in: the hurricane tie-downs, the hurricane-proof windows with exterior shutters special-ordered from Florida. She pointed out that the main floor was ten feet above the maximum high-tide line.

"OK, great," Jazz had said, "but it's still 3,000 square feet for one rich bastard."

She had definitely not meant to say that last part out loud. But still she was surprised by how quickly Kisala rose to Dan's defense. "He is not a bastard," she said, "he's really a nice guy. He says he wants to finance some affordable housing projects when this is done." That's when Jazz should have known.

"Oh, Kisala, he really has you sucked into this, doesn't he? Do you really believe him? Is this who you've become?" Jazz was hurt, and not just about Kisala working on a project for a rich guy.

But Kisala had refused to agree, refused to attack him, making Jazz think for sure that there was more to the story. Obviously, Cody knew this as well. And anyway, Jazz had heard that Cody had a new girlfriend, Charlotte, who lived on The Corridor.

Jazz knew that Cody had had a thing for Kisala ever since he met her at UNH when they were all freshmen. Well, frankly, everyone who met Kisala was attracted to her. And then Cody and Kisala had worked closely all those years since college, and now he had her on speed-dial texting, and was helping on her projects? Jazz was both worried and jealous. She had had an on-and-off affair with Cody herself, back in college.

When Jazz had left Kirk and Alaska, she had lived at Everlee for a month or two, but then, after her boys went back to Alaska, she realized that what she really needed was independence. She got an apartment in Dover, but truth be told she was still at loose ends in the relationship department. Or was it more that she was happier being by herself? But this was no time to worry about who was hooking up with whom.

She and Kisala had been so young—a college fling, really. She had left New Hampshire, and Kisala had gone to architecture school at MIT and stayed on in Boston. Kisala had had a few other relationships while developing her career, and now she mostly worked on affordable housing projects. There were always many such projects under construction, ever since the New New England regional compact had declared a housing emergency just as Jazz and Kisala were graduating and started to seriously work on creating housing. The result, for Kisala's career, had been an endless stream of affordable-housing multi-unit projects or innovative cottage communities, in both central and outlying areas of Boston. All of them were mandated to be energy-conserving, solar, net-zero buildings that produced as much energy as they used.

Kisala still loved to come back to New Hampshire, even though there were fewer project than there were in the Boston area. Still, the public supportive housing for veterans or seniors that she worked on often included connected microgrids, and that's the part she often worked on with Cody and Solar New Hampshire. She had also worked on many of the buildings in The Corridor: the first of the dorms, then the first of the market-rate housing, and then the affordable housing on The Corridor east of Dover when they had extended it out there. She sometimes worked for developers on trendy high-end condos in Portsmouth, to which she applied her spot-on sense of design.

Portsmouth and neighboring Rye were the high-roller areas of the region. Portsmouth had always been hip and trendy. Wealthy people from Boston had started moving up to Portsmouth even before the pandemic. After that, the influx got completely out of hand, driving up property values and driving out the workers who kept the trendy restaurants and shops going. And Rye? Rye wasn't even trendy—just wealthy. It had started in the 1880s as a retreat for well-to-do Bostonians, and even for Midwestern industrialists who could afford

that a gold-plated Kohler bath fixture will pay off. They would rather pay for that and the latest rain-shower and two dishwashers than a battery back-up system or geothermal heat."

Jazz could tell she was touchy about the whole thing.

"And you should talk," Kisala had shot back. "You were the one who moved back to god-damned Alaska and married an oil worker and lived off oil dollars. And then left your kids."

Ouch. That was a body blow. Kisala really knew how to twist the knife. And the most vulnerable spot.

"God, Kisala. I really don't care why you're doing this. You have done tons of good projects—more than your share. And, yeah, I left Alaska. And my kids."

The truth was that Kisala and Jazz had been arguing about affordable housing forever, just like everyone they knew in Dover and Durham. Jazz's position was that it was completely unethical to build anything BUT affordable housing, as long as there were people unhoused or living in inadequate housing. Kisala wasn't such a purist; she couldn't really afford to be. Partly because she knew that some of her business would always be market rate housing. But partly because, raised in a 125-year-old overcrowded apartment, she had to admit that she wanted more.

After the 2008 housing crash, developers had spent fifteen years building luxury condos and McMansions everywhere when banks pulled back mortgage dollars for the less well-to-do. The eviction crisis that followed the pandemic had finally turned public opinion around. And the Green New Deal funding that followed had included money for publicly financed housing that was near public transit. But there were still arguments about how much technology could be included. Low budgets and the high cost of energy-efficiency seemed to often rule out advanced features like battery storage.

Kisala, as an architect and developer, had been totally committed to affordable housing. She had done her share of projects, and she could agree that set-asides were a good idea—like Boston's, in which every housing project had to include 15% affordable units. But a moratorium on market-rate projects? She didn't like the ultra-luxury projects, and rarely got involved, but she tried to design for a middle ground. Twenty years before, folks had still been arguing about solar panels: Could anyone afford solar panels on their house? Should the government subsidize them? And they argued about energy-efficient building codes; builders said they would make houses too expensive. They never argued about whether the latest rain-shower fixture or granite countertop would make houses too expensive; that's what buyers wanted, they said.

But the rooftop solar panels on individual houses that were Solar NH's bread and butter were just the tip of the iceberg. The larger issues in the environment and with climate change became more and more obvious, especially to Chip. When reports came out, they always emphasized the fact that a third of the energy use in the region was for transportation, and another third was used for home heating, or actually wasted with insufficient insulation. As the 2010s came to an end, housing—especially affordable housing—became another flashpoint. But the two could not be separated. People couldn't afford existing housing, but they also couldn't find affordable housing that did not require them to have a car. Planners in Durham, Dover, and the county, as well as at the university, all began talking about smart growth. But what was that, and how were they going to get there?

After the housing crash in 2008, developers almost stopped building houses altogether, and banks stopped lending to people with lower credit scores. With New Hampshire cutting aid to UNH and student tuition rising, millennials were triply burdened with student loans, high costs of housing, and a lack of affordable childcare to boot.

10 | THE RUMP CAUCUS

Monday evening, September 17, 2040, 8:00 PM:
Hurricane Mitch off the coast of Florida, moving NE at 40 mph

As the Rump Caucus continued their Monday night meetings, discussing the tangled knot of issues, they came back to the interconnectedness of energy production, transportation, and housing which had to be tackled together. As they thought about the issues, they sought out more expertise, and gradually added folks to the caucus. The transition to renewables to produce electricity was the simplest place to start and was already underway, but there was still work to be done on modernizing the grid. So, they recruited Ahmed, the electrical engineering professor who ran the microgrid controls lab in the engineering department at the University. Microgrids and new controls were a key piece that would be needed to integrate renewable energy into the grid.

As it became clear that transportation was the key, they went further afield for expertise. Their friend Fiona Lake, who had been at UNH with them, now studied transportation in a joint project between the planning and engineering departments at MIT. She started coming to all the meetings, and told them about her projects, and then brought Mimi Farquhar, her professor, who was hoping to develop a center for alternate transportation. Mimi came to a few meetings, and then brainstormed with them, too.

Mimi and her students at MIT were working on various forms of transportation, including optimizing mass transit and bus systems, and electric vehicles. But of course, as people moved to electric vehicles, there would still be traffic, and gas or electric, everyone commuting in individual vehicles would never be an efficient use of energy. That's why the lab was looking at various forms of mass transit. The problem was that outside of Boston, people all over New Hampshire and New England lived in far flung and widely dispersed towns, and rural homes and subdivisions. Throughout the late twentieth century, and even the beginning of the twenty-first building in rural areas continued.

Transportation was maybe the most difficult issue, because adding light rail or bus rapid transit was going to be expensive, and there was still a lot of resistance. But the transportation issues were really also housing issues. New Hampshire liked to think of itself as a rural state, with most people living a rural or semi-rural lifestyle. But despite that, if you really counted, many people were already living in apartments. But the apartments were not necessarily near transportation, in fact, most of them were built on rural parcels, or off of commercial strip developments. It seemed that if new apartments could be built closer to transportation, it might change the equation. Of course, new forms of transportation would have to be developed as well.

Nic had worked in the lab of Magdalena Urbina, director of the MIT planning department. Her lab specialized in transportation-oriented development, which had been an important topic in the planning world for more than a few years. The idea was that new housing developments should be built along transportation corridors, and as mass transit was developed, then housing should follow at the nodes, or stations on the subway, bus, or light rail lines. This was exactly what the Rump Caucus team was thinking, so, they invited Magdalena to the next meeting of the Rump Caucus.

Fiona had in mind that if there were new forms of transportation, new cars, new kinds of trains, it would accelerate their implementation. While other universities and private enterprises were working on various forms of automatically driven cars, Mimi was more interested in new form factors for light rail and other rail transport.

Mimi and Magdalena had actually informally discussed the idea that these forms of rail would be attractive as anchors, or connectors, within new corridors of development. But it did not take long for them to discover that they shared a vision. Barney, Katrina, and Chip got out their maps and aerial photos of Dover and Durham. Mimi and Magdalena were especially intrigued, because they realized that the project of the connector between Durham and Dover could be a perfect, not too large, demonstration project that could get funded as an example. And possibly, ready to get built as a shovel ready project if funding ever materialized.

After a few months, they grew bolder and invited the planning officials from the university, and the engineering dean. Katrina led them all through a strategic planning process, and together they came up with a strategy. Mimi and Magdalena would offer a cooperative seminar at MIT, and endeavor to get their students to work on the plan for the connector and the corridor. Meanwhile, the university officials would work to advance the plan: working through channels, and then working to develop an institute to further them. They would all work on fundraising for the first three to five years of the institute, to hire someone to lead it and write grants, in conjunction with the MIT departments. Once there was a professor, students could work jointly with MIT. The project to remake the communities of Dover and Durham required a new outlook on planning and development. For too long, development had emphasized convenience for people in cars. Far flung subdivisions with oversize lots were routinely approved.

A year later, the students in the combined lab came back with their presentation. The lack of affordable housing really presented an opportunity to remake the communities of Dover and Durham with a new outlook on planning and development. The students had taken elements of many new initiatives and combined them. The presentation was the genesis of the Corridor, a light rail line on the Amtrak right of way, with all new affordable housing built in new developments in a three to five block wide strip, so that it was all accessible to the new line. Furthermore, the University could build all new dorms on the line as well. The whole six miles would be a new connecting town, where no one needed a car.

Students in the lab continued to work on various aspects of the project, even though it was unclear where the money would come from to actually build it.

11 | GREAT GRIDLOCK 1

When traffic into downtown Boston hit gridlock at 10:00 AM on a Wednesday morning in the late spring of 2023, it caught nearly everyone off guard. Many people had predicted that after the 2020-2022 pandemic, most workers would continue to work from home. Pundits predicted that traffic would never return to what it had been. Boston's MBTA began cutting service, anticipating that no one would want to get on a crowded rail car again. But they were all wrong. They failed to account for how fed up everyone was from staying home for nearly two years. Many office workers were only too glad to return to the lively downtown scene. As restaurants and offices reopened and people came back, traffic came roaring back as bad as before.

On that fateful Wednesday morning, the weather was not a factor; it was clear and warm, no rain in sight. By that point, Boston's famous rush hour lasted from 6:00 AM to 8:00 PM almost every day. It didn't happen at a particular time; it was rush hour at just about any time of the day or night. It was like watching a storm coming—but there was no storm, and no end in sight.

The gridlock began with a series of accidents on Storrow Drive, heading both east and west. Soon traffic was backed up coming off I-93 from the south, through the tunnels, off of I-93 from the north, and from the bridges to the east. Once I-93 was backed up, and all of the

Big Dig entrances from downtown were at a standstill, the gridlock spread to the Mass Pike.

Of course, once you were on the Zakim Bridge, or in the tunnels, or on the Mass Pike, there was no exiting and no turning around. It only took forty minutes for traffic in all directions to come to a complete standstill. People were stuck for hours. Emergency vehicles could not get through. Thank god no one had a heart attack. How to unspool the big jam became the problem. First, they put up barriers to prevent any more cars from entering I-93, the Mass Pike, Storrow Drive, or the tunnels. Of course, this meant no one could get to or from the airport, either, including the pilots and crews. Traffic officers had to walk into the tunnels and out onto the bridge and climb down the embankments onto the Mass Pike to direct people onto the shoulders.

Eventually, with all the radio coverage and the GPS emergency notices, people on the roads realized what they were in for; those who could still move found another route or turned around and went home. Traffic backed up to Andover to the north, and all the way to Framingham to the west.

After that, the subject of the Great Gridlock, as it came to be called, came up at nearly every Rump Caucus meeting.

"Oh yeah," said Magdalena, who had moved to Boston just as Boston transportation planners were beginning yet another improvement plan, "remember when Uber and Lyft started? And they claimed they were improving transportation for everyone?"

"That turned out to be the Big Lie," said Mimi. "Far from solving problems, Uber and Lyft only created more problems. It took years for the City to acknowledge that ride services increased congestion when Boston was almost at gridlock already. With ride services, everyone was still traveling in an individual car. Just because it was driven by someone else didn't mean the cars didn't clog up traffic and drop-off points."

"Exactly right," said Chip.

"Uber and Lyft together almost doubled the traffic to the airport," said Mimi. "Somehow, everyone thought driving was bad but taking a Lyft by yourself was good. Strange, strange. And they were so convenient, that was the thing. No one wanted to ban them. And how could they? It was a regulatory Wild West, and deep-pocketed hedge funds were dumping money on Uber. They had attorneys up the wazoo."

"Still, I know that when given the chance, I always used to call a Lyft to get to the airport anyway," said Chip. "It was so damn convenient; it was like crack. So damn easy."

"And I always thought that whatever it was that I had to do, it was important enough that I had to use the quickest form of transportation, not the cheapest."

"Multiply that by a million, and you get a disaster."

"You'd get to the airport and it would be nearly gridlock all over again."

"Just like the airlines' pitch that 'you're special.' Special enough to demand more leg room, or Class-A loading. What a world."

"Yup."

There was just too much traffic. Everyone had known that for years. But the loudest voices had come from those who saw free public transit as a benefit only to transit riders. They entirely failed to see that every transit rider decreased traffic. If one looked at the effects of forty years of policies and budgets, it was clear that drivers came first in every calculation.

But in the end, the Great Gridlock turned out to be the Great Turning Point. First, it turned up the heat on talks to create the New New England Compact—to tackle all these ideas regionally. And then, by great good fortune, coincidence, or just sheer necessity, the Green New Deal came to fruition and accelerated funding for research and implementation of new ideas in transportation, housing, energy, and planning. Especially transportation. It was the moment to finally get funding for The Connector.

Folks in Western Massachusetts had been clamoring for a direct train to Boston for decades, and with connections south from

Springfield Mass south to Hartford and New Haven Connecticut. A train that ran frequently from Boston south to Providence was a necessity, along with more frequent trains running north to Nashua, Manchester, and Concord, New Hampshire. Of course, Durham and Dover already had the Downeaster—the Amtrak service that continued to Maine—but it was far from convenient as a commuter train. Only by committing to build out all regions at once could the New New England compact agree to the budget for increased service on the MTA in Boston, balanced by the expanded rail system. Trains were started on existing tracks from Boston north to Manchester and Nashua, west to Worcester, and south to Providence. To keep Western Massachusetts and Vermont tied in, the rail lines they had been begging for from North Hampton to Hartford, and from Pittsfield, Springfield, and Worcester were added. The old commuter train system was incorporated into the MBTA in Boston, which was now all-electric. All public transportation in the city was free, and outside the city prices were reduced.

MIT became the designated regional center for research on transportation, with cooperating and associated labs on the UNH campus in Durham. MIT and UNH together set up a new lab in Berlin, in New Hampshire's North Woods, as an experimental site for Mass Timber, a new fireproof building system utilizing cross laminated and glued wood timbers that minimized the use of energy-consuming steel and concrete. Truthfully, even back in 2020 these were not new ideas; Canadians had already built large developments with the new systems.

With the Green New Deal funding in hand, New New England was ready to attack the transportation issues. All of New England had been talking about increasing and improving train service, for what seemed like forever. For Massachusetts, it was fast and frequent east-west connections from Boston to Worcester, Springfield, and the Berkshires, and south from Worcester to Hartford and the rest of Connecticut. Rhode Island and Maine wanted a faster, more frequent connection to Boston. And New Hampshire wanted a rail link from

Concord, Manchester, and Nashua to Boston. With the New New England Transportation Commission on board, a compact was signed that regionalized all rail decisions, and monies from the regional funds were used to create and enhance rail transportation. Nashua and Manchester got their rail service, just as the cities were growing.

That's when the Rump Caucus organized citizen lobbying for transportation in the Dover-Durham-Portsmouth corridor. They started by demanding that the regional COAST buses run frequently enough that people could rely on them. On the seacoast routes connecting Durham, Dover, and Portsmouth, that meant running buses every fifteen minutes, instead of every hour, and providing service until 1:00 or 2:00 AM to serve the hospitality workers in Portsmouth who were priced out of housing in Portsmouth itself. The Rump Caucus was in a good position; New New England already had a compact to decrease the carbon output of transportation in the whole region. And UNH was already moving along the path of sustainability in energy generation.

With funding coming from the Green New Deal via New New England for all regional transportation issues, the Dover-Durham-Portsmouth bus system was quickly improved.

And Durham-Dover got the green light for their enhanced light-rail package, which included an every-ten-minute commuter service between the two towns, with quick stops along the route. Exeter, the wealthier community to the south, claimed they weren't interested until a few years into the experiment. When they saw how successful it was and evaluated traffic issues they demanded to be let into the deal. And in just a few years it was extended north into Berwick Maine.

At the Durham end, the university had already made the potential rail line a focus of development for new dorms and other university facilities. The DART really cemented The Corridor as the county axis. One of the biggest things the county did was to locate new sports facilities along The Corridor, including, most importantly, a new ice arena. Now anyone who wanted to play ice hockey or practice skating could take the train. At the Dover end, the light rail became the center of development for housing, retail, and new business.

Of course, all of these improvements depended on advances in technology. Without the progress in battery storage for electrified transportation and electrical grid storage, the electric vehicles (EVs) and the microgrids could not have been developed. But the biggest disruption was the evolution of reliable and safe Autonomous Electric Vehicles, introduced as a new era of transportation-as-a-service along the lines of Uber and Lyft but driverless, and thus far cheaper and available as a subscription. In the old model, every individual or family had to own a car or truck, or multiple cars. The true cost in the tens of thousands of dollars was something that people really didn't think about because they didn't see an alternative. The system was like an octopus encompassing car dealers, repair shops, gas stations, and occupying hundreds of acres for parking lots.

Once alternative transportation was reliable, people could rely on public transportation and they came out and voted. They voted to support housing initiatives, regional housing programs, non-profit investments—anything to increase the amount of housing and services available, especially in proximity to the bus and train lines. People finally realized that the cost of housing was not just rent and utilities, but the cost of transportation as well.

12 | THE REAL LEAP FORWARD

The real leap forward for Dover, Durham, and the Rump Caucus came courtesy of MIT, when Mimi Farquhar finally snagged funding for the Alternative Transportation Lab. Mimi had been working on transportation for more than ten years by then, constantly jockeying for funding and recognition. It was both amazing and shameful, she thought, how Boston's vaunted tech scene was so micro-focused. Researchers in biotech labs were working on nanoparticles and gene editing, splicing one gene into a new drug that would potentially help ten people with a rare disease. All well and good, but they couldn't even get to work because the traffic was so bad; public transportation operated within a system conceived literally in the nineteenth century. Park Street Station, one of the busiest transfer stops on the MBTA, had opened in 1898. The Cambridge Tunnel, which would later become the Red Line, had opened in 1912. And the bus lines! Buses themselves had changed only incrementally since the 1960s. One can almost hear the universe calling out "Helllloooo" in that 1990s singsong cliché wake-up call.

Finally, in the early 2020s with the advent of automatic, self-driving EVs and auto-driving EVs, AEVs on the horizon, Mimi saw an opening. When the Great Gridlock hit in 2023, her lab was well positioned to receive the flow of funding from the Green New Deal to really make over the transportation system.

Mimi gathered all those high school nerds who'd been making MBTA apps in their bedrooms, first to try to make sense of it all, then to track every train in real time, and finally rethink the transportation system from the ground up. She brought in a brilliant group of motivated grad students and post-docs, so her lab was well positioned for the flow of funding from the Green New Deal to really makeover transportation. Many of her students were from UNH, and some completed internships in Dover and Durham. They frequently attended Rump Caucus meetings, and they participated in developing a strategic plan. They worked on improving the MBTA, but also on creating new vehicle types: smaller, sexier buses, and autonomous trams with new form factors that could run on the city streets—not exactly a light rail train, but slimmer and less cumbersome than the typical bus. By this time, everyone knew that electric vehicles were going to be the standard. But what kind of vehicles? Surely this would go beyond just a copy of those dirty old diesel buses.

That's how Durham and Dover got funding to build a demonstration commuter light-rail connector between their two growing towns. The key was collaboration between the MIT lab, the UNH planning department, community planners, and activists like Barney, Chip, and Katrina. Their mission was not just to build the rail connector, but also to plan new buildings along the corridor created by the new rail line.

All they had to do was persuade the various planning boards and zoning commissions. Ha. "All they had to do"! It was a tall order, no matter how you sliced it. UNH had been on board with the Rump Caucus's sustainability initiatives before the 2020 elections, but it took another five years to get support in the communities—and more like ten years to get anything built.

When the University finally approved the establishment of a new transportation lab at UNH to work on transportation solutions for New Hampshire and other rural areas, it was only natural for Fiona Lake to move from Boston to Durham to head it up, and UNH immediately began working on joint projects with MIT.

13 | THE CONNECTOR AND THE CORRIDOR

The whole idea of the DART light rail connector and linear development making up The Corridor had seemed fanciful to most people. How could the entire pattern of development be changed in ten years—or even twenty years? But this skepticism overlooked the fact that the university already had money allocated for building new dorms, and that research funding from the Green New Deal and New New England would fund new labs as well. Ultimately, it only takes a few years to build a series of dorms, new labs, or a townhouse development.

Transportation planners for years had been evaluating and debating the merits of electric bus rapid transit vs. light rail commuter service, an arcane choice to many. What was the difference? Electric buses would not need expensive track, just guided and dedicated lanes on existing roads, and better bus stop facilities. But they still looked like the same old buses and could get caught in traffic. Light rail would be, let's face it, sexier. It looked like something sleek and up to date in a European city. UNH and MIT, led by Mimi Farquhar's Transportation Lab—had been developing models to help make just these kinds of decisions. Fiona Lake had led the team in developing algorithms to compare efficiency, cost, and scheduling. Which system would lead to the most frequent and convenient service for passengers—and at the lowest cost with the least maintenance?

Which would be the best investment long-term? Fiona's research was instrumental in making the decision for the light rail Connector, now known as the DART. Light rail could use the existing Amtrak right of way through an area that did not have existing road, providing an opportunity to create The Corridor of new buildings where thousands of residents could live and work with lower-carbon lifestyle without even owning cars. Adding tracks for a parallel light rail would provide faster, smoother service. The light-rail train would be able to stop and start more quickly than buses, would be more energy-efficient, as well as more enticing and attractive to passengers.

A native of Boston, Fiona had moved to Durham when she was hired at UNH to head up the new Transport Lab. Coming from Mimi's lab at MIT, everyone expected great things from her, and she did not disappoint. She had gotten a large grant to develop the criteria for The Connector while still at MIT. And she had quickly networked with all of the transportation activists in the area. It was a truism of the early 2020s that real change could only happen with pressure from the inside, combined with pressure from outside the establishment. For years, Monday nights at Barney's had provided the continuing opportunity for everyone to get together and discuss progress and new initiatives.

After her appointment as a professor at UNH and director of the Transport Lab, Fiona had been under a lot of pressure to actually move to Durham. So, she had moved in the midst of the housing shortage of the early 2020s and had to rent an apartment a few miles from campus—an arrangement she found less than optimal. She would have to drive to campus, a situation she knew would change when new developments on The Corridor were completed. Meanwhile, Fiona's husband Paul had been promised a position at UNH as an associate professor of math, but with disabilities that prevented him from driving, he was offended at the idea of moving from lively Somerville to the sticks—which is how he viewed living in a cluster of ordinary, four-story apartment buildings. He refused to move from Boston until the new development was complete.

14 | PLANNING

Back in 2022, as the pandemic waned, affordable housing, or total lack of it, became a pressing political and economic issue all over the country. It was finally clear, after a decade of builders building only luxury condos, that the free market was not going to solve the housing problem. For decades developers made decisions about where and when to build housing, with cities and counties mostly providing a rubber stamp. But as 2022 came around, activists urged the powers that be to acknowledge that the free market had produced nothing but more and more luxury homes and condos, and little or no affordable housing, and it was folly to expect the free market to produce anything other than more of the same. They would never produce affordable housing—at least not without significant incentives.

Chip, Barney, Katrina, and the whole Rump Caucus encouraged the cities of Dover and Durham to get together, become more proactive, and invest creatively. Their proposal for a light-rail corridor between the two cities was not theirs alone; it incorporated ideas from activists and housing agencies around the region.

Nic had been hired to lead the Housing and Planning Development office at UNH, which had been designated the lead office for developing The Corridor. The DART light-rail commuter line and The Corridor had been planned together; while Fiona and her team were working on the light rail, Nic and his team formulated a solid plan to begin construction on the University end of The Corridor.

The advantage of starting at the university end of The Corridor was that the university had complete control. UNH had already been planning to build new dormitories, faculty housing, and labs. Now they planned to build all these new buildings along The Corridor, which was being designated as a three, four or five-block-deep strip along the DART line.

Under Nic's direction, the housing office planned Alton Street as a demonstration, starting with new dorms for incoming freshmen. Knowing that the vitality of the Alton Street demonstration depended on including all the amenities, Nic made sure that the square at the DART station featured a small café and corner grocery. In addition, all of the dorms and apartment buildings had co-working space on the ground floor, along with small offices, interspersed with amenities like dance studios, workout gyms, art studios, and maker spaces.

The tree-lined and landscaped wide pedestrian boulevards leading down the three or four blocks from the DART tracks would have designated lanes for all manner of transport, except private cars: foot traffic, bikes, electric scooters, and skateboards—called micromobility. Two designated lanes would accommodate LaMAs, disability transportation, and emergency vehicles. But there would be no parked cars, no parking lots. Buildings on the next street, Belmont, would be separated by forested park-like greenspace, with winding walking and bike paths that led out to routes to other areas of the University. As a concession to those who insisted on owning individual cars, there would be limited parking at the very end of the street.

Fiona and Paul were among the first to move into a townhouse in the faculty housing section. At the ends of the main streets, the narrow townhouses were in one of the clusters built on narrow streets—terraces—curving off the end blocks of the main streets. Each townhouse had a spacious front porch, and a tiny front yard. The front porches encouraged neighborliness, and the circular streets connected back to the main streets at each end made safe spaces for kids to play. Residents enjoyed spacious porches on the back, facing the linear park that ran between blocks. For Fiona and Paul, it had been the perfect place to begin their family, finally: disabled access, bike access to campus, and in easy walking distance to the DART and the train. The real selling point for Paul was that he would be closer to skiing.

Now, sitting at Barney's, Fiona still remembered walking the kids to the daycare center and preschool on her block, then to the elementary school a few streets over. Now the kids were in high school and took the DART by themselves. Fiona still liked to ride her bicycle through the campus to the various labs and workspaces she supervised.

15 | TRANSPORTATION

Fiona was still not satisfied. The expanded train service certainly helped Manchester, Nashua, and Concord. But there was still no transportation from outlying towns, and there were still places where trains didn't go, like to Hampton Beach or Portsmouth. The trains bypassed the growing I-93 corridor through Salem, Londonderry, and Derry altogether. Folks on those routes were still dependent on buses.

Boston had a phenomenal regional bus system that took passengers from every town in New England to the big Boston Logan airport, and too and from downtown Boston via South Station. But Fiona had had always been dissatisfied with the buses and South Station. The whole system was annoying, as far as Fiona and her team were concerned. Buses were not sexy, they did not attract riders, and the routes they took seemed slow and circuitous.

She still remembered the period when she and her colleagues had followed transit riders around Boston. They waited with them at cold, uncovered bus stops in the wind, wondering where the bus was. They followed them down flights of stairs and through mazes of tunnels into subway stops. Finally, they rightly pointed out that transit riders should have a bill of rights, insisting that riders should be guaranteed frequent service, covered bus stops and walkways, timely information on wait times, working escalators with no "extra stairs," moving sidewalks where they had to walk long distances, and elevators everywhere. Of course, some of these features were incorporated already into newer stations, but a shocking number of riders waited out in the cold.

Fiona remembered the crazy entrance to the South Station, the major bus station in Boston, that required taking an escalator up a level to the bus platform and into the large open station, where you had to buy a ticket from a separate window for each bus line. From there, doors opened into a semi-enclosed busway that reeked of diesel fumes. Once on board, the bus seemed to go in circles back down to street level. What was that about? And to add insult to bus passengers, there were not even bus lanes—so the buses immediately got stuck in traffic. It seemed that bus riders were supposed to be grateful that there was even a semi-direct bus. But what use was it if it got stuck in traffic for an extra hour any time after 3 PM?

By the mid-2020s, the bus systems companies had made some improvements; most of the buses were now electric, which at least reduced the diesel fumes. And the City of Boston dredged up money to rebuild South Station by selling the rights to build a high-rise on top.

Finally, governors, state legislators, and business leaders recognized that every bus passenger meant one fewer car on the clogged roadways, and that while building out rail was essential, it was not enough. As far as Fiona was concerned, there was still a need for expeditious travel up the freeways. Planners just had not thought about how passengers actually used bus transportation. Live in Derry and have a doctor's appointment at 4:00 PM in Boston? Get on the bus at 1:30 PM for the trip that should take an hour and fifteen minutes, because if you take the 2:30 bus you might be late. And who knew how long it might take if the bus got stuck in traffic, because there were no bus lanes.

Fiona had started the research while at Mimi's lab at MIT, and she continued when she got to UNH. Transportation authorities finally implemented bus lanes in the early 2020s so that buses didn't get stuck in traffic, despite not wanting to do anything to further inconvenience drivers in their gas-guzzling, carbon-spewing individual cars and SUVs. They also increased service to every fifteen minutes or less, instead of every hour. And all of the bus lines were mandated to go electric by 2030.

It was a start, but there were still issues. Each time the bus made an intermediate stop at a park-and-ride, it had to take the exit off the interstate, loop onto a side road and into the station, park, and then reverse course to get back on the interstate. Maybe it only took four minutes each way—in fact Fiona had timed it—but still, it didn't give commuters the feeling that they were on any kind of rapid transit.

Fiona was the kind of obsessive person who actually spent all of her time thinking about these things. In her mind, there needed to at least be a new kind of vehicle, a low profile, smaller kind of combined bus-tram, sometimes called microtransit. There was no need to use the raised profile of the old-model intercity buses like a long-distance Greyhound bus that needed room underneath for luggage. But if the bus-trams were a component of a regional transportation system, then the whole form factor could be reconceptualized. Self-driving, electric, with a sleek form factor, maybe doubled cars, trams that came every ten minutes. Bus-trams would travel a straight line on the highway shoulder, stops would be under the overpasses, and the passengers would take escalators and moving sidewalks to a designated LaMA pick-up and maybe a token parking area for anyone who still drove a car. The autonomous driving LaMAs would transport people from the station to their home. Expensive to build? Yes, but so necessary if commuters were to be lured out of their cars.

But that had always been the big question, hadn't it? How many people would really give up their cars? The culture of cars—in films, on TV, in ads—had been front and center for decades, for entire lifetimes. The entire landscape of subdivisions, highway strip developments, destination shopping malls, and freeways had been designed for individual cars. It was hard enough to imagine deconstructing it and imagining what that new world could look like.

It was even more difficult to project how long it would take for this new landscape to be constructed and for individuals to make the transition.

That was really the brilliance of The Corridor concept. The rural subdivisions and strip malls would not have to be reimagined or rebuilt—at least not at first. Instead, the new Corridor would provide an alternative, and be built mostly on undeveloped land along the train tracks. People would truly have a choice. No more developers declaring that homebuyers wanted a 3,000-square-foot home with a three-car garage and an acre of lawn on a cul-de-sac.

The first time Fiona had actually lived in a semi-rural area was when she moved to Durham. Still, on the New Hampshire scale, Durham and Dover were relatively large towns; Dover still had a population of only 32,000 people in 2020. But they were surrounded by a dense web of smaller towns and villages, and thousands of people living on the connecting two-lane roads who prized their rural lifestyle, complete with two cars in the driveway for the commute to work or a quick trip to the market—or to pick up the kids from school and take them to hockey or baseball or ballet practice. Would they actually give up cars? How many of these trips could be replaced by LaMAs? Actually, all of them could be… but still, would people be willing to give up their cars?

Some people argued that commuters should not have to transfer from one mode of transportation to another. People could still choose to take an AEV for the whole trip. But would it be more expensive? Would the AEVs be able to travel on the shoulder with the bus-trams? How much regular traffic would there still be in twenty years? It had been up to Fiona's lab to provide research on which to base these decisions. As it turned out, The Corridor was a big success. Many people chose not to move to rural subdivisions. They valued the new community along The Corridor and chose to spend their time on recreational activities instead of maintaining a large house and property.

As for The LaMAs, they caught on immediately with those on The

Corridor, as well as with folks still living in the old apartment complexes, who used them for quick trips to the grocery or to the University. The rural dwellers in the single-family homes were slower to give up their prestige cars, but they transitioned to using LaMAs for the kids, instead of buying them a car when they turned sixteen. The self-driving electric bus-trams on route I-93, now called Freeway Flyers, took more time to develop because, with Fiona's plan, first they had to dedicate bus lanes, and then infrastructure had to be constructed at every highway overpass. Before that could happen, commuters started LaMA-pooling to arrange transportation direct to home.

17 | WIND AND WAVES RISING

Monday evening, September 17, 2040, 6:00 PM:
Hurricane Mitch off the coast of Florida, moving NE at 40 mph

By 6:00, Rump Caucus members were beginning to arrive for their weekly meeting, despite the fact that this evening was in no way regular. They were settled into tables or lounging in the more comfortable chairs by the windows. Avery, now the official town planner for Dover, was sitting at the bar. Nic and his husband Henri were at a table near the window, and their two-year-old was playing in the toy corner. Ahmed, the electrical engineering professor, had arrived, and Cody was sitting with him; the pair were focused on Cody's computer, waiting to see how sites in the south that used their microgrid technology would fare in the storm. And Jazz and Jeff had come in after their work.

They were gathered because they'd held Rump Caucus meetings every Monday night for years, but also because Barney's was the best place to watch the latest storm news with friends—and on the big-screen TV behind the bar—with Barney's great beer and food.

This storm would be a major test for the Rump Caucus: Would their innovations protect the residents of The Corridor? Would microgrids with Ahmed and Cody's controls work to protect the area from power outages? And what would happen on the coast, where residents had not adopted these innovations? Barney and Avery were part of the county Emergency Response team, and many of their buddies had also shown up at the bar. Some had been doing their regular jobs working remotely from the back rooms all afternoon.

By this time, Hurricane Mitch was glancing off northern Florida. It was far enough out that it wasn't going to make a direct hit on Florida, but still stirring up waves and storm surge and bringing rain that would cause flooding. But by 2040, rain and flooding were almost normal in Florida.

On the Climate Channel, Richard was anchoring the news desk for the afternoon, continuing the coverage from areas farther south that were already under assault, or that expected the hurricane to hit them imminently. "The next twelve hours are likely to bring Mitch up the coast to North Carolina," he said. "Maryland, Delaware, and Virginia are under evacuation notices. New Jersey coast residents are evacuating, as are residents of Long Island. The Mayor of New York City announced implementation of the Coastal Emergency Plan. And, the Governor of Delaware had declared an emergency

"Let's go to that right now."

The screen switched to Governor Belknap, surrounded by his emergency team, at a press conference in the capitol in Dover. "Folks, I know you've heard many emergency declarations and storm warnings over the last few years," he began. "But, please, take this seriously. We are facing the worst hurricane since Sandy in 2012."

"Now, as you know," he continued, "our predictions are not perfect, but all indications are that this storm will ride just off our coast. It will produce unprecedented waves, flooding, winds, rain, and storm surge. I urge all of you in Evacuation Zones A and B to leave immediately. We will have buses running all along the Delaware shore, through Dewey Beach and Rehoboth, beginning now and every half hour through tomorrow. If you need to be picked up off the main routes, please use your Shoreline Emergency Text App to text your address; you will get a confirmed response with a pick-up time. Use the app to let us know if you have pets and bring them in a kennel if you have one. Bring your go-bag with medications, identification, and emergency paperwork, and a duffle with bedding if you can. If you have any questions, call your local fire department."

Richard cut to Jeremy, on the coast at Rehoboth, one of the most popular beach towns on the East Coast.

"Big waves and wind here, Richard. But the surfers are still out. I'm talking here to Chief Enderley of the local fire department. Chief, tell me how your evacuation process going?"

"We are really urging people to evacuate, and evacuate now, Jeremy," replied the chief. "But, as you can see, we still have a lot of sightseers and surfers. I know some folks think they can get out tomorrow afternoon and beat the storm, but they're just not thinking about how long it will take to pick up everyone in buses, or for people to drive, given the traffic heading away from the coast. I really hope people are not planning on hunkering down in their homes. You can expect to lose power. You can expect to be flooded and surrounded by water—and that's if your home even survives. I hope you show that footage from Sandy, Jeremy, and I hope folks watch it before deciding to stay in their homes."

"Thanks, Chief Enderley," said Jeremy. "A solemn warning for folks along the coast. Now back to you, Richard."

Richard repeated the emergency and evacuation announcements from New Jersey, Long Island, and New York City. Officials in every state warned that folks could expect power lines to go down, leaving whole communities without power. Maya came onscreen and showed the traditional photos of utility trucks heading east to make repairs once the storms were over.

"Enough with New Jersey," shouted Avery.

"Yeah, Barney, switch to the local news," echoed the others. The growing crowd at Barney's was waiting for the 6:00 news from Boston, with the local forecast from Eric in Gray, Maine. Barney dutifully changed to the local news channel and their usually cheery anchor, Penny Matthews.

"Welcome to the 6:00 news. We're going to go right to our hurricane coverage." Penny did not sound cheerful at all; in fact, her mood was decidedly grim. "The Governor of Massachusetts and the

Mayor of Boston will start their press conference very shortly. We're going over to that now with Lakshima who is there. Lakshima?"

"Yes, Penny. I have to say, the mood here is somber; I would say everyone is extremely worried. As you know, the Governor announced evacuation plans earlier this morning. OK, here are the Governor, the Mayor, and I believe that is Mordechai Levinson, the Governor's Emergency Services Manager."

Levinson stepped up to the mic, and he did not mince words. "We can't emphasize this enough, folks. This hurricane is definitely coming for us.

"Particularly if you are watching from Cape Cod or for those of you in coastal Rhode Island, you should be evacuating right now. I repeat. If you are planning to self-evacuate in a private car, you should plan to leave immediately. Tonight, at the latest. If you aren't right on the coast, at least be making your preparations. You know traffic is going to be a disaster tomorrow, and Wednesday will be too late. Now, Collette Query, our Cape Emergency Services Director will be here to review your car, bus, and mass transit options, as well as your shelter options."

Morty was right. This wasn't looking good. He knew that many on the Cape still depended on their own cars. They hated the idea of giving them up. Even though they knew how horrendous the traffic was getting on and off the Cape even on ordinary summer weekends. Emergency authorities had known for years that evacuating everyone from the Cape would be close to impossible in an emergency. Those signs on Route 6, the spine of the Cape, that said EVACUATION ROUTE? Everyone knew that getting over the bridges would be impossible.

"So, here is our Cape Emergency Services Manager, Colette Query."

"Thank you, Morty. I'm going to review our shelter options."

Back at Barney's, Jason chimed in from his barstool: "Their plan has always been the 'Bangladesh Plan.'" A former Cape Cod reporter, Jason was a heavyset guy with a dry sense of humor and a critical perspective some called just cynical. When he'd relocated to Durham as the communications director for the planning team, he became a regular at Barney's and a valuable member of the Rump Caucus.

The "Bangladesh Plan" was named after the shelter-in-place solution adopted by Bangladesh, a country with millions of people living just a few feet above sea level. Faced with storms rapidly increasing in intensity, rainfall, and flooding potential, Bangladesh officials saw that evacuating millions of people wasn't feasible. They began building raised storm refuges in every neighborhood; the plan seemed to be working for them.

Colette was explaining that Barnstable County had been building all new schools as shelters since 2023 and strengthening and reinforcing all existing schools and hospitals. Now, the emergency buses would pick people up in their neighborhoods and take them to the shelters.

"Yeah, but what they aren't saying," said Jason, "is that each shelter, maybe all of twenty-five of them, can only accommodate 1,000 or 2,000 people at the most. Think about it: The high schools accommodate about 2,000 students. So, all those people on cots? And there are more than 200,000 people living on the Cape. What's going to happen to the rest?"

Colette continued to run-down the options for residents of the Cape, echoing the Governor of Delaware, earlier.

"You can consult the emergency map we send out every year," Colette continued. "Or, you can see the emergency zones on our website, as well as emergency bus routes and pickup spots in every town. Or you can consult our CAPE-OUT Emergency App. We will have buses running through every town, going to the shelters, tonight, beginning now until midnight, and then starting at 5:00 AM tomorrow and running every half hour. If you need to be picked up off the main routes, please use your CAPE-OUT App to text your address. You will get a confirmed response with a pick-up time. You may also bring pets. Use the app to let us know if you have pets and bring them in a kennel if you have one. And don't forget the kids.

Bring your go-bag with drugs, identification and emergency
paperwork, a duffle with bedding. If you have any questions, call your
local fire department.

"Those of you sheltering in place can expect to lose power,"
Colette continued. "Stock up with seven days of food, and a gallon of
water per day per person. Also, not to be too grim, but this is
important: Write on your front door the number of people and pets
inside your house; a phone number for your next of kin, and write
your name and social security number on your arm with a sharpie
marking pen."

This was obviously the evacuation protocol that had been adopted
in the 2030s across the country after too many cities, especially in
hurricane-prone North and South Carolina, had failed to make
provisions for people unable to self-evacuate. And now, since the
Green New Deal had mandated a move to a low-carbon future and
people had been giving up individual cars, it had become necessary
to institute new procedures.

"It's going to be a shit show," said Jason, "mark my words."

Barney and the emergency techs agreed with him, but the mood
was grim; there was nothing they could do.

Just then, Cody walked in with Ethan and Jody, ready for dinner
after tying things up at the job sites. The Rump Caucus members
looked away from the screen for a moment to greet Cody and the
boys, then turned back to watch the hurricane coverage.

18 | CODY AND ENERGY

Monday evening, September 17, 2040, 6:00 PM:
Hurricane Mitch off the coast of Florida, moving NE at 40 mph

Growing up with Solar New Hampshire, driving the backroads and helping his dad, Cody had become unusually attuned to the landscape of energy transmission in New Hampshire and throughout New England. He noticed all the wide cuts for transmission lines through the rural landscapes of forests, neighborhoods and farmland, transmission towers marching across the countryside. Power lines along every road, through every neighborhood. When he was bored as a kid, he liked to follow the transmission lines on the satellite view on online maps on his tablet through town and country to the power plants we never see from the road. Driving with his parents, he began to notice the substations, those collections of transformers, wires, and equipment behind barbed-wire fences bearing signs that said "DANGER."

"We assume that that's how things have always been," Chip always used to say, "and that it's how things will always be if we want to get electricity. And no one doubts that we all rely on electricity. But every god-damned time—every time there's a hurricane, or windstorm, or ice storm—we get ready for power outages from trees down, or tree limbs blown across power lines, or even fires started by downed lines."

"Yeah," Cody said out loud, coming out of his reverie and continuing a Chip rant he knew by heart, "Hurricane Sandy way back in 2012, was supposed to be a wake-up call after New York was without power for days and days."

"Hell, the entire grid went down," added Harrison, who had worked as a lineman for more than thirty years. "Every tree-fall or god forbid a blown substation meant there'd be a wild, cascading failure that might cripple a whole region."

"Year after year, things hardly changed," continued Cody. "Instead of addressing the root problem, the utility companies advertised that they were massing armies of linemen at the border, ready to move in and rebuild downed power lines, every part connected to every other."

"And the mainstream media swallowed it hook, line, and sinker," added Ahmed, "dutifully showing photos of the linemen and their trucks, as if they were the do-gooders in a story with no alternative endings—as if they weren't advertising their own total failure as a system."

Chip picked up the thread: "And besides that the utilities bought up as many legislators as they could afford and flooded state legislatures with lobbyists. Utilities control everything; they refuse to change. I mean, for gods sakes, the Atlanta airport had an eleven-hour power outage in 2017. The airport! Eleven hours!"

Now Jazz chimed in; electricity was her thing. "Yeah, I studied that. The electrical system was so poorly configured that a fire in an underground electrical facility damaged two substations and brought down the whole airport, including their so-called redundant system that should have provided backup power."

Ahmed joined back in with one of his famous backgrounders. "Remember the summer of 2019, when a transformer fire caused a power outage in New York City? The middle of hot summer, 70,000 people without power. And it was all due to a simple small transformer fire that cascaded out to the whole system before they could contain it. Then, in California, after two or three disastrous fire

years, PG&E, the giant northern California power monopoly, admitted that it was stray power from their lines that had caused the disastrous Paradise Fire and others in 2018. Then, in 2019, their solution was to cut power in their lines every time a triggering Santa Ana windstorm was predicted. Cut power, suddenly, to everyone in specific areas."

"Oh yeah," said Harrison. "I sure remember that. People who depended on electricity for life support systems like oxygen generators, were left without power. What a disaster!"

Chip continued with the whole backstory, which he had mostly learned from Katrina who was an expert on public utilities and finance. "Yeah, the whole problem was that utilities were profit making monopolies. People thought that the utilities main job was to make sure people had electricity, but really their main goal was to generate profits. The less maintenance they did, the more money they could return to shareholders. And they couldn't generate profits by letting everyone have their own solar system on their roof. All of the profit-making utilities make a guaranteed rate of return on their capital investments in new power plants.

"While we're at it," continued Chip, digging in, "we might as well try to explain explained the whole Northern Pass imbroglio for folks who weren't around at the time, right Barney?"

Barney hardly ever contributed to the conversation at the bar. But the fight against Northern Pass was an effort he had been personally involved in.

"Yeah, as all this was going on New England's major power company thought the solution was to cut through the forests for another high-power transmission line they called Northern Pass.

"Let's see," he continued, "I still have this explainer," and he dredged up a brochure from behind the bar, and began reading it out loud:

"Northern Pass was a corporate partnership between Eversource and Hydro-Quebec to construct a 192-mile, high-voltage transmission line from Canada through New Hampshire to bring

electricity to load centers in greater Boston."

"Yeah," said Chip again, "they wanted to retire their coal fired plants, and decided that a high energy transmission line from Quebec Hydro was the way to go.

"Oh boy was it unpopular," add Chip. "No one, and I mean no one wanted 192 miles of high energy transmission lines cutting through New Hampshire forests. And the worst of it was that most of the energy was going to go to Massachusetts."

And Barney continued, "We had petitions, we had bumper stickers, and signs for businesses."

"I remember that from coming up skiing, said Ahmed. "There was a 'No Northern Pass' sign in every general store and diner north of Concord."

"Yup," said Barney, "and something like thirty towns along the proposed route voted to oppose the project at town meetings."

"The project was finally killed by some kind of regulatory action in 2019," Chip said. "Katrina explained it to me, but it was pretty arcane."

"You know," explained Ahmed, "the whole Northern Pass debacle came at the tail end of the reliance on centralized power plants and long-range transmission lines. Just as new options were finally becoming feasible."

"The major power companies had always, always, swatted down rooftop solar systems by using their lobbying power to oppose net-metering. Even in Florida, even in Arizona," Ahmed tried to explain. "But it was so damned complicated. Most people had no idea what the issue was."

"They said that compensating owners of solar rooftop installations would just make poorer people pay more."

"Of course, that turned out not to be true. Or you could say, it was a big lie."

"As if they really cared about poor people," Chip almost snorted in his beer.

"Ok," said Ahmed, "pay attention, I'm just going to explain this

once. Net-metering is a formula for compensating owners of solar arrays for energy they produce at the retail price per kilowatt hour, in effect, the same price they pay for energy they consume from the grid. Of course, the utilities didn't want to pay, so they created a cut-off for how much power they would have to pay for in their overall working area. Only homeowners could be compensated, they said, not owners of large arrays. This left New Hampshire towns, fire stations, school districts, and even neighborhoods clamoring for permission to build solar arrays and sell power into the grid."

"The real problem, then, was not the technology; it was the reluctance of the power companies to give up their monopolies, and the legislatures and public utility commissions protected them. Renewable energy and energy storage had all been affordable for years, but power companies and the utility industry continued to define the terms of the debate, calling renewables 'unreliable.'"

Chip picked up the story. "In New York, after Hurricane Sandy, the Public Services Commission actually admitted that the regulatory system was broken, and that the monopoly power system was oversized in order to meet just a few hours a day of peak demand. Furthermore, they said, the transmission and distribution system had annual losses of nearly 9%. And, despite the vaunted capitalist free market, the commission admitted that commodity markets were inefficient.

"New York's Governor Cuomo had every intention of addressing these issues directly by overhauling the entire utility regulatory system. He asked the utility commission to completely shift the regulations in order to create incentives for a more distributed, consumer-focused energy system with an interconnected, modernized power grid. New utility rules would incentivize and subsidize microgrids that could "island" (separate themselves from the grid), so that they could take over and provide power in case of a grid failure. A microgrid with backup power could allow gas stations to continue to function in the case of a region-wide power outage; a microgrid could ensure that airports continued to function; a

microgrid could power a hospital complex.

"But Cuomo faced massive pushback from the utilities, which were still dependent on and profiting from their dinosaur power plants. The utility companies fought back for another five years. But they had doomed themselves to playing catch-up, even as they were losing huge segments of their market."

While all this was going on, Jazz was texting with Kisala.

"Kisala says her friends are coming to Dover tonight," Jazz exclaimed out loud. "She wants me to meet them and take care of them?"

"Wow, I didn't really believe we would have storm refugees here."

"They got on the train in Boston at 4:00 PM, but who knows how long it will take them to get here."

19 | REFUGEES: JONETTA AND DESHAUNA

Monday evening, September 17, 10:00 PM:
Hurricane Mitch is off the coast, heading for the border
between Florida and Georgia, moving NE at 40 mph

The TV at Barney's was back on the Climate Channel, and Morty Levinson was back with details on Boston. "And now an update on the evacuations in Boston. We have started evacuating low-lying areas of Boston today. We started with folks with health problems, as identified by their healthcare centers. We have been evacuating them to centers out of the area, many to Worcester and Springfield, where they can be assured of getting their needs met."

"As we said earlier, we do have a plan in place. You can find routes for emergency buses on the maps we have been distributing on your refrigerator, you will see the routes for our emergency buses. Or you can get on our app. If you live in an apartment building, you will see the instructions for your building posted near the front door. Information is also posted at every bus stop."

In fact, twenty years earlier, as the planning committees, city council, and emergency response teams were planning their emergency response, they realized that there was going to be no way to evacuate everyone. So, Boston adopted their own version of the Bangladesh Plan. Boston planners had mandated that every new multi-family apartment or condo building have community rooms

with kitchens and rec rooms for kids on one of the upper floors. In an emergency, these would be the refuge rooms for the building's residents, and more important, also for those in the surrounding neighborhood in less secure housing. Even market-rate housing was mandated to adopt these configurations, and to accept all evacuees into the buildings in case of an emergency. The planners had also mandated installation of all of the electric and other mechanical and HVAC equipment on higher floors, rather than in basements where they would be in danger of flooding. In addition, all new buildings were required to connect to a microgrid that could be islanded, with battery storage so that elevators and mechanical equipment would continue to function. All new schools and city buildings were configured as shelters, and some older schools had been retrofitted for emergency service. It was these demands for microgrids in new and different configurations that had kept Ahmed's electrical engineering lab at UNH busy for years.

Jonetta and DeShauna were aware of all these plans and facilities, but they also knew that the shelters would inevitably be overcrowded. Since they were able to organize evacuating on their own, they decided it was a good time to get out of town.

"OK. Well, Kisala's friends are on their way from Boston," said Jazz, looking up from her phone in the middle of the evacuation announcements. "They got on the train about 4:00 o'clock, they think they'll be here about 10:30."

Kisala had become close to Jonetta and DeShauna while building numerous projects in Dorchester and Roxbury. One or the other frequently served on the neighborhood stakeholder committees, and they had both developed some expertise in building walk-throughs, where folks made final checklists for the builders. They grew even closer after she decided to move into one of the market-rate units in the Dorchester project. Kisala was for some reason still in Dorchester as she texted with Jazz, but she had told Jonetta and DeShauna that if they needed to get out of the low-lying area they should get on the train and head for Barney's in Dover. So they were. Kisala texted Jazz

to greet the evacuees.

Kisala: Jonetta and DeShauna and their families are coming, Jazz, you gotta look out for them.

Jazz: Of course.

Kisala: I'm gonna loop Jonetta in here.

Jonetta: We're coming! Hope it's still OK.

Jazz: Of course, keep me posted.

Jonetta: We heard they're pulling people off the trains to take them to shelters.

Kisala: Just insist on staying on till Dover.

Jazz: I'll meet you at the station.

Jazz grabbed an e-cart for the baggage from Barney's back room. Walking to the station with a cart for baggage was standard operating procedure in Dover.

It seemed like 200 people from Boston got off at the Dover station. They were met by emergency workers ready to bus people to the shelters., except the system they had set up to allocate people to shelters was already going haywire. Despite all the planning, it seemed that many of the shelters were almost filled. The buses were going to schools and community centers in outlying towns, twenty or thirty minutes away on a good day. Of the fifteen or twenty shelters, most were in schools, despite longstanding guidance directing that schools should reopen as soon as possible after an emergency, to return a sense of normalcy.

When Jonetta, DeShauna, and their families finally rolled into

Barney's, they were semi-exhausted from the trip but elated to have finally arrived. All told, there were eleven of them: Jonetta, her fourteen-year-old son Johnnie and two smaller kids, her friend DeShauna and her two sons (twelve and eight), DeShauna's younger sisters Shayla and Sharice, and Jonetta's brothers Hakeem and Kenton. Barney offered stiff drinks for the adults, and hot chocolate for the kids, as the Boston crew unspooled the whole story.

Jonetta and DeShauna were lucky; they owned their own dress shop in Boston's Nubian Square, which was always closed on Mondays, so they were able to declare the shop closed for the rest of the week. Not everyone was so fortunate; many people were reluctant to give up pay for Monday and Tuesday.

At every street corner in Dorchester, teams of firefighters, cops, and city volunteers were insisting that people evacuate if they lived on the first floor or in low-lying areas. In the downtown med district, teams of EMTs and nurses were already evacuating the hospitals.

The firefighters said that buses would soon be available, but no one knew exactly where the buses were going—just out, away from the city to a shelter somewhere. How would people be able to keep their families together? Meanwhile, staying in the city wasn't a great idea either. Anyone who didn't evacuate would face chaos: groceries in short supply, shelters crowded, and streets possibly flooding.

Jonetta and DeShauna wanted their families to stay together and did not look forward to a shelter. Who knew how chaotic that would be? So, they chose to make their way to Dover.

Barney and Chip and the volunteer firefighters at the bar had been talking about evacuations. How many people would Boston shelter in its own suburbs? Ethan, who had come in after hockey practice, did some calculations: the capacity at any one shelter was supposed to be no more than 500. 100 shelters for 50,000 people. The Emergency Services teams would have to operate 200 shelters. OK, maybe that was an underestimate, maybe there were 1,000 shelters. Well, that would have to be it. It was a fact that most people didn't actually evacuate.

"We weren't even sure we should evacuate," said Jonetta.

"We went back and forth for a while Monday morning," continued DeShauna. "We didn't know how bad it would be. No one knew."

"Yeah, no one knew what was going to happen back there," added Hakeem. "People were running every which way. No one has a car. Anyone who had family farther out of the city was getting on buses and trains. Oh yeah, buses were showing up to help people get out. But everyone was crowding in, not sure if there would be enough buses."

"When we realized that public transportation would actually shut down on Tuesday night," said DeShauna," and that panic would set in on Tuesday, that's when we knew we had to get out, and right away."

"So," said Jonetta, "we talked to Kisala, and then we decided to do just what she had suggested. We took the T to the Back Bay Station this afternoon and got on the train to Dover before the whole thing got to be a mess."

"We knew a lot of folks who were heading north to Lowell, on the train," added DeShauna, "or to Salem, NH, and Manchester on buses up I-93. But that was mostly people who knew someone or were willing to brave whatever shelter would be offered."

All of the towns and cities along the route had pledged transportation from the stations to the shelters, but how crowded would it be? How efficient? How long the waits?

"That's why we decided to just go ahead and come on to Dover," said Jonetta, "just like Kisala said. What with getting the whole family packed up and ready, we didn't get to the Back Bay Station until about 4:00 o'clock. By then it was rush hour. People were trying to get out. The station was mobbed."

"They said they had put on more train cars, and were running extra trains north," said Hakeem.

"Yeah," said Jason, "but there's a limit on how many cars Amtrak has available."

"Yeah, we had to wait," said DeShauna. "We finally got on a train

at 7:00 PM. It was supposed to be just an hour and fifteen. But that turned out to be just the beginning. The train was crowded, every car was full, people standing up. People who had friends or relatives, some people just taking their chances on getting to a shelter."

"Then," said Hakeem, "at every stop, there were emergency people waiting—getting on the train, calling for anyone who did not have a place to go—but they were working with allocations: 300 people in Andover, 200 people in Exeter. It was confusing. People got off, got counted, some got back on. That's why the train didn't get here until after 10:00."

Finally, everyone settled down. "We're going to take you and the kids to Alyssa's farm," Jazz said. "She's opened the farmhouse and barn especially for families with kids; the kids will be happier there. They will love the animals."

Then Chip looked at Hakeem, who was twenty-four, and Kenton. "The thing is," explained Chip, "during evacuations most people are passive acceptors of aid. Looks like you two might be happier having something to do. So, what do you all do?"

Turned out Hakeem was an IT guy; his skills would be wasted out on the farm, so he was detailed to the Dover Emergency HQ. Kenton, still in high school, wanted to be an IT guy too, so he stayed behind to help wherever he could be useful.

"I could have stayed and worked from home anyway," said Hakeem. "But I was just worried that I would lose all connections if the power went out, or if the cell towers went down. And, besides, I thought if Jonetta and the kids were going, I wanted to make sure to go with them. Good excuse to get out of town, right? So, if I can help you guys out, you let me know. Kenton here, he's learning coding too, so just hook him in as an intern for a few days or something."

"Ok, then," said Chip, "you and Kenton can stay here. Accommodations aren't great, but you can help us out here. Let us know when you want to crash and well find you some sleeping bags and pillows."

While Ethan was glued to his tablet, making calculations on

evacuations and wind speed and rainfall in different places nobody noticed that eight-year-old Jody, listening wide-eyed to the evacuation stories, was starting to get scared. So, he called his mother, Alyssa.

"I'm scared, I want to go home to the farm," he said.

"OK," said Alyssa, "I'll come get you in the morning, OK?"

"I wish you would come get me now," he pleaded.

But Alyssa really did not want to make the trip down to Dover at 10:00 o'clock at night.

"I'll come and get you in the morning," she said.

Alyssa was furious. She had wanted the boys at the farm all along, but Cody had talked her out of it. "Put your dad on the phone," she said.

"Cody, Jody is scared," she said. "I told you they should be here."

"It's not like it's safer, Alyssa. The Corridor is perfectly safe; we won't have our electricity cut off, and we have all the services we need. The farm might have a microgrid, but you could be cut off by falling trees, or culvert washouts, or whatever, I don't know."

"Well, the farm is perfectly safe, and besides, Jody just wants to be with me," said Alyssa.

"OK," Cody agreed, "OK."

"But Ethan wants to stay here and help, right Ethan?" he called out.

"Yeah," said Ethan, "yeah, I want to stay with you."

"Well," said Barney, "that settles it. We'll round up a van and I'll take Jody with everyone else out to Little River."

20 | LITTLE RIVER FARM

Monday evening, September 17, 2040, 11:00 PM:
Hurricane Mitch off the coast of Florida, moving NE at 40 mph

Barney had bought Little River Farm after his divorce. All the time he had spent getting the brewpub up and running had probably destroyed his marriage, but by the time of the divorce the brewpub was profitable and running almost by itself, with a master brewer. So, he spent a lot of time driving around on back roads, with the excuse that he was looking for a farm but then he had seen Little River and decided to buy it. In the back of his mind, he had very strict specifications: a house that had not been renovated into a fancy trophy farmhouse, and a good-sized barn. It would be a plus if it already had stalls for cows, and a milking barn; expansive fields to grow hay and pasture the cows; a sizable area for growing vegetables, a forest for firewood, and for wildlife. It would be an extra plus if it were on a river or pond, and a had south-facing hillside that could be converted to solar energy production. Little River checked all the boxes and was only fifteen miles from Dover, on the Maine side of the river that divided Maine from New Hampshire.

When Barney and his wife had split, she got their small house in town, and he'd ended up living in an apartment above his brewery. He figured he could hire a farm manager, and maybe spend weekends on his farm.

Barney had always been into resilience and sustainability, and he wanted the farm to become a center for all of these efforts. First, he added solar panels to the farmhouse, then devoted a vacant field to a solar array as well. He pictured a few goats for goat cheese, and a few cows for fresh mozzarella. And wanted high tunnels that would extend the seasons so he could grow greens year-round. The woodlot would supply firewood not only for the wood stoves in the house, but also for fireplaces at the restaurant and the brewpub.

Things developed slowly. The solar panel system wasn't hard to get going; Chip took care of all of that, it was just technology. But the farm was a bit more difficult. At first, he leased out the fields to his neighbors to graze cows and grow hay. He always hoped that his farm could produce vegetables for his restaurant, but after going through a series of managers, he had not found someone who was a good fit.

When Alyssa and Cody split, and Alyssa made up her mind to leave Everlee, it was natural for Barney to scoop her up to run his farm. He had watched as his friends Chip and Katrina grew their farm expansively. As Katrina got busier with the Solar NH business, she had found and trained Alyssa who was eventually managing Everlee almost by herself.

So, when Alyssa told Barney she needed to fix up the house, he listened. Soon it had all new windows, a new kitchen, and a geothermal heat pump to replace the old noisy, smelly oil boiler, all improvements which Barney had just never bothered with. Then she added her own touches, until she created the shabby-chic, cozy farmhouse she'd always wanted, with cottage fabrics and the bric-a-brac that Cody had always hated. And that's how Barney himself was won over. He started spending more and more time there.

Truth was, despite their age difference, Alyssa and Barney had a lot in common: their hard-working spirits, their attitude—nothing fancy, but the best of everything in the way of tools and renewable energy, as long as it was truly useful. Barney was happy to spring for anything Alyssa wanted, as long as it was for the good of the farm.

As Alyssa's interest in cheesemaking grew, they added to the goat

herd and finally brought in the cows that Barney had always wanted for fresh cow's milk, cheese, and yoghurt. They completely renovated the milking parlor and built a brand-new cheese facility, with all-new equipment: marble tabletops, walk-in cooler, and smoker for the smoked mozzarella and gouda they both loved, which was now a favorite at the brewpub.

* * * *

When Barney arrived at Little River with the van, Alyssa was totally relieved to see her boy, Jody. And she greeted Barney and the families from Dorchester warmly. After such a long trip from the city, they were overwhelmed with the cozy house, the woodstove with a small fall fire defined warmth. The kids went over to pet the dog.

Barney was tempted to stay, but he had a feeling. On the way over, the hurricane news on the radio had been getting even more dire: wind speeds increasing; the speed of the hurricane itself uncertain, but possibly picking up; the trajectory uncertain. Would rain bands come in over Dover? Sustained winds? He felt like he should stay and button up things at the farm, but then he realized that Alyssa had plenty of help and would have everything under control. So, he headed back to town to hold down the fort there.

TUESDAY

21 | TO THE SEACOAST

Tuesday, September 18, 7:00 AM:
Hurricane Mitch has moved 300 miles north/northeast
and is off the coast of North Carolina, moving at 28 mph

Kisala had been at her office in Boston on Monday. She'd returned to her apartment for the night when Dan called about *Seabourne*, the house that Kisala was designing for him on the Seacoast, which was still under construction.

"Kisala, we gotta go up there and close up *Seabourne*."

"Why do we need to go up there?" she asked. "You have the whole crew there. Can't you just video chat with them?"

"I'm going to ride out the storm there. I want you to stay too."

Kisala didn't say so, but she was petrified at the idea of riding out the storm in the house. But like eight-year-old Jody, she tried to act brave. In the back of her mind, she figured she could go up with Dan, see how she felt, then bail out if she needed to.

As usual, Dan insisted on driving his oversized e-pickup truck. Not that he had much to bring; he just liked the high view and — let's be frank — the sense of prestige. He picked up Kisala at her apartment, and they headed up I-95. I-95 hadn't changed much over the last twenty years, despite the efforts of planners to change malls into mixed-use neighborhoods. The same car culture which had built the interstate system in the 1950s and 1960s and had spawned the

malls and the suburbs seemed to still be the defining geography. They passed the same exits, with their curlicue designs and overpasses, and there was still traffic. Despite all the efforts of Fiona and her fellow planners to institute Freeway Flyers, there was still traffic. It seemed like there would always be traffic.

They exited the interstate at Alfred's Corner on Route 1 in Rye. Route 1 had evolved from the old road that ran north-south about five miles inland from the coast, into one of those obnoxious commercial strip routes with endless businesses and strip malls that took a car to navigate. Alfred's was one of the major grocery chains in New England. At least they thought of themselves as a grocery chain. But after the pandemic of 2020 began, after everyone started to order their groceries online for home delivery, the company realized that they had to rethink their paradigm. They woke up to the fact that their prime asset was real estate. At the same time, the states of New England woke up to the same realization. The grocery chains controlled important real estate along major transportation routes, with a lot of land wasted on one-story strip development and acres of surface parking that would be virtually unnecessary in a future with fewer individual cars.

With more people preferring to get their groceries delivered, Alfred's needed something to bring people into their stores. They remodeled many of them, adding a café, a tap house, and a sit-down spot with Wi-Fi — the so-called third space beyond home and office where people could hang out, work, or connect with each other. Truthfully, most urban grocery stores had already made that step. Now they were going to remake their businesses in more rural areas.

Alfred's also realized that with Wi-Fi and a microgrid their stores would have a role to play in the weather-related emergencies that were becoming more and more frequent, and indeed inevitable as climate change brought more storms. Then housing and transportation became the overriding concerns. With transportation generating over one-third of carbon emissions, the whole sector was deeply in need of change. But if housing continued to be spread out

in rural developments, transportation reform would continue to be piecemeal.

The solution was new affordable housing near transportation routes. Finally, local governments, prodded by New New England, realized that there were things they did in fact have control over, in particular land-use zoning. Following models developed regionally, many towns followed through, re-zoned the land along their strip highways to Mixed-Use, and changed required parking regulations to scale down those huge parking lots. In any case, with the advent of AEVs and LaMAs, and more efficient bus systems, big parking lots weren't really needed. New New England funded incentives and loan funds to construct affordable housing in place of old one-story strip malls and parking lots.

In their quest to remain relevant and profitable, Alfred's had first installed solar arrays on all their stores to save energy on their extensive refrigerators, freezers, and lights. Then they added Electric Vehicle Charging stations for their customers. Then, in the mid-2020s, as storms got worse and the county began to focus on emergency planning, Alfred's connected their solar-electric systems into their own microgrid and battery storage systems, with a natural-gas-fueled generator for backup power. Over the next fifteen years, they added more battery storage, which now would sustain the complexes for up to a week. Alfred's took advantage of this, and now each of its old stores had become a transportation node with housing, transit stop, and multiple micromobility stations for e-bikes and scooters. And the store and its services could remain operational and available in the event of power outages.

With the advent of the regional compact, New England began to address the whole issue that had developed after World War II: our social geography was plotted around cars. The auto companies had sold Americans a bill of goods, with decades of those insidious advertisements on TV that we needed to own a car, and that the car was an expression of our personality and our individuality. Small kids played with tiny cars, and when they got older, parents bought battery

powered play cars that the kids could actually drive. Learning to drive was a rite of passage. A car was a sixteenth-birthday present, or a graduation present. A car was a first date, and the back seat. A car was a road trip. A car was Thelma and Louise. A car was freedom, and individuality, and your personality, and towing your boat to the lake. In the end, Americans couldn't separate American culture from car culture. And that was just as much of a problem as ubiquitous freeways and interstates and commercial strip developments and suburbs with curving streets and cul-de-sacs. It was nearly impossible to drive down an interstate and imagine the landscape as anything other than what it was.

Families might need an SUV to tow a boat to the lake, but no one needs an SUV with an internal combustion engine to drive into Boston and park all day. You might want an SUV to take the kids to their suburban school, but the kids would rather be able to get to school on their own. And school buses might have been the most inefficient form of transportation of all: big, hulky, unsafe, and running on diesel. Diesel? Besides poisoning the atmosphere, diesel fumes made half the kids sick while the buses drove around on endlessly curving suburban roads, picking up thirty kids at a time.

It turns out that there are three ways to change the impact of carbon-emitting transportation: public transportation, meaning fewer cars; electric vehicles (EVs), which only generate less carbon if renewable energy is used to charge the vehicle; or shorter commutes, with people able to live closer to where they work and shop. The New New England states pledged themselves to all three, and Alfred's Corner in Rye was the prime example.

Then came the autonomous vehicle revolution. People did not realize how suddenly it would disrupt everything. Why own a car— especially one type of car for every purpose? It was expensive to buy, expensive to maintain, and expensive to replace. And with everything being delivered, and autonomous vehicles that could be summoned with a cell phone, owning a car ceased to make economic sense. Nevertheless, especially in New England's rural areas, there were still

people who were attached to their cars and wanted to see their car sitting there in their driveway. Most of those people were the suburban wealthy now, and they at least had electric vehicles and solar arrays of their own.

The algorithms used by the AEVs, whether public or private, worked out the best route for three or four people, guaranteeing a maximum of a five-minute wait. With no one driving individually owned cars to stores, there was no need for giant parking lots. Most of the big indoor shopping malls from the 1980s and 1990s had gone bankrupt in the 2010s and 2020s; many had actually been abandoned. Now they were being redeveloped into housing complexes.

Rural New Hampshire never had real malls, only strip malls. New New England mandated that strip malls and surface parking lots be transformed into other uses, with the help of generous grants and low-cost loans. The locations on major traffic routes—now repurposed as bus or tram routes—made them prime spots for concentrated development. Where there had previously been a one-story strip mall, now the ground level of each complex housed a grocery store and a suite of retail stores, a gym, a dry cleaner, a drug store, a café, and neighborhood restaurants, with two floors of apartments and condos above. These were surrounded by clusters of townhouses. What parking lots were needed, were now behind the stores.

Dan and Kisala stopped at Alfred's for last-minute supplies. Then they went to the fish store to pick up lobsters and clams for a celebratory dinner. Now they were committed. Kisala was more scared than she let on, but she wanted to keep up a brave face for Dan and didn't want to say anything to him. She texted Jazz to let her know they were going out to the house.

22 | ON THE CAPE

Tuesday, September 18, 7:00 AM:
Hurricane Mitch is off the coast of North Carolina,
moving at 28 mph

Jazz woke up on Tuesday, got dressed quickly in her usual overalls and summer tank top, and made her way to Barney's with a feeling of dread. She had purposefully waited to hear the storm news until she got there, surrounded by people to talk with. She was reassured to see Barney in his usual place behind the bar. She settled in with coffee, ordered a mozzarella omelette with hash browns, and turned her attention to the TV. The storm was east of North Carolina, and all of the storm analysis models were still predicting it would follow the coast.

On the Climate Channel, Maya was reviewing damage in Florida and North Carolina, and then jumping to her colleagues spread out in the northeast, waiting.

"OK, let's go to Marie in Hyannis."

"Yes, Maya. I am here at Hyannis this morning. The shelters are filling up. The traffic is still horrendous. You can see behind me buses, loaded up, arriving at the shelters."

"Thank you, Marie. And now on the Cape, we have Cheryl who has been out to Chatham. Cheryl?"

"That's right, Marie, Maya. I've been here in Chatham," said

Cheryl, standing at the overlook for the mostly empty harbor. "You can see that most of the boats are gone. The fishermen have run them up the coast as far as Maine to try to escape the storm. And most everyone has, indeed, evacuated. And the Governor has sent in the National Guard to patrol the empty towns. OK, here comes a National Guard high-water vehicle. But it's still relatively calm; the winds are expected to pick up around 6:00 PM."

"Thanks, Cheryl. Now let's go to Doreen, at the roundabout near the Bourne Bridge. Doreen?"

"Well, you can see, Maya, that the traffic is backed up for miles. And you can see that there is a bus lane on Route 6 heading onto the bridge. If you are planning to leave the Cape by car, emergency managers are telling us that you should expect an eight-hour wait to get over the bridge. If you are not on the road now, you should probably go to a shelter. Back to you, Maya."

"OK, Doreen, thanks. And let's go to Jaren, at a shelter in Wellfleet."

"Hello, Doreen and Maya. I'm here at the high school in Wellfleet. The parking lot is full, and buses are still pulling in. Let's talk to the shelter manager, Mike.

"Are there a lot of folks in the shelters already, sir?"

"Well, thanks, Jaren. There's quite a crowd here. We are a little surprised. Most of our planning assumed that more people would either shelter in place or leave the Cape. But with so little time, and the storm predictions so dire, many more people are here."

"Are you expecting to exceed capacity?"

"We very well might. We might run out of cots, but we have enough food and supplies — and, of course, with the microgrid and system batteries installed some ten years ago, we will be able to maintain power. So, this will be safe shelter during the storm. Of course, if too many houses are destroyed, I am not sure what will happen after the storm."

"Thank you, sir," said Jaren. "I wish you all the best. Now I'm going to talk to one of the folks here. This is Elton." Jaren turned her

attention to an older gentleman in a grey sweatsuit. "Good morning. I see you're walking your dogs. When did you arrive here at the shelter? And did you try to leave the Cape?"

"We arrived early this morning. We looked at the forecasts, the traffic reports; we boarded up the house, which incidentally faces the water. We knew we couldn't stay there. And we have pets. We knew we didn't want to be on the road, in the car with the dogs for possibly eight hours. That's what the traffic reports were saying. So, although we are anxious about the house, we are a lot less anxious here. It's safe, the electricity won't go out. We will have a warm place to sleep. They have food. We brought good coffee, some cake that my wife Maryanne baked yesterday. I guess you could say we're settled in for the duration. Maryanne is inside helping entertain the kids."

"OK, thanks for speaking with me Elton, we wish you and Maryanne the best."

"OK. Thanks, Jaren, thanks Cheryl," said Maya. And the Climate Channel went to a commercial.

23 | E-OPS

Tuesday, September 18, 11:00 AM:
Hurricane Mitch is off the coast of North Carolina,
moving at 28 mph

In the back room at Barney's, the members of the County Emergency Planning Board were briefing interested folks. Pamela, the County Emergency Services Director, and Rene, the Dover Emergency Manager, were briefing the committee. Pamela gave the rundown: "Dover-Durham-Rochester—we're in pretty good shape. I know you think it's because we're not on the coast. True, we won't face storm surge. But we have spent the last twelve hours reviewing the patterns of previous storms. Downtown Dover has flooded in the past, from storms with a lot of rain upstream. And there is a tidal effect, too, measured at the Cocheco tidal station. If the river goes over flood stage and the bay is in flood from King Tides and storm surge, the river water will have nowhere to go, and the flooding will back up from the bay.

"But we've been preparing for years," Pamela continued. "More than half the population of the county lives within half a mile of The Corridor. We have set up our microgrids and energy storage so that we can island—cut ourselves off from the main grid—if need be. And that includes the university buildings, so no one in those areas will lose power."

"And we are getting ready to announce that in conjunction with the Red Cross, and the university, we will open up some of the public spaces on The Corridor itself for shelters.

"If the power is reduced, we're going to ask folks to voluntarily cut their power usage. That means don't use the dryer or the dishwasher and cut the air conditioning as much as is comfortable. Close up rooms you're not using if you can. But everyone's refrigerators will keep running, and everyone will be able to cook.

"Now, downtown Dover and Durham: They have some connections to microgrids. Of course, the pub here has its own microgrid. The Dover Main Fire Station is set up as a hub that will power the Emergency Services building, where we have our Emergency Operations hub. This was one of the first systems built with new control systems designed by Cody and Ahmed, a product of Ahmed's lab. And the Emergency Services Department has funded solar arrays and battery storage for a number of key service stations, to provide fuel for people who are evacuating with legacy gas or diesel vehicles, as well as people who still have legacy diesel or gas generators. And the library will also be powered, in case people need a place to charge up or hang out.

"So, our major efforts will be to prepare for evacuees from areas both here and in Rockingham County, and possibly even from Boston. Our schools are set up as their own microgrids, with cogeneration, solar, and energy storage. We are getting ready right now to set them up as shelters. We are seeing people arriving already. We know we will see people from Portsmouth and the Seacoast. But we don't know how big this thing is going to be. Suppose it hits Boston hard? And not only Boston, but all the towns in the surrounding Metro? Feeding all the people at shelters will be another problem. Of course, the Red Cross has a certain amount of food stocked. We are preparing to canvass the county for all the fruits and vegetables folks may have stocked up: the apple orchards, the grocery warehouses, the bakeries. We are working with the Maine counties on this as well.

"But, really, how big will this thing be?" Pamela's voice trailed off as Cody walked in in the middle of the discussion.

"I think you guys should set up an insta-link with Mrs. Estes' classes over at the Middle School," Cody said. "Ethan seems to have as good a handle on this as the weather service. I mean, the weather service is broadcasting the big picture, but Ethan and his class have access to almost all the same information, and they're drilling down through the data to look at what might happen hyper-locally."

* * * *

All of the East Coast, from South Carolina to Maine, was now under emergency warnings and evacuations. The hurricane hadn't hit Florida, but the storm and high tides had created dramatic and dangerous rip currents and storm surges.

Of course, Florida had already been suffering from bimonthly high tides that flooded streets and entire downtowns. They had "learned to live with it." In other words, the officials refused to take any action, leaving every town, every property owner, to act on their own. It was not a successful strategy. Still, after every storm, the state begged the federal government for money to rebuild, in exactly the same places. Rising payouts led insurance companies to raise flood insurance premiums which were now at the level that most people couldn't afford. Since the banks required insurance in order to get a mortgage, most poor and middle-class people were forced to sell. By now, all the coastal properties were owned by the uber-wealthy, just as the entire coast of New England had long been gentrified.

From Cape Cod to Maine, only the wealthy owners of coastal properties could afford flood insurance, and they could also afford lawyers to shake down the insurance companies and FEMA who often disputed claims. Many wealthy property owners simply chose to "self-insure," ready to rebuild another multimillion-dollar house if anything happened.

That was now the case on the whole coast: Florida, Georgia, South and North Carolina, all the way to New Jersey, Connecticut, Massachusetts, Rhode Island, and the short eighteen miles of New Hampshire coast. Seacoast properties had been bid up to the point where there were no poor, or even middle-class, people on the whole coastline.

* * * *

After breakfast at Barney's, Chip and the Emergency Management staff made their way over to the E-Ops-Center, taking along Hakeem and Kenton. First, they stopped at the high school shelter to talk with Sherry, the shelter manager, and find out how things were going.

"Pretty calm here," said Sherry. "Many people — people with cars, that is — self-evacuated from the coast last night or this morning. I know that folks who live along the DART line in Dover-Durham forget, but a lot of people in New Hampshire are not keen on giving up their cars, especially folks in rural areas, and the surrounding areas here are still rural. Most folks here are from the coast: Hampton Beach, Seabrook. They figured we would be more prepared than some of the smaller towns. COAST started running buses after school yesterday to all of the multi-family housing developments east of Route 1, and some in low-lying areas near Portsmouth. Those will be the areas threatened by storm surge. But, of course, people from outlying areas will be losing power and everything. So, we'll be seeing more people trickling in."

"We're already manning the phones for evacuations of those folks," said Caleb, the Emergency Operations Center manager. "The end-of-the-road folks. We know who they are; we need to call them and see if we can get them to evacuate, maybe go get them. If we get more rain, and more major gusts, we're going to get a lot of trees down on the power lines."

Despite the progress with solar, energy storage, and microgrids, many people still depended on power lines — and power lines were, of course, still vulnerable to storms.

"We've been monitoring all the emergency channels," said Caleb. "No injuries in our section yet; keep your fingers crossed."

They stopped at the small building containing the microgrid control center, where Caleb explained the microgrid to Hakeem.

Caleb pointed to a couple of control panels and explained, "In addition to the E-Ops center itself and the fire station, our microgrid is connected to the high school and half a dozen other buildings, including the senior center and the senior housing across the road."

He showed Hakeem and Keith the controllers and demonstrated on his tablet how to link to them.

"Yeah, we're familiar with microgrids," said Hakeem. "Our building in Dorchester is connected to one, and I got some training on the controls there. Of course, the controls here are a bit different."

Then they headed into the E-Ops center itself, a room on the second floor of the City Public Safety Building next to the Fire Service living quarters. The room was outfitted with a dozen computers and screens, as well as a central projection screen, and numerous maps on the walls. In the center was a table, with lots of comfortable office chairs. There were two or three people there, who had been there all night.

"Take a break, you guys," said Caleb. "Take a nap, and we'll wake you up if anything happens."

"So, here is our HQ," said Caleb to Hakeem and Kenton. "Comfortable chairs, in case we have to sit for hours, and you can always go over to firefighters' quarters for a snack, or to take a nap on the couch.

"First, let's look at the survey of the shelters in the county, and reports from Portsmouth, the Hamptons, and Exeter," he said, firing up one of the computers.

"Here's Exeter," he said, pointing to it on the map. "They're not on the coast, but they are on a river, so, again, if it's raining, they could see some flooding down there. Same with Newmarket." They scrolled through the list of community shelters in schools, churches, and community centers on their database.

"So, Kenton," Caleb continued, "here's a job for you as we get going. You can monitor the shelter numbers and conditions. The shelter workers are supposed to update once every two hours. So, the numbers and conditions on our screen should update automatically. But you can monitor and put in calls to some shelters to see how things are going and make sure the list is up to date. When a shelter is full, we need to make sure the dispatchers know. That way we won't have to remember to check. Just let someone here know if there is an emergency we have to respond to at one of the shelters, or if they need anything."

"Wow," said Kenton. "Sure, and thanks. That's a cool system. And you bet I'm glad to have something to do."

"Now let's look at the outages map," said Caleb. He went over to another computer and brought up a screen showing not only dots for the people who were out of electricity, but the utility companies' own maps of the grid, showing where the actual breaks were, as well as the energized and failed lines.

"Not so many outages, now," said Caleb. "But, Hakeem, I'll show you how to do this, and then you can monitor outages for us. First, I think we should do a map survey of where the electricity is out."

Caleb and Hakeem sat down at another computer and pulled up the power company website.

"We've had this microgrid technology for almost twenty years," Caleb explained to Hakeem. "It was one of the first projects to come out of Ahmed's lab. Over the years, they've used it as a project to do continued upgrade on the technology. Nearly everything in the denser part of Dover is connected to the microgrid. We won't see any power outages here. And you would think that the power company would have buried the power lines or something out in the rural areas of the county, but they continue to say that it's too expensive, and just not worth it. They would rather wait till the lines go down. After all, it's all on the consumers at that point. And the regulatory commission keeps giving them a pass.

"So the wealthier people in the county live out in these newer subdivisions," Caleb continued, pointing out the winding rural subdivision roads on the satellite view map with houses spaced out on two- and five-acre lots. "These folks have gone ahead and gotten their own generators. Some of them have solar panels, too, and storage batteries. But most of them just have generators.

"So that leaves the poorer folks kind of stuck out there in the older homes. Can't really afford to move, can't afford a generator. There were some programs for them to go solar, but a lot of them haven't."

"And a lot of them live along those little creeks and streams that you just know are going to come up and flood if there's a lot of rain," added Caleb's assistant Meighan. "But it won't necessarily happen today if the rain is upstream. It may even be a few days after the storm before the creeks rise to flood stage."

"Right you are, Meighan," Caleb agreed. "They will call the power company when the power goes out, but we'll be hearing from them after the storm."

24 | LITTLE RIVER

Tuesday, September 18, 8:30 AM:
Hurricane Mitch is off the coast of North Carolina,
moving at 28 mph

When Jazz got the text from Jeff, she walked out of Barney's and waited for him to pick her up. They were off to inspect Solar New Hampshire installations and make sure everything was properly protected from the coming storm. Their first stop was out at Little River, just to make sure everything there was working properly. Jazz was nervous about the storm, anxious. She'd been through storms in Kenai. She was a relentless studier of historic storm surge maps and had been down to the coast with Kisala many times. She was worried.

Alyssa, on the other hand, had only worried because everyone else was worried. She didn't naturally gravitate to the worst possibility. The farm seemed like a reasonably safe place to be. Still, she wanted to be prepared, and she wanted to be able to help others. And now she was doing both.

Alyssa and Barney had heard that many people along the coast, even as far south as Boston, were looking for a place to evacuate to. They'd talked it over and decided that there would be room at Little River. It was, after all, a four-bedroom farmhouse, with a few rooms for workers in the attic of the ell. Alyssa had collected food, water, cots, blankets, and sleeping bags from the neighborhood for any evacuees who showed up. She'd made sure the old outhouse was functional. And Barney was the kind of guy who always stockpiled food. He wasn't exactly a disaster prepper, but he did like to be prepared.

It was a beautiful morning, still not raining, with only a few cirrus clouds in the east. When Jazz and Jeff arrived at Little River, Jonetta and De Shauna were making breakfast: bacon and eggs, toast, coffee, oatmeal, yoghurt, and a cheese plate — a real farm breakfast for Alyssa and the farm help who had just come in from doing the chores. Jazz was sorry she had already eaten. Jonetta and De Shauna were glad to be out of the chaos in Boston, but they were beginning to admit to some dismay at finding themselves in the unfamiliar environment of the farm. They all sat down to breakfast, a major meal.

Evacuation took different forms for different people. The well-off coastal residents were already booked into hotels, motels, inns, and vacation condos as far away as the New Hampshire mountains and the Lakes Region. Meanwhile, the Central New England Emergency Planning Board had a comprehensive list of official Red Cross Shelters, including schools, gyms, and community centers. But these were limited, and in no way adequate to accommodate the thousands of people expected to actually evacuate.

To fill the gaps, the local emergency boards had lists of farms, and homes where people might take in other evacuees. The Little River farm was on the tail end of the chain of these evacuation centers. Everyone expected that they'd only need to evacuate for a few days— but who knew how long it would really be?

Suddenly Alyssa got a call on her emergency landline. Could she take in another family with children? "The more the merrier," said Alyssa.

Half an hour later, the Phillips family arrived: Jackson and Rosemary from Hampton Beach, and three kids under ten.

"We are so grateful to you," said Jackson. "We just moved to Hampton Beach. We bought an inn. What incredibly bad timing. And we must be the only people in town without relatives somewhere in New Hampshire. But we just didn't think we could handle the three kids in a shelter."

"It is so wonderful to be on a real farm," said Rosemary. "And we'd be happy to help out."

"Grab some plates and help yourselves to breakfast," said Alyssa, "and then we'll work things out."

So far, so good. Little River could handle one or two extra families. They had plenty of food. After breakfast, Alyssa and the farm crew cajoled the adults into going out and learning how to harvest lettuce, baby spinach, and mixed greens. It had to be done as soon as possible; without the sheltering hoop houses, the greens would not survive the storm. The two older girls, Shayla and Sharice, took the younger kids out to explore the barn and meet the animals.

Having satisfied themselves that the Solar NH equipment at Little River was well protected, Jazz and Jeff were off to the next houses on the Maine side of the border. Jazz drove while Jeff watched on his tablet, as Mitch hurled winds and rain up on the North Carolina Outer Banks. Anyone who had not left was going to be soggy toast.

Mostly, the systems they visited were in order. In a few places, where wires in a damp basement had corroded, or connections had come loose, they were able to make quick repairs. In a few cases, they decided that the panels were not anchored solidly enough, and they called in a repair team. It was hard to really perceive it as an emergency, because, like the last few days, it was a perfect, sunny, calm fall day, with the leaves just beginning to change colors. The sheep, cows, goats, and occasional llama or alpaca were grazing in green fields, and the countryside was calm. Only tuning into the Climate Channel kept them keyed up.

By early afternoon, as Jazz and Jeff navigated down another long drive to an isolated old farmhouse, the Climate Channel was announcing storm surge already onshore along the North Carolina coast, disaster warnings had been declared for Virginia, and New York announced that the subway system was shutting down in just a few hours. They checked out the large solar array behind the barn and all the connections, finding everything in working order.

Their next stop was a cottage community, thirty or so small houses on two or three streets, with systems installed about five years before. With houses close together, they could afford a complex system with a small microgrid and battery storage. As a new system, all the controls were centrally located. Everything looked tidy and in order. As they drove out of the neighborhood, they enjoyed seeing kids playing in the cul-de-sacs and on the swings in the tot-park.

But as they headed back over the Salmon Falls River from Maine into New Hampshire, Jazz and Jeff were listening to the governors of Virginia and Maryland issuing emergency declarations. The river was low and calm, with just a few small falls burbling over exposed rocks. But could it really flood if there were too much rain upstream? It was hard to imagine. Another five or ten places were all they could squeeze into the rest of the afternoon, before they drove back to Everlee.

25 | KATRINA AND THE GRID

Tuesday, September 18, 7:00 AM:
Hurricane Mitch is off the coast of North Carolina,
moving at 28 mph

Katrina could hardly sleep when they got home from Barney's Monday night, trying to imagine what the storm would bring. She got up early on Tuesday; it was easier to watch Maya on the Climate Channel and see the destruction on the Florida coast than try to imagine what was going to happen to Boston or Durham.

Katrina was one of the few people who understood the language of the grid and the ISO New England, the Independent System Operator for the New England Electrical Grid: distributed PV forecasting, future system load, Forward Capacity Markets, Non-FCM Energy-Only Resources (EOR) and Generators, gross load forecast. She could speak their language, and over the years she had appeared at legislative hearings on the need for delimiting net metering. But most important, she had provided the resources and language for Chip when he served in the legislature.

Few people really understood how the grid was organized and structured to accommodate the peculiarities of electrical transmission. In short, every electron generated had to be sent over a wire and find a home the second it was generated. There was no slack. The ISO balanced production and demand at every second. It was a system that had at first been cobbled together, joining many regional electrical generating and transmission systems. In New England, the come-to-Jesus moment had been the Northeast Blackout of 1965, which shut down power for thirty million customers. That shock to the system spurred broader systemic thinking, and increased integration across state lines.

Over the years, the ISO had been created to organize and coordinate the regional electrical grid. But still, electrons generated had to be balanced with electricity demand in real time. The introduction of batteries to the power grid changed everything, and in short order. A change the energy gurus called a major disruption. At first, people had thought of the batteries as backup for individual homeowners. They had not imagined them as a regulator on the entire system. If there was a backup, then there would be no need for peak power generation. Peakers, as they were known, were power plants that could start up in real time to meet a high demand load, like millions of air conditioners turning on during a hot a summer afternoon. In fact, some utilities actually charged customers not for their actual electricity used, but for their maximum demand. With batteries, all these calculations became null and void, like a huge formula being erased from a whiteboard, or a display of plastic numbers cracking, falling apart, and falling down into a pool of water and dissolving. Electrical energy could be stored and spooled out as needed. Batteries also allowed the system to balance the contributions of solar and wind power, to avoid the oft-cited problem that the wind did not always blow, or the sun always shine.

In New Hampshire, the major utilities were unwilling to allow for net metering on large arrays at factories. This had led businesses, once they had backup batteries, to disconnect from the grid altogether, destabilizing it and leaving those still connected to pay. The major utility had trotted out the threat of leaving those "poorer" customers in the lurch, but now it was happening anyway. Now the rich had solar arrays and batteries, disconnected from the grid, and the "poor" had utility bills and were stuck with a grid that frequently went down.

On this Tuesday morning, Katrina thought, as always, about the big picture. What would the storm and all its potential destruction mean for their solar business, and for the farm? And what could they do to help?

Luckily, after Alyssa had left Everlee for Little River, Katrina had found another capable farm manager in her niece Ellie. Ellie had worked on the farm as a teenager; she worshipped Alyssa and followed her by going off to Unity College for a degree in sustainable agriculture. Even though UNH offered the same degree program, Ellie, like Alyssa, preferred to be on the much smaller campus, away from the crowds. By the time Ellie graduated, many farm-to-table operations had become much more efficient and profitable, due to better management practices and more automatic controls. Katrina considered herself lucky that Ellie had agreed to come back to Everlee, having been offered a number of other jobs. Ellie now lived with her boyfriend Travis, a solar system installer, in the cottage once occupied by Cody and Alyssa.

Ellie and Katrina met every morning over coffee to go over plans. This morning Chip joined them, and there was more tension in the air.

"We'll have to take the high tunnels down," said Ellie, "which is a shame, because it will expose the crops. But I don't see what else we can do. We can't afford to lose them."

They agreed that Ellie would call in all of her high school and college help, take down the plastic, and harvest as much as possible, then store it in the walk-in coolers. They didn't have the animals that Alyssa had at Little River, so they were spared that problem.

Ellie, Katrina, and Chip brainstormed about making room in the barn for evacuees. Then Katrina suggested that they wire up all the solar panels they had on hand and use them to charge electric car batteries. Early in the electric-car development cycle, solar energy companies had realized that even after batteries lost their ability to charge to the 100% needed for car operation, they were still perfectly good for solar storage. Chip had been buying the used batteries in bulk on the wholesale market ever since, and there was always a stockpile in the barn. Microgrid and battery developers had realized that, if the grid went down, people with electric cars dependent on the grid to charge their cars were going to be stuck. At the same time, fully charged electric cars could be used to provide backup power for homes in the event of power outages. Of course, the microgrids configured to be able to use EV battery power were the ideal solution. But in the meantime, those outside of the range of a microgrid could at least use a solar panel to charge a battery and then use that to charge a cell phone or run necessary medical equipment.

Like Alyssa, Chip and Katrina had spent Monday setting up the farm for evacuees. Long ago, they had built several rooms in the attic of the large ell that joined the house to the barn. Even historically, these kinds of spaces had been used to house farmworkers, which is what Katrina had done at Everlee. Lately, she had rented them out from time to time, to students, or campaign workers during campaign season, but now they were conveniently unoccupied. Like Alyssa, Katrina and Chip had been collecting bedding and camping pads for whoever showed up. Now they dug out those old sheets and towels. The farm was set to welcome evacuees who were fleeing the low-lying areas around Portsmouth.

Theirs was such an established destination, and they had so many friends, that the rooms in the barn were spoken for by Monday. It seemed like at least ten people were expected. They had already dedicated one room to their own IT and logistics people—Lianna on logistics, and Holly on IT—who would move in and share a room for the duration. Lianna and Holly would make sure that Everlee stayed connected in the chain of emergency management, ready to relay messages. The guest rooms in the house went to relatives: Katrina's sister Val, her wife Sylvia, and their two kids. The kids were doubled up with Sylvia's sister Drew's kids, while Drew and her husband Adam, who had left their own inn in nearby York Beach, claimed the final guest room. All were arriving mid-day Tuesday.

"When we heard about the storm," Drew explained, "we just had a feeling it could be the big one. I mean, maybe not, but we've all seen those evacuation videos from North Carolina. We wanted to stay at our place as long as possible. It seemed like we had so much to do: storm shutters, putting away the outdoor furniture. But if we stayed too long, there would be the traffic."

"The whole reason we bought our place," said Adam, "is because it's right on the coast. Thank God we're up on the bluff, and not down on Ogunquit Beach." He was talking about one of the few long sand beaches in Maine — one of the lowest spots in the state.

"But I've seen photos," he continued, "of fifty-foot waves coming up over the bluffs. If that happens, there won't be anything we can do. It just wasn't worth risking our family."

"And the crowds shopping!" Drew interjected. "You should have seen the parking lot at the Shop 'n Save in Kittery. It was just hard to know what to do. Stay and board up the house? Spend two hours in line to get bottled water at the Market Basket? We prioritized and just stopped at the bakery in Kittery. Their breads would keep dozens of people going; they were rationing, only ten loaves per customer."

As a planner, always a planner, Katrina had delegated Kara, one of her installers who lived farther west and out of the storm path, to shop for carloads of groceries in Manchester, where there would be no lines and no shortages. Kara showed up with a van full of beans, rice, flour, bread, cold cuts, cheese, cereal, eggs, milk, donuts, and cookies, coffee, tea, and more for people who showed up at the farm, or to give to the shelters.

26 | KISALA, DAN, AND JAZZ

Tuesday, September 18, 4:00 PM:
Hurricane Mitch has crossed the North Carolina/Virginia border
and is off the coast of Virginia, moving at 28 mph

Jazz hadn't heard much from Kisala, so she was surprised when Kisala messaged:

"Please, come down and help me and Dan close up the house."

She sensed it was important, so after she dropped Jeff off, Jazz drove the company e-truck down to Rye before the storm. Were they really worried about the big house? When she got there, she saw Dan for only the second time. She could see the attraction: not a tech bro, not a nerd, really just a nice guy: tall, glasses, light fuzzy curly hair, medium build, tight North Face T-shirt — and a take-charge attitude.

Kisala had designed Dan's new house as a showplace: energy efficient and storm resistant, with all the latest bells and whistles for controls. It was built on concrete-and-steel piles, so that the main level was ten feet above the road which elevated it over the projected storm surge, and as a bonus, gave it a nice view over the gravel-and-rock barrier wall and the harbor towards the ocean. Folding glass doors on the ocean side towards the East caught breezes and provided access to the deck, but could be protected with rolling hurricane-proof shutters. The inside of the house was still bare studs, no insulation or sheetrock. The floors were still plywood, since the final hemp-plank flooring had yet to be installed. Thankfully the windows were in, and the house was buttoned up. Still, it was far from finished. Of course, there were no curtains or shades; they looked out on a deserted row of houses, with no lights in any direction.

The guest bedrooms to the back of the house all had angled windows and decks facing the ocean — a condo-design cliché, for sure, but a practical one. On the second floor, the main bedroom faced the ocean, with enormous sliding doors leading to a deck that shaded the dining deck below. And there was a roof deck with a shade sail anchored with steel cables, altogether giving the whole house the look of a sailing ship. The house faced east to the ocean, so the solar collectors were on the side of the house facing south and on the back, facing west, to better provide electricity for cooling now that summers had gotten hot. The outside of the house looked completely finished now, but it was unfinished on the inside.

Dan was calmly in command, with three or four workers on hand. They really only needed Jazz for another look, to see if there were any loose ends to tie up that they hadn't seen.

But really, as it turned out, it was a call for help from Kisala. And Jazz came, because she wanted to see Kisala, to check on Kisala.

But what she said was, "Let me check the connections on your energy storage system," completely avoiding the tension in the air.

"Yeah, Kisala and I are riding out the storm here," said Dan, "right Kisala?" Kisala said nothing, but she looked nauseous.

"Really?" asked Jazz. But it was obvious he was serious; he looked so pleased with himself.

"We sure are," said Dan. "I'm stocked up, everything is shipshape; I can't wait to see how the house performs. Come on, I'll show you my command headquarters."

He led them into the large bathroom on the main level, behind the kitchen. He had outfitted it with two cots and sleeping bags. Of course, with the battery storage he wasn't going to be without electricity, so he had a radio, and a TV, and a small induction hotplate on the bathroom counter. He had stocked a supply of high-end freeze-dried camp food. Dan was more than eager for the adventure. Jazz felt her stomach churn, but she swallowed her fears.

"Great," said Jazz, "looks like everything is shipshape indeed."

While Dan futzed with last-minute preparations, Jazz invited Kisala for a final walk on the beach. The night before the storm was due to arrive, it was still calm, clear, and beautiful, with the low clouds in the east reflecting the sunset in the west.

But the ocean was angry, with waves rearing up out beyond the sandbars and crashing onto the beach, already pushing foam up beyond wrack line of seaweed outlining the extent of the last high tide. They walked up to the curve on the beach, the spot where the nineteenth century Grand Hotel came into view. Flags waved from the steps in front, and the hotel loomed grandly on its peninsula, its four-story pristine white façade reflecting the pink-and-orange evening light.

With the hotel's lights on, they could see the staff removing all the furniture in the glass-walled dining room, while more workers boarded up the windows. The lights were still lit on the walkway from the hotel down to the marina, illuminating the deck and the docks. Trucks rolled up one after another to pull the remaining boats out of the water.

Jazz and Kisala turned and walked to the line of waves, where they wandered, heads down for a bit, as if they were looking for shells. After a while, they headed back to Dan's. The house came into view, standing like a sailing ship, rising above all the other houses over the beach dunes.

"Dan's excited about staying through the storm," Kisala finally said, "and he wants me to stay too. But I'm scared."

"Did you tell him that?"

"I told him, but he just said that I was the one who designed the house, and he had complete confidence."

"Ummmm."

"I mean, it's not that I don't have confidence, but it's not finished yet. I'm really hoping the guys can have the stormproof shutters operable by the time the storm hits. But even if it were done, I wouldn't want to stay. I mean, what's the point?

"We do have the extra-strength impact resistant glass," she continued, "and that wasn't cheap. But I'm just scared of storms. I don't want to be sitting for hours in the dark. Of course, it doesn't have to be dark. We have emergency energy systems. But given everything, it would be stupid to turn on more than one emergency light. We'll be sitting in the safe room, the bathroom, with one emergency light."

"Yikes," said Jazz, "not fun. You should come home with me. I insist. Please. I'd feel so much better. If you stay, I'll be worrying about you."

"Yeah," said Kisala, expelling her breath, "that's what I'd like to do. That's why I called you. I knew you would come and help me make sense of things." She squeezed Jazz's hand, and Jazz felt a special kind of chill.

"I tell you what, Dan has planned a big dinner for tonight — a special celebration of the house. He's brought down a special bottle of wine, we got some lobsters, clams, corn, the works, and Dan always gets more than we can eat. Stay for dinner."

"OK," said Jazz. Even though the storm was building, it seemed safe enough to stay a few more hours.

They could see that the waves were building out on the Isle of Shoals; the surfers knew, too, because they were beginning to gather on Rye Beach, testing the waves, determining the direction, trying to guess when they would build on the beach. Wisps of cirrus clouds were already forming on the horizon. Jazz and Kisala walked the beach together, and then — anticipating the storm to come — they held hands to comfort each other, like in the old days, when they were together. So much had happened, so much had come between them since, but, really, they still cared for each other.

They stood by the water for a few more minutes, watching the tide come in. Then they turned, picking up shells from the wrack line of seaweed, and headed over the dunes to the house.

When they got back, the workers had gone home to prep their own places. Dan was in what was going to be the kitchen, where he had set up a few pieces of plywood on sawhorses. He had gotten a small refrigerator for temporary use, and there was a sink cut into the plywood counter, with a bucket underneath. A five-gallon plastic jug supplied water. He had a big lobster pot heating on a propane camp stove. It was actually a lot like camping; a multimillion-dollar house, and it was like camping.

Still, Dan was determined to stay. "It'll be fun," Dan said excitedly. "This is exactly why I wanted a house on the coast. I love storms. And Kisala and her engineers have designed this to withstand anything."

Dan got the lobsters out of the cooler, along with some corn, butter, and a loaf of fresh bread he'd picked up from the bakery next to Alfred's in Rye. He dropped the lobsters and corn in the boiling water, then he opened the bottle of wine and found some actual wine glasses in one of the boxes under the counter.

When the lobsters and corn were done and the butter was melted, the three of them sat around a folding table in vintage aluminum folding chairs with green-and white-strapping, just like the ones Dan's parents used to take to the beach. The setup was funky and comfortable, even though the night's chill on the beach breeze was creeping into the unfinished house. As they quietly picked apart the lobsters, they could hear the wind picking up.

"Look, I know you think I'm crazy," said Dan. "But before I bought this property, I spent a lot of time looking at maps of sea-level rise and storm surge. Then I had Kisala go over it all. You know she's the best. She's studied all the surge maps from north of Boston to Portland, Maine.

"It's surprising to a lot of people," he went on, "but the problem is not going to come from the ocean; it's going to be from the marshes and bays in back of us. The storm surge will raise the water level, and then when the wind picks up, it'll drive the water up behind the houses. But, you know, even ten years ago it was becoming obvious

that New Hampshire was not going to give up on its eighteen miles
of coastal road." Jazz and Kisala both new he was talking about famed
NH Route 1, Ocean Boulevard, which snaked along the length of the
coast. It provided access to all the beaches, and the coastal homes
and was a tourist attraction in and of itself.

"All the big houses on the coast are now owned by the wealthiest
people in New Hampshire," Dan continued. "You don't think they
are going to allow the state to just have a hearing and decide to
abandon it in a coastal retreat plan, do you?"

He was right, they knew. For decades, Ocean Boulevard — the
coast road — had been a political football: expensive to maintain, and
impossible to abandon. Whenever abandoning it was brought up,
coastal residents with a lot of political pull agreed to funding for buses
to get people to work or some other compromise. "New Hampshire
has and will continue to maintain and upgrade the coast road," Dan
added.

"So that's why you felt so secure in buying and building on this
oceanfront property?" asked Jazz.

"Yup," said Dan. "Rich people are risk-takers, and they have
enough money to cover their bets if they're wrong. So, they're betting
the Big One doesn't come for a while — enough time for them to
enjoy their ocean views for another twenty years. Like that famous
billionaire on Martha's Vineyard. He built too close to an ocean bluff
which was threatening to destroy the house. Then he badgered the
island government until they let him move his — get this — 8,000-
square-foot house back from the bluff. Massive operation. Cost
millions. That's rich people for you. And now I'm one of them."

So, with the confidence of the wealthy, Dan had bought one of the
few remaining older cottages right across the highway from Rye
Harbor. And torn it down.

Finally, Kisala blurted out, "Dan, I'm going back to Dover with
Jazz. I know I told you I might stay. I know you want me to stay. But
I can't. I'm scared."

Scared, yes, but Jazz knew how much courage it had taken for

Kisala to admit she was scared.

Dan looked crestfallen, his eyebrows wrinkling, his mouth in a pout.

"Come with us, Dan," said Jazz. "There's room at my place, or we can take you to Alyssa's, or Chip and Katrina's. They're all preparing for evacuees."

But they knew this was futile. Dan was determined to stay.

"It will probably fizzle out after it crosses Cape Cod," said Dan.

"But suppose it doesn't?" Kisala challenged him. "No, I'm not going there. I know you're determined to stay."

"So, do you have enough food?" Jazz asked. "Food you don't have to cook?"

"Yeah, plenty of food. And don't be silly, plenty of power from the batteries and a hot plate to cook on. Lights and a radio hooked up to that giant solar-system battery. I'll be fine."

"You're going to message me for as long as you can? Right?" asked Kisala.

"Right," he said, even though they both knew that if the cell towers went down, his messages wouldn't get anywhere.

All of a sudden it became clear that Kisala cared for both Jazz and Dan. She would worry about him; she might have even preferred to stay with him, if not for her fear of the storm. Calm and confident, Dan assured them that all was well, he would be fine.

By the time Jazz and Kisala got out to the truck, the wind was definitely picking up — more than a breeze from the northeast. The new moon, so clear when it had been rising a few hours ago, was now partially obscured by hazy clouds. It was hard to drive away and leave Dan but staying was just not possible for either of them.

For old times' sake, and to see the beaches one last time, Jazz and Kisala drove up along the coast, getting out of the truck from time to time to stand on top of the levees — concrete sea walls built more than fifty years before. Would the walls hold this time? What would change before they saw these beaches again? Then Jazz turned inland.

They drove the rural New Hampshire back roads past farms and suburban houses, many of them set into hollows near creeks or ponds—so low they were sure to be inundated if the storm reached the worst-case scenario. And everywhere were the overhead wires, and the trees, the grand trees of New Hampshire's mixed-hardwood forests, interspersed with tall, stately pines. All of them were now at risk from ferocious storm winds.

27 | HURRICANE COMING

Tuesday, September 18, 6:00 PM:
Hurricane Mitch is offshore of the DelMarVa Peninsula,
the Delaware/Maryland/Virginia coast, still moving at 28 mph

It was still eerily calm in Dover, fifteen miles from the coast with the sun setting in the west under colorful, only partly cloudy skies. The crowd at Barney's now included Spencer, Avery, Nic, and Alex. They had once been the youngsters — right out of college, hanging with the crowd. Now there was an even younger group as well, including Hakeem and Kenton, college students, Barney's crew, farmworkers from some of the local farms, and even new professors in their thirties who lived in the condos and still looked like kids.

Barney got out some of the sausages he had stockpiled and served them in the custom potato flour buns he always had the local bakery make for him, with their special mustard and green tomato relish.

"Have some of our green tomato relish," he said. "They're making extra right now."

"Yeah, did you see the lines at the grocery stores?" asked Spencer. "I mean, there isn't that much to worry about where we are — at least, I hope not. But what if the storm makes a direct hit on Boston?"

"It doesn't have to make a direct hit on Boston to get people nervous; people only have to fear that it will," said Avery.

Barney turned the TV to the local station, and at 6:00 PM Eric came on with the latest forecast from their local National Weather

Station in Maine. This is what the crew at Barney's had been waiting for, and the room grew suddenly quiet.

"OK, folks," Eric began, "here's the latest update: Hurricane Mitch is headed directly toward the Cape. Yes, this is the worst-case scenario we've feared. The winds are already coming ashore. The storm will cross the Cape.

"We've been wondering whether the hurricane would deteriorate before crossing the Cape, or whether the eye would hold," Eric continued. "Unfortunately, we are seeing some real low pressures, and the eye wall is rebuilding. We are now expecting the eye to cross the Cape between Yarmouth and Harwich, probably right through Dennis, right around noon tomorrow. And, yes, this will be at high tide. I sure hope folks have evacuated."

The mood around the bar was somber as everyone took this in, remembering trips to the Cape, all their times on the Seacoast, all of their favorite places.

"And, sorry to say this," said Eric, "but you've probably guessed and as you can see from the map here: the hurricane is expected to track directly between Martha's Vineyard and Nantucket. The winds are picking up there already, and we are expecting a lot of destruction on the islands. But you folks over there, you've been through this before. Be sure to get to the shelters as soon as possible and settle in. And the emergency folks there on the Islands want to remind you that, yes, you can bring your pets; there will be facilities for pets."

"After crossing the Cape, Mitch will probably deteriorate into an extratropical storm. But that's not necessarily good news; it means the storm will spread out, with extensive winds and rain bands, sending tides and winds into Boston Harbor. Effects will be felt here in our region—New Hampshire and the Southern Coast of Maine— beginning mid-morning Wednesday. In fact, some of the outer bands are already being felt. Waves are picking up in Hampton Beach."

The screen switched to a shot of surfers at Hampton Beach. Everyone could see the wild, angry waves building up.

"God, I sure hope those guys are getting ready to get out," said someone.

"We are expecting the storm to push the sea level higher," Eric continued, "in conjunction with our expected high tide at Hampton Harbor at 10:05 PM — the highest of the tides today. But tomorrow morning will be even higher. We can expect extreme flooding from the bay. Tonight, after 10:00 PM, the storm will still be raising swells from an already rising sea level. So, I sure hope that everyone has evacuated."

At the end of Eric's report, Barney turned back to the Climate Channel. Richard and Maya were holding down the desk as cameras panned the outer banks of North Carolina, lined with all those enormous houses on the barrier beaches, which were now boarded up and deserted. Despite the dangers, people kept rebuilding them after every storm. They were saved again this time by the fact that the storm was tracking parallel to the coast but still offshore.

Of course, a few intrepid weather reporters were walking the beaches in front of their camera operators or hanging out on a pier in front of a "safe" concrete-reinforced hotel. The cameras cut to Virginia Beach, already inundated, as it often was. The Navy had not managed to convince Congress to fund relocation of the Newport News Naval Station until ten years before, and the contracting process took so long that they had barely gotten started.

Now the climate analysts were going back over the speed of the hurricane, the cone of predictions.

"It's a worst-case scenario, folks," said Maya. "The jet stream has taken a southward dip around a high that's stationed over the Great Lakes. Now it's keeping the hurricane offshore, which is the good news: it won't actually make landfall tonight or tomorrow in Maryland, Delaware, New Jersey, or, with luck, Long Island."

"But the bad news," Richard continued, "is that Mitch is tracking the warm waters of the Gulf Stream, increasing in breadth. Soon we expect it to be over 500 miles across. And as it gains in width, those ferocious northeast winds on the north side of the storm will be pushing storm surge into every coast and harbor from New Jersey to

Maine."

"Oh my God," said Alex. "You know Boston has planned for a total flood, and so has New York. They've all planned as if they were going to get resources from outside the region. But what if the storm hits the whole coast? That's going to spread resources really thin."

Even as Alex said that the screen showed long lines of electrical repair trucks heading east from Ohio and Indiana.

"I can't believe that some of these areas are still relying on overhead wires," remarked Harrison. "Stupid, stupid."

Then Cody came in with Ethan

"At least folks on The Corridor will be in good shape with our microgrids," he said, a bit smugly, after watching the some of the coverage.

"Yeah, and New York," he continued, "they completely overhauled their utility commission; their whole coastal area is set up with microgrids that can island off the main grid and still function if the grid goes down. Too bad it took a devastating disaster like Sandy to make that happen, but I guess that's what it takes.

"They'll be OK after a few days, but Connecticut, Rhode Island? Small states, they never had the money or the political will."

"Hey, New Hampshire has never had the political will to spend the money either," said Spencer, who was always cynical after ten years spent in the New Hampshire legislature. "Those electrical utility monopolies kept fighting and fighting to keep their markets, save them from collapse."

"Yeah, at the expense of all the rest of us," added Alex.

"On the other hand," Cody interjected, "Maine started adding renewables at scale in the early 2020s, when they got a Democratic governor, and they never stopped."

"Well, we showed them that if we all get together regionally, we can beat them," Barney chimed in as he wiped down the bar.

So, it looked like Mitch was going to continue to track up the East Coast. Ethan had his tablet and kept up a running commentary of statistics.

"So, Hurricane Mitch is traveling at twenty-eight miles per hour. Center now is east of North Carolina, so about 800 miles… that's 28 hours till it gets to Boston. Of course, it might slow down after crossing Cape Cod…." Ethan did some more calculations. "Let's see, it's almost 7:00 PM Tuesday, so 28 hours out… twenty-four hours would be 7:00 PM Wednesday, plus 4 hours… that's like 11:00 PM on Thursday. On the other hand, Mitch could speed up."

"Now, about the speed," said Maya on TV, "look for the storm to speed up. All the Atlantic hurricanes that have tracked the East Coast have gained tremendous speed. The Hurricane of 1938 was moving at 40 miles per hour."

"Oh my god," said Cody, as a collective gasp went up. "That's… twenty hours to Boston? 2:00 PM tomorrow??"

"And high tide on Wednesday is going to be nine feet at 10:43 AM — nine feet," said Ethan, quickly consulting the charts, "and then again ten feet at 11:00 PM."

"OK," said Maya, "we're going to Massachusetts now, where they're getting ready for the storm." The camera cut to Governor Garcia of Massachusetts again, who introduced the Director of Emergency Management, Mordechai "Morty" Levinson with a direct message for people still on Cape Cod.

"Folks, if you can hear me, you've got to go to the nearest shelter on Cape Cod. If you trying to drive off the Cape and you are still on Route 6, you are not going to be able to get over the bridge. If you have passed Hyannis, please go to Sandwich High School. We have officers directing folks to the Barnstable High School or Cape Cod Community College. And for those of you who are still on the outer Cape, I implore you to go to the Dennis-Yarmouth Regional High School. I repeat: Please, head for the nearest shelter."

On the TV, reporters shouted out their questions to Levinson: "Sir, are the high schools prepared to receive these evacuees?"

"Yes, Frank, our legislature began preparing for an emergency like this fifteen years ago," said Governor Levinson. "We have strengthened the school buildings, and all of them have a safe area.

We have emergency supplies, and personnel setting up there now."

"How many refugees — I mean evacuees — do you anticipate?"

"We just don't know. In past events only 20 or 25% of people have evacuated. But we have not had a storm like this. We sincerely hope more people evacuate this time for their own safety."

"And what about the folks who don't have cars?"

"Yes, we have plans. I'm going to refer your question to Cape Emergency Manager, Colette Morgan. Colette?"

"Thank you, Morty. Yes, we do have emergency buses. We have brought them in from all over the state. You can go online to see the schedule, or you can use our CAPE-OUT Emergency App to schedule a pick-up. Or especially if you have someone who is disabled, call your local fire station. I repeat, call your local fire station in cases of disability, or if you have an emergency."

Indeed, the news had shown fleets of buses heading down to the Cape on Monday afternoon to evacuate people, and then all day Tuesday. But the Cape wasn't the only problem. There was also the threat to the towns on the South Shore.

"There are a million people on the coast under evacuation orders," piped up Ethan back at Barney's. "Let's see, if they were all in cars, that would be 250,000 cars," he said, looking at the traffic maps and doing the math. "Yup," he added, looking at the onscreen map, "traffic is already crawling up I-95 from the North Shore and heading west, inland, from the South Shore."

"That's why we have been encouraging people to take buses and trains, and to evacuate to the west, out of the range of the storm," Colette continued, seeming to directly answer Ethan. "In fact, as of 2:00 PM, *all* the lanes of the Mass Pike will be for westward travel only."

The Massachusetts Governor returned to the mic. "Thank you," said Governor Garcia, "and now we have the mayors of Worcester, Springfield, and Lowell."

One by one, the mayors stepped up to the podium to detail the plans they had made, the shelters that were available, and a hot-line number to call their region directly.

"Where are they all going to go, Ethan?" asked Cody.

"Well, I checked the hotel booking sites. Every hotel room in the whole region is already booked up. I don't know where they'll go. Maybe they can go to Vermont, or Albany?"

"Yup, folks with money can," said Barney from behind the bar. "They've already booked up every hotel room in the region outside of Boston, including most of the inns and hotels in the Lakes Region—which were probably full already with reservations from leaf peepers."

"Shelters?" continued Ethan. "Each shelter holds maybe 500 people. So, they'd need 2,000 shelters. Are there 2,000 emergency shelters in Massachusetts? There certainly aren't enough shelters."

Maya, on the Climate Channel was going over the expected path of the storm and it didn't look good.

"Let me remind you, this is still pretty close to the track of Hurricane Bob almost fifty years ago," she said as a graphic of Bob's track came up on the screen. "And, of course, we know that our sea level has risen more than three inches since Bob, and storms have intensified. So, we've got a higher sea level, coupled with storm surge, added to King Tides — and a storm moving at forty miles an hour. That's why we're calling this a worst-case scenario, folks."

"And just to review," Maya continued: "An estimated 2.5-3.7 million people fled prior to Rita's landfall, because it came just weeks after Katrina devastated New Orleans."

A list of major evacuations due to hurricanes flashed on the screen:

"September, 1999: The size of Hurricane Floyd, its intensity and its track prompted public officials to launch the largest evacuation in US history, with an estimated three million people fleeing the storm.

"September, 2004: Evacuation orders were issued for over 2.8 million residents in advance of Hurricane Frances, potentially the largest in Florida's history.

"August, 2008: At least 1.9 million people were evacuated from coastal Louisiana, including New Orleans, for Hurricane Gustav. In western Cuba, at least 300,000 people were evacuated.

"October, 2016: More than 2.5 million people were told to evacuate in Florida, Georgia, and South Carolina due to the approach of Hurricane Matthew, becoming the tenth most destructive in US history

"September, 2017: One week after Hurricane Harvey rampaged through coastal Texas and Louisiana, seven million people in Florida, Georgia, and South Carolina were told to evacuate due to Hurricane Irma. A low estimate of the actual number of evacuees is 700,000 people.

"2019: Hurricane Dorian strengthened again to a Category 4 as it approached the coast of Florida after nearly wiping out the Bahamas as a Category 5, and at King Tide. Florida, Georgia, South Carolina, North Carolina, and Virginia all declared a state of emergency. Coastal counties from Florida to North Carolina issued mandatory evacuation orders, even though the eye of the hurricane stayed 100 miles off the coast; it was extremely slow-moving, dumping more than eight inches of rain when it made landfall at Cape Hatteras.

"Kyle in 2020 and Faye in 2024 hit North and South Carolina. Then came Mindy and Terry back-to-back in 2026, almost a repeat of Harvey and Irma, dumping rain on coastal Texas and Louisiana. Again, millions of people were told to evacuate Florida, Georgia, and South Carolina."

The southern states, despite these repeated ravages — and despite the disastrous efforts to evacuate — seemed unable to come up with alternative plans or realities. It seemed they didn't want to spend any money to create more shelters, and they didn't want to spend money either statewide or regionally for buses to evacuate those without cars. They stuck to the ideology of "everyone on your own."

The next decade brought Teresa in 2030; Victor in 2031, a very late storm that nevertheless devastated South Carolina and North Carolina coasts; and Wanda in 2032, another very late storm. In 2034, José had threatened North and South Carolina, and then the

DelMarVa Peninsula. Then Margo, in 2035, had been a quick, fast-moving storm, looking like it was aiming directly for Miami and the Everglades. At the last minute, it veered north, sparing the region a direct hit, yet inundating it with rain and flooding. Luckily, most of the direct impact was at lower tides. Still, hundreds of thousands of people attempted to evacuate, and despite a new regional north-south rail line, drivers were stuck on the interstates for hours. If the hurricane had actually hit, it would have been a total disaster. Oscar in 2036 was followed by Ernesto in 2037, Henry in 2038, and then Fiona in 2039. Again, and again, people saw the lines of cars evacuating. It was hell if you stayed, hell if you left.

* * * *

Of course, people on the Cape knew they had to evacuate. And most did so as soon as the evacuation was announced, not wanting to get caught in the inevitable traffic jam. Martha's Vineyard and Nantucket, the islands off the Cape, were some of the oldest settlements on the East Coast. They had been dealing with hurricanes for hundreds of years. People on the Islands knew they would not be able to evacuate, and the Islands' emergency services had built up and stocked a robust system of shelters.

But this time, the hurricane threatened not only the Cape and South Coast, but downtown Boston itself. The goal was to avoid the horrendous scenes of mass evacuations seen in Houston as Hurricane Rita threatened in 2005, when Texas officials tried to evacuate 2.5 million people. The emergency authorities had set up evacuation routes, but hundreds of thousands of people were stranded on the highways leaving town. Officials had waited much too long to change traffic patterns to allow people to use both sides of the highway to evacuate.

Emergency planners knew that the scene leaving Boston had the potential to be just as chaotic. They had spent years on a plan to avoid that possibility. People from the inner metro would not be allowed to use I-95 North to evacuate; they would have to flee to the west, leaving the road open for those from the North Coast: Revere, Salem, Peabody. There would be hundreds of thousands of people just in those areas. But anyone who was still commuting by car in Boston knew that those routes west could be a disaster even on an ordinary day.

The problem in New Hampshire would be accommodating those thousands coming from Boston and the North Shore of Massachusetts, in addition to those evacuating the coast of New Hampshire. The airport at the former Pease Air Force Base would have to accommodate emergency supplies coming into the region in case the low-lying Boston airport shut down, which now seemed more than likely. But it was very likely that the Route 16 Bridge from Portsmouth to Dover — the major route over the Piscataqua River and its tidelands — would have to be shut down before the hurricane arrived. That would certainly disrupt things.

Despite promises and meetings, the light-rail DART had never been extended to Portsmouth, only thirteen miles from Dover. Instead, the powers that be had decided to revamp the COAST bus line, using electric buses and more frequent service — a situation Fiona found inadequate, as there were still no dedicated bus lanes. Down in Durham, the entire university campus could become an evacuee village, including the use of gyms, cafeterias, and dormitory public spaces — all on the microgrid that had been established in the 2020s.

Of course, Barney's Brewpub itself would be a refuge in the storm, well stocked with supplies and, of course, beer. Remembering the catastrophic floods that had come down the Cocheco River in recent years, Barney had relocated all the important grain storage, batteries, and electrical and control systems to the second floor when he built his own microgrid with solar panels on the roof.

The crew at Barney's continued to watch the storm coverage on the Climate Channel, and study maps and statistics on their laptops.

"You people are all looking at the storm surge maps," put in

Avery, "but you haven't been thinking about the rain."

"Yeah," said Spencer, the Dover City Councilman, "if the storm comes with a lot of rain upstream, like the one in 1938 or like Sandy, we're going to be looking at soggy, wet soils long before the hurricane even gets here. That was what did them in in 1938," he continued. "It had already been raining. The National Weather Service was so inept, they didn't even know about the hurricane almost until it hit. Then all the rain from the hurricane had nowhere to go but to run off into streams and rivers.

"It's a good thing we were actually thinking about emergency management when we were planning and building The Corridor," Spencer continued. "Remember how many of the old guard said, 'Why bother?'"

Just then, some of Barney's friends from Boston walked in, carrying duffle bags. Barney had forgotten all about them, even though they had texted hours earlier.

"Man, the traffic getting out of Boston," Harry said. "It took us four hours!"

Everyone crowded around them.

"How many people are leaving?"

"Are they driving?

"Are the Freeway Flyers running up I-93?" The auto-piloted electric bus-trams on route I-93 had finally been started ten years before, after the gridlock in Boston. Thankfully, they were running now, along with the trains to Nashua, Manchester, and on to Concord.

"Well, there were four of us, and Randy here has an e-van, so we picked up a few more friends and drove. Driving may have been a mistake. By the time we got going, it was 4:00. The traffic was horrendous."

"If we'd been on a bus or a Freeway Flyer, we would have been in the bus lanes. At least those were moving," said Phil.

"But to get a Freeway Flyer, we would have had to go to one of the bus stations — and people were waiting in line for hours there," added Owen.

"Yeah, and in theory we could have called Uber or Lyft, but we couldn't get through on the app. I guess there just aren't enough of them."

"But once we were out of town," Harry continued, "there was no way to switch. Most of the old park-and-rides are gone, and the ones that are left were all full to overcrowded. People were parked a mile away."

"You would have thought that eighteen years after the great gridlock, this would be easier," said Fiona, shaking her head.

Now that it was dark, there were no new images of the storm on the Climate Channel, only reruns from earlier in the day. The crew at the Climate Channel began discussing how many people had already lost power from the storm. They reviewed the history of power outages in previous storms — almost unbelievable, but what were the alternatives in the early 21st century?

"Didn't anyone think about this before?" asked Ethan. "I can't believe no one thought about any of this."

"Yeah," said Avery. "What kind of business advertises its services with images of lines of service repair trucks lined up to fix things when they inevitably fail?"

"Well," said Ahmed. They could all tell he was getting ready to launch into one of his monologues to explain something no one else understood. "Hurricane Sandy, in 2012, was the wake-up call for New York. Nine subway tunnels flooded; their equipment fried. Pumps had to be deployed to pump out millions of gallons of seawater. Miles of electrical lines had to be replaced," he continued. He was really getting going now. "Hospitals in lower Manhattan still had their electrical utilities in the basement, and of course they all flooded. The hospitals had to be evacuated, with the public watching TV shots of nurses and orderlies pushing patients on stretchers through the streets. Tens of thousands of residents of public housing projects were stranded in buildings with no electricity. People in outlying areas who lost electricity in their homes found that they could not get gas to go to the grocery store or run their generators because the gas stations did not have electricity.

"After Sandy," Ahmed continued, "New York woke up and realized that their energy policies actually discouraged long-term thinking. All electricity was generated in central generating stations, like nuclear and coal-fired plants, and distributed via high-voltage transmission lines, then stepped down to above-ground power lines— ubiquitous power lines; power lines that were highly prone to failure in every storm. Tens of thousands of people in New York were without power for days after Sandy, some for weeks as the entire grid went down. Every part connected to every other.

"And it wasn't just households out of power, people couldn't fuel up their cars or generators because gas stations were without power as well.

"Despite the 21st century 'innovation economy,' there was no real innovation in how electricity was supplied," said Ahmed.

"Why? Because the entrenched interests — utilities, their stockholders and suppliers, and the utility workers — had too much invested, they made too much money off the system as it was, and they had too much money to spend on lobbyists. Only in the brief period after Sandy did New York muster the political will to change and provide incentives to move towards reconfiguring the power system into small, independent power grids that could be cut off from the main grid and keep individual neighborhoods up and running despite the storms.

"Despite efforts, not much changed for most people. In the winter of 2018, a Nor'easter wiped out power for more than two million people on the East Coast. A power plant exploded in 2018, and then a transformer fire caused a power outage in NYC in the summer of 2019. Then, at Halloween in 2019, a completely unremarkable storm cut power to 800,000 people.

"And even airports were susceptible. In 2017 there was an eleven-hour power outage at the Atlanta airport that stopped all air traffic, and that is huge hub airport.

"And people just normalized all of this. 'That's just the way it is.

This is our power system. We must strengthen the grid.' They kept saying it over and over, while doing next to nothing. Altogether, it's totally amazing how many excuses cities and states accepted from power companies.

"New York tried to address these issues with an overhaul of the entire utility regulatory system. All well and good, but of course the utilities fought back, big time. They had a lot of profits to protect. Big changes were slow to come.

"That's why I got into microgrids. At first it was just small, incremental, experimental systems: hospitals, emergency services. New York and New Jersey realized the need for backup power at gas stations. The more microgrids that were completed, the faster the technology evolved; by 2020, there were engineering firms with expertise in configuring the grids, and there were many companies offering the specialized technology and software. Everything was set... except. The Sandy debacle sparked a lot of discussion about resilience, but like a storm channeled on a path out to sea by an upper-level high, the upper level of resistance of Republican conservatives and fossil-fuel interests meant that the whole discussion was channeled out into oblivion. Planning and action were left to states and municipalities."

That was one thing that had sparked the creation of New New England: the realization that the cavalry was not coming to save anyone. That and the transportation problems and the housing problems. It was all connected. Barney and friends realized that even if they could not win the overall war nationally, they could win locally.

"California finally came to its senses after PG&E power lines caused so many fires in 2017-2019. When called on to pay for damages, they instead instituted rolling blackouts meant to prevent fires. It was a shit show, I mean really," added Cody.

Harrison, who had been an IBEW union lineman in the old days, picked up the story: "Oh yeah, I remember the outages in the past; every damn time a storm went through, we would get trees down on the power lines. We'd have to go out there and clear the trees, reconnect the power lines. And then there were always people at the ends of the lines. Like the person in the house across the street could have a line that came from behind them; they would have power, and yours would still be off. People were without power for days. 'That's life,' the power companies said, as they continued to send dividends to stockholders and get a fat guaranteed interest rate on their investments in coal plants."

Spencer, who had been in the legislature through some of the teens and twenties, got into the political side. "After Sandy, New York was fed up. Finally, enough political will was channeled after the outages in '18 and '19 and that mess; that's why their plan to reconfigure the policy incentives was finally passed. The plan was started just after Sandy, but the utilities never gave up fighting it. They continued to put up obstructions."

28 | LATE NIGHT AT BARNEY'S

Tuesday, September 18, 10:00 PM:
Hurricane Mitch is moving off, picking up speed.
Rain and wind are beginning to hit the Cape.

When Kisala and Jazz got back to Dover, and walked into Barney's Tuesday night, everyone around the bar was still glued to the Climate Channel. Now that it was dark, the images were of the storm hitting the coast of Florida earlier. The aptly named Noah Brinkman was standing in waves almost up to his hips on the front terrace of a hotel in Daytona Beach, a thirty-five-mile-an-hour wind blowing his stylishly tousled hair.

Maya and Richard were at the desk in the studio, and Maya was saying, "Mitch did not make landfall in Florida, but it did make that slight turn to the northeast we were talking about."

"Right, Maya," Richard chimed in, "but Florida did not get off scot-free. Those northeast winds raked the coast, especially where they hit at high tide. Now that the storm has mostly passed by Florida, we're beginning to see those offshore winds coming from the west, on the bottom of the storm, and it's still raining. That's giving a little relief to those on the coast, but it's wreaking havoc on Florida's bays and canals."

Maya continued, following the map on the screen, "We saw those winds pick up in Georgia and South Carolina," Maya continued, following the map on the screen. "You know, we mostly worry about where the hurricane is going to make landfall, but we've seen storms over the last dozen years that have brought heavy rainfall even when they never made landfall."

"Remember how Florence, back in 2018, dropped thirty-five inches of rain in North Carolina?" asked Richard.

"Yup," said Maya, "that was just the first of the big-rain-event storms."

"You know," said Spencer, sitting at the bar, "I remember seeing images of those big evacuations twenty or thirty years ago, with the big houses on the coast getting blown down. Remember, Barney, when we said they'd surely have enough sense to abandon those spots?"

"Oh yeah," said Avery. "Just like I used to say that all those big mansions in Rye would soon be cut up into condos. Hasn't happened. All those wealthy people just keep rebuilding and rebuilding, and somehow persuading the government to rebuild the roads and bridges too." And they all shook their heads.

Barney turned his attention to Kisala and Jazz now warming up at the bar with Hot Toddies.

"We just came from Rye," said Jazz. "Not much happening at all there. Looks like almost everyone has left. Just a few lights on."

"Dan is staying, though," reported Kisala. "I made him promise to text me with updates."

"But crossing over I-95, it looked like a lot of traffic," said Jazz. "Whole lotta traffic for Tuesday night at 10 PM. Wonder if the hotels are filling up. Radio said they're evacuating the whole coast."

"Yeah," said Avery, "for the eighth time tonight, they ran that corny simulation of a twelve-foot storm surge overcoming a one-story house, trying to scare people into really leaving. But no matter how many times they run it, some people are just gonna stay in those houses. I don't know why. Guess they think it's fake news."

"And then," added Spencer, "they're gonna call 911 from their attic in the middle of the storm and expect someone to come rescue them."

"Yup," agreed Avery. "They've gone ahead and built new housing above the flood lines, but they just have not had the guts to tell everyone they have to abandon their property. And so, on it goes."

"Why the hell don't they get out when they have a chance?" asked Meighan, a younger EMT. She had been on her share of these call but was still not as jaded as the older guys. "The county has been running bus routes down there for two days."

"People are still stubborn," Avery responded. "If I've heard it once, I have heard it a hundred times: 'Mom wouldn't leave, so I decided to stay with her.' Or 'I was afraid looters would get in.' These are always the people who have nothing to loot anyway."

Back on the TV, Richard was saying, "The Virginia Beach and Newport News areas have been hit especially hard," while the screen filled with images of cars lined up on the interstates, trying to evacuate.

Really, they were all waiting for the 11:00 PM New England forecast to tell them what was predicted to happen to Rhode Island and Cape Cod and the Mass coast.

Everyone at Barney's knew that the storm itself wouldn't hit New England until morning at the earliest, but they couldn't tear themselves away from the TV — disaster porn.

Ethan was watching the forecast on his laptop before Eric came on TV with it. The storm was offshore, but the center was passing off New York Harbor and the southern tip of Long Island, traveling now at 30 miles an hour.

"Let's see," said Ethan, "Virginia Beach to Rye Beach, 530 miles, as the crow flies, 18 hours."

"Eighteen hours folks," said Eric.

"Eighteen hours, that's 4 PM tomorrow night."

"Check the tides, Ethan," said Barney.

"OK, let's see, high tides Wednesday, 11:01 PM at 10 feet, and then Thursday at 5:38 AM at -0.86 feet."

Now the crew at Barney's was torn between being voyeurs of the disaster unfolding farther south and preparing for whatever was going to happen close to home.

"Shouldn't be too bad on the Tuesday night tides," said Cody, looking over Ethan's shoulder. The storm was still pretty far away, but the higher tides were coming in just as the storm moved north along the coast.

Wednesday at 11:30 AM would be high tide in Chatham, on the "elbow of the cape," just as the storm was moving in. But, worse yet, just before midnight on Wednesday would be one of the highest tides of the year.

Kisala was getting interested; she had the tide tables open on her own laptop just as Eric on the TV was pointing out the same thing: Wednesday at 7:24 AM would be high tide at Woods Hole, on the Cape. "There are so many small beach houses on the bays there," she said. "Not sure how they've survived this long. Boy oh boy, I sure hope people have evacuated."

"And the people in Sandwich and Scituate always get knocked out; they'll be getting hammered big time," Cody said.

"But suppose the storm goes right over the Cape?" asked Avery.

Now they were all silently begging Eric, Maya, and Richard to predict: Would it or wouldn't it? If Mitch did make landfall, all the towns on the Cape would be devastated — but it would probably cause the storm itself to dissipate, possibly sparing areas farther north.

If Mitch veered to the east, sparing the Cape, it would maintain its strength, probably bringing stronger winds and higher tides to the North Shore of Massachusetts and the New Hampshire beaches. Either way, a disaster unfolding.

"Looks like Cape Cod will take a direct hit," said Maya solemnly. They cut to Cheryl out on the Chatham bluff overlooking the harbor, who was almost too stunned to say anything; she was virtually writing an obituary on the spot, speaking to the tune of a funeral dirge.

"I'm getting ready to leave as we speak, Maya," said Cheryl "The wind is picking up, we're starting to get the thirty and forty mile an hour gusts, and it's just starting to rain. We're heading back to Hyannis."

"Ok, folks, Mitch is expected to make a direct hit, landfall on Cape Cod, between Harwich and Barnstable, at roughly noon on Wednesday," said Maya solemnly. "And, yes, that's just about at high tide. No one on the Cape will be spared."

As soon as Maya delivered the news, Barney's emergency landline phone rang. Chip answered it.

"Yup," said Chip. "Yes, we know, and we're about as ready as we can be here. Yes, we are doing a survey of emergency beds. Yeah, ok, I sent you a list earlier today. Yes, we're updating it. We have fewer than 1,000 shelter spaces.

"Yes, I know Rockingham County will be trying to accommodate their own folks from Hampton Beach. Yes, I know. We're expecting folks from Portsmouth. Of course, there's the UNH campus; you've checked with them, right? Their dorms are full, but they do have cafeterias, classrooms, gyms. OK, check in with you later. I'm going to stay over here at Barney's to coordinate. Barney isn't up at his farm, but there will be some room there, and the farm will be a gathering place for collecting food and supplies from that area up in Maine. Now, yes, the food, all food will have to come in from the west, of course. Of course."

Chip hung up, then turned to address the crowd. "OK, folks," he said, "that was the county. The storm will take about two hours to get to the Boston Harbor after crossing over the Cape."

Barney switched to the local channel, now featuring Eric explaining what to expect: "But again, it's not the hurricane eye we're worried about. There probably won't be an eye by the time it gets to our Seacoast. We expect it to break up into an extratropical storm. But that's not the problem, folks; the problem will be the sustained winds and rain, pushing all that water from the ocean up into the bays. Tremendous storm surge. And coming at high tides. Stay tuned, folks."

"Wow," everyone murmured. It seemed inconceivable. Especially inconceivable was that the storm would not actually make landfall till the next day — yet, sitting there, there was really nothing they could do.

Were they all going to stay up? There really wasn't much to see; it was too dark. And the highest of the tides wasn't expected until the next day.

And even Dover had some low-lying places. It now seemed more than likely that the Cocheco River winding through town would flood. And the lowest areas were along Highway 16, the Spaulding Turnpike, the most direct route to and from Portsmouth.

Central Portsmouth itself was probably safe; the main parts of town, the oldest, were on something of a hill, but there were many low-lying areas that would certainly flood. And who knew how much damage the winds would do?

"I wonder if people are staying in their homes in New Castle?" asked Spencer. New Castle was on an island off Portsmouth; one of the wealthiest enclaves on the coast, it was connected to the mainland by causeways. Parts of New Castle itself were high enough, but there were many houses facing the coast, and the island would be entirely cut off when the causeways flooded. And for how long? How soon before the causeways could be repaired? They certainly would not be high priorities. Of course, everyone there probably had a generator, and enough money to stock up.

But if there was one place Jazz wouldn't want to be, it was the old Grand Hotel that she and Kisala had seen over the bay from the end of Rye Beach, an enormous four story tall Victorian wood-frame pile, one of the few grand hotels left from the tourist boom of the 1890s. She could just imagine how that would shiver and shake, maybe tearing itself apart in the face of the hurricane.

29 | WAITING

Tuesday, September 18, 11:00 PM:
Hurricane Mitch off NY harbor and South Long Island;
rain and wind are already raking Martha's Vineyard and Nantucket
and are beginning to gain strength over the Cape

Now there was nothing to do but wait. Some of the younger folks wanted to hear, again, how Chip, Katrina, Barney, and the rest of the Rump Caucus had actually gotten the DART and The Corridor built.

"Tell us the story again, Uncle Chip," some of Barney's crew asked.

"You know," Chip said," in the beginning, Katrina and Barney and I thought that everyone would want to get out of their cars and live in a more convenient environment like The Corridor. And it's true that more and more people are moving to the more urban parts of the state."

"How did you get them to build the DART and The Corridor?" asked Ashley.

"Well, I started to tell you," said Chip. "Really, it all started long before the Great Gridlock in Boston. I mean, anyone with half a brain could see it was coming. The leading lights in Boston had been talking about the problems in transportation for a decade. The freeways and roads were getting more crowded, the Big Dig was in the rear-view mirror.

"Here in New Hampshire, we had Amtrak. They had maintained a minimal Amtrak rail. And the county maintained a really deficient bus system, COAST. Conventional wisdom said we couldn't afford bus service. Meanwhile, year after year they seemed to come up with millions to work on roads. And on the interstates. Then housing became unaffordable, and then just plain unavailable, and workers couldn't afford to live in Portsmouth, and couldn't get to their jobs unless they had a car. And then students at UNH in Durham were having trouble finding housing. They were all living in these spread out housing complexes, and they had to have cars, too. So, then we had 30% of developed land devoted to parking lots."

"And anyway," added Barney, "we knew it was going to get more and more crowded, and that the university was inevitably going to have to build more dorms and apartments, and Dover was going to be building housing for workers from Portsmouth. We knew that light rail was a solution. We watched as politicians talked and began to throw around ideas for a Green New Deal. But we knew that we couldn't just sit around and wait. Whether they ever solved problems in Boston or anywhere else, we figured we would solve our own problems.

"Katrina, always the planner, always the visionary, put together the idea for the Rump Caucus, really kind of a stealth, behind the scenes planning board and then guided us through developing a strategic plan. We recruited the transportation lab, and architects and planners from MIT to use it as a project. We could see the state and the Feds were not going to come in and make a plan. So, meeting every week, we had a plan all ready to go by the time the Great Gridlock finally loosened up some money."

"Wait, they probably don't even know what the Big Dig was all about," said Harrison.

So, Chip continued: "I know it's hard to fathom now, but they thought that digging those enormous tunnels under Boston to bury the freeways would solve their transportation problems. It was kind of, at least almost, the last gasp of the automobile era. And of course, since cars still burned gasoline, they had a huge ventilation problem on their hands, too.

"But no matter how many lanes they added, more people drove more cars. Obviously they needed to improve the T, the trains, the buses, but it would all cost big money. Spend state funds? Raise gas taxes? Go ahead with bonding? They talked and they talked. And they talked some more. In hindsight, they should have gone ahead with all three. But by the time they got started, even that would have been too little too late. The politicians could not see the public transportation riders as their constituents, the state legislators on the hill in Boston did not know anyone who took the bus. They did not see the point that every person who rode public transportation decreased the traffic. They saw it as subsidizing transit riders. People had been begging for a train from Boston to Nashua, and to Manchester. But the Republican governor at the time asked why we should pay for transportation for 'them'? I don't know who he thought 'they' were. Every person who took the train would have made for less traffic on I-93, the main north-south route between New Hampshire and Boston. By 2020, even the buses were getting held up in the traffic, and still they dithered."

"Oh, yeah," chimed in Cody, Jazz, and Kisala, who had all been in college at the time.

"By that point, rush hour lasted all day. In fact, The Great Gridlock happened at 10 AM on a sunny day. Just one accident started it and led to a series of accidents. Pretty soon traffic was backed up in all the tunnels."

"Yet, when it was all untangled, instead of going all in on efforts to enable biking and walking, and more mass transit, the first step was to declare that automobiles would all have to go all electric. That helped with the pollution, but not the congestion. But even with that, they had to implement congestion pricing in Boston, a charge for every car that drove into town."

"Yeah, but they ignored the fact that that wouldn't work unless they had alternatives," chimed in Fiona who had just walked in. "Even though Lyft and Uber were the first to adopt driverless electric vehicles, it still wasn't enough to calm traffic in the city."

"They finally had to ban Lyft and Uber and all individual transport in the city, and to the airport. No special treatment. Except for disabled people. And seniors."

"But wait," said Liam interrupting, "I'm confused, what does all this happening in Boston have to do with the Rump Caucus and all of your strategic plans?"

"Like we were saying, we could see all of this going down, we could see a kind of disaster on the horizon, and we wanted a solution up here, for ourselves. But we knew that transportation was the key, and that as far as transportation goes, we were just a link in the wider area whose hub is Boston, and that it would be hard to shake any money loose until Boston was hurting.

"It wasn't until the Great Gridlock that the New New England compact finally decided to fund widespread efforts, everywhere in the region."

"Yah, like, they thought that no one wanted to ride buses, that they needed something faster," said Fiona. "Until the folks at the MIT Transport lab pointed to the analysis. Buses carried the most people, in the least space. They were the fastest. So, you know the rest. After the Great Gridlock, they finally listened to our experts in the Transit Lab, made buses free, and ran them on a closer schedule and in dedicated bus lanes, and instigated congestion tolling for cars coming into the city."

"And then, instead of light rail on I-93," said Magdalena, "Fiona and her team devised a sexier, lighter, smaller electric tram service, the Freeway Flyers. The LaMAs were supposed to be just last mile service, but more and more people tried to take them on longer trips."

But the transportation issue was just one part of the equation. Power generation and housing were all related. Fortuitously, UNH was already leaning into renewable energy, and already planning the first microgrid in the area. The Oyster River Clean Innovation

Project, announced in 2019 by UNH, the major utility, and the town of Durham, used solar and battery technology for distributed energy, with the capability for islanding and continuing to provide power for both the town and the campus in case of emergencies.

While announced with great fanfare, the project did not include major innovations. The only innovative thing was that it was finally happening in New Hampshire — and with the major utility, a company that had previously been all in on major transmission lines from Canada.

Was the major utility company finally seeing the sunlight? Hopefully. Of course, there were already microgrid innovation labs at any number of universities, including Dartmouth and MIT. So UNH was not the first, but certainly did not want to get left behind.

Once the University committed to the microgrid, Durham and UNH began working on the transportation and housing issues. And following their collaborative moves, they began trying to establish The Corridor.

Timing wise, they were lucky that this happened just as Boston hit gridlock, and the entire New New England compact turned to mass transportation, energy, and housing as triple focuses, each one dependent on the others. Both transportation and buildings were major contributors to energy use. If housing continued to be spread out in far flung suburban subdivisions, the transportation problems would never be solved. And of course, if cars, trains, buses, and trucks transformed to EVs, and houses went all-electric, then electricity production and distribution would be a major focus by itself. New New England resolved that there was enough suburban single-family housing, but too little housing for middle- and low-income residents that was close to mass transportation. Builders continued to say that the suburban housing was "what consumers wanted." But the truth was that often that was all that was available.

With the New New England commitment and new focus, the entire region saw more housing units, like the ones that Kisala had worked on: affordable apartments and townhouses near mass transit, with very low or no utility costs.

The focus of the crowd turned back to Maya on the Climate Channel, who was now talking about power outages. Waiting for the storm, not knowing what could happen next, she scrolled through a list of power-disruption disasters.

Ethan was paying close attention, and began reading off the screen:

2018

March 2: A major Nor'easter left over two million people without power on the East Coast.

April 18: all of Puerto Rico lost power when they were trying to repair damage from Hurricane Maria in 2017. And right before that, 870,000 customers lost power when a tree fell on a major power line.

October 10: Thousands of households in Florida lost power for ten days when Hurricane Michael hit the Gulf Coast.

2019

June 9: A severe thunderstorm downed hundreds of trees, leaving 350,000 people without power in Dallas County, Texas.

July 19: Storms and high winds caused loss of power for 600,000 to 800,000 customers in Michigan for up to six days.

July 19 - 20: Severe thunderstorms, tornadoes, and floods

caused power outages, leaving 277,000 customers without power, some for more than a week.

July 22: In New Jersey, 300,000 people were without power

Nov. 1: A major storm left nearly two million people without power throughout New England and Quebec.

"Why did anyone put up with all these outages, Dad?" asked Ethan.

"Because they were told that there were no good alternatives," answered Katrina, who had just walked in as Ethan began reading about the power outages.

"Really, renewable energy sources were competitive long before that," she continued, "but the US continued to subsidize fossil fuel companies, and the utility industry had so much invested in their power plants and their transmission lines."

"And in their lobbyists," added Barney. "It was an almost impossible lobby to break."

"Yeah, but all that was just prelude," Katrina continued. "It was nothing compared to what PG&E did to screw the state of California. In November of 2018, wires that PG&E hadn't maintained started the Camp Fire, which destroyed the town of Paradise in Northern California, killing ninety-five people and displacing hundreds more."

"A truly ironic name," chimed in Chip under his breath.

"Indeed." Katrina agreed. "And, after they finally accepted blame, PG&E decided the solution for the next fire season was to just shut off the power when weather conditions seemed threatening. Never mind the folks who depended on power to operate life-saving equipment, like home oxygen generators. The first time they did this, PG&E hardly gave any notice at all. Everyone in California was up in arms, but what could they do? PG&E had a total monopoly on half the state, and they controlled the legislature. They brooked no competition.

"Eventually, like after a few years," Katrina continued, "and several investigations and court cases, PG&E was found liable for the damage from the Camp Fire and a few others. So, of course, they declared bankruptcy, and the whole fiasco wound through the courts until an ordinary person couldn't possibly keep track of the action. Then, just when it looked like the Governor might finally wrest control and set up a public utility, lo and behold, PG&E rose like a phoenix from the ashes again as a public, investor-owned company."

"Yeah, I always thought that was weird," said Barney. "The way I remember it, they said the total cost to repair the electrical grid in California, and to maybe underground everything, was so high that only a publicly funded company could afford it. Is that right, Katrina?"

"That's what they said, Barney," answered Katrina. She found the whole memory was so disquieting that she asked for a White Russian from the bar even though she rarely drank anything but beer.

"By this time, the technology for microgrids was well developed and proven," said Ahmed, jumping into the discussion. "The only thing holding them back was the stubborn insistence of PG&E. They always feared they would lose market control if people could generate their own power. But finally, finally, finally, in 2021, opposition forced them to begin to build local microgrids so that people would have uninterruptible power. And that was huge. Because, once California began building microgrids…. Well, California is the ninth largest economy in the world. The equipment and controls then came down in price and began to be standardized off the shelf."

Cody had thought a lot about power lines. "I've been hearing this debate my whole life," he said, "ever since the two-week power outage at the lake when I was still a kid; I was twelve or thirteen and just beginning to think about power distribution systems. How could it be that everyone had so many electronic devices, that people said the US was an innovation economy, and yet the whole country was still dependent on wire lines on poles to bring electricity to houses?

And all the lines in a town — in the whole area — could be downed by trees in a gust of wind? And it could take a week to get the whole system up and running again? It just seemed crazy.

"When I was working for Mom and Dad," Cody continued, "I thought that solar collectors on everyone's roof would solve the problem. It took me a while to figure out that, even with solar panels, most houses were still connected to the electrical grid. The grid functioned as their backup, and with a system called net-metering, the power company paid the homeowner for the extra power generated by the system. If the homeowners hadn't invested in a battery backup system, they had no power when the grid was down.

"I was so lucky that when I got to college, Ahmed was already there with his microgrid lab. I mean, a lot of the kids in the Electrical Engineering Department were there for computer engineering."

"Yeah," said Ahmed, "by the time you got there, the university had already gone to all renewables. We made ourselves a center of microgrid research by working in conjunction with the power company."

"I was really lucky I got to spend all of college in Ahmed's lab."

On the TV screen, the litany of power outages was continuing in the background behind the climate desk. Ethan continued reading:

"2021: February 14–15 and 17–18, giant winter storms caused over five million inhabitants to lose power across the United States. 4.3 million people in Texas lost power."

"Oh my god, yes," shouted Ahmed, jumping up and beating on the table. "Remember that? Texas was so stubborn they'd disconnected their grid from everyone else, and their whole grid—controlled by a corrupt state agency called ERCOT—went down totally. They tried to blame it on wind generators, when the real problem was that controls on the gas wells froze because no one ever required them to invest in freeze-proofing. Gas prices went through the roof. It was an absolute disaster, but the Republicans in Texas kind of brushed it off and then arranged for the gas companies to be paid off by the same ratepayers who had lost power for a week. What a fiasco."

"Yeah," added Chip, "it took a few years, but eventually the voters turned on the Republicans and threw them all out. Now Texas is connected to the grid again, and generating more wind power than it even needs."

The discussion of power outages of the past was interrupted by Ethan, who had already gotten bored and found online a map of current power outages due to Mitch.

"Check out this map!" Ethan interjected, expanding the map on his tablet.

"Let's show it to everyone," said Barney and in a minute, they'd put the map up on the large-screen TV, leaving behind more scenes of tides and destruction on the Climate Channel.

On the map, Ethan zoomed in on metro NYC. The areas that still had electricity stood out as lit-up dots and grids, on the black background of areas where the power was out, with faint grey lines tracing the transmission lines. The dots and grids appeared all over the Metro New York area — except when you got to New Jersey.

The lit-up dots were microgrids, where power storage had been installed. Sometimes the microgrids were at the electric substations themselves, those fenced-in conglomerations of equipment and wires where the electricity from the high-voltage lines was stepped down to the current needed by the neighborhood. When utilities had installed batteries at substations in the 2020s, they'd also installed sophisticated switching devices that could de-couple from the main grid and power the neighborhood by itself. The switching also allowed the neighborhood to share in any solar electricity generated by neighborhood arrays.

Sometimes the center of the microgrid and power storage was at a local hospital, nursing home, senior home, fire station, or school. For more than fifteen years, New York had been building all new schools, libraries, and public facilities with power storage and microgrid technologies. Then the surrounding neighborhood could be hooked in as well. Everyone at Barney's could see these grids and lit-up dots on the map now.

In contrast, New Jersey, still under the control of the utility interests and their lobbyists, had been slow to undertake any kind of reform. In 2028, the state had finally mandated the addition of backup power storage in hospital remodels, in new senior facilities, and in emergency facilities. These appeared as tiny, isolated dots on the map. But that was about all. Folks in New Jersey still thought that backup natural-gas generators at gas stations was the way to go. Eastern Pennsylvania had made more headway under Governor Fetterman in the early 2020s, followed by his successors. Some individual entities had adopted microgrids for their own facilities. You could see them on the map as Ethan scrolled out, then zoomed in to New Jersey and the Philadelphia area. There were lighted dots at a couple of universities, a few hospitals — all surrounded by blackness, with light grey lines tracing the power lines that were out.

"People forget the really major power outages," said Cody. "It's truly amazing how long people and politicians put up with these outrageous outages. Why? Because utility interests paid lobbyists to represent their interests in PUC hearings and in the legislature."

"Like I said," Ahmed interjected, "the deadlock was only broken in New York after Hurricane Sandy blew up substations in Manhattan, near the Financial District. Then it was suddenly clear how much the destruction was costing the Manhattan economy. Do you think these changes would have happened if it was only those folks on Staten Island? Or Far Rockaway? Or in the projects? Of course not.

"A lot of people thought we could just add solar and wind power," Ahmed went on. "But not so simple. Power companies built the big wind projects in the pass east of Los Angeles, starting in the 1980s, sixty years ago, hundreds of wind generators. But they're just another centralized power-production site that needs to be supported by the larger grid. Same for the large commercial solar-electricity arrays. Smart people with big money to invest thought that was the way to go. Utilities liked these arrays because they got a fixed rate of return;

that means whatever they spent, they got a guaranteed 9% return, courtesy of you and me. The utility commissions, the PUCs, through their rate-setting authority, just asked the utility companies how much they had to spend for that new power plant, and then virtually cut a check from you and me."

"What a scam!" Cody was revving up for a rant. And why not; he had a captive audience, and the Climate Channel visuals were repeating on an endless loop now that it was too dark for more live video. "Economists call it rent seeking," he fumed, "though it has nothing to do with actually renting anything. It means getting a government body to grant you a monopoly right — a franchise — to collect payments, called rents, from everyone, everyone! And all for a service you can't do without."

"In the early 1900s," Chip jumped in to explain, "this rent seeking by utilities was a hugely corrupt enterprise. You can see how profitable it would be to just buy a legislature — actually, you only have to buy one-half-plus-one of the party in power to get yourself this monopoly — and, bingo, 8 or 9% rate of return — forever! And politicians sold it as a way for little old grandmothers to invest — an income investment that paid dividends. Everyone was happy, supposedly. Except for the ratepayers, who were left holding the bag for outdated coal plants, nuclear plants that cost ten times what was expected. And transmission lines that started fires."

Now Cody took a breath before he went on: "But the main point was that the systems weren't even reliable, and there was no requirement for the big utilities to install the controls needed to integrate independently produced renewable power.

"So, New York's restructuring after Sandy was huge, even though most people didn't really know about it at the time. They figured out a way to reward utilities for reductions in carbon emission. We mostly take this stuff for granted now, finally, but you have no idea what an uphill climb it was."

Of course, the older folks had heard this all, but the younger crowd listened intently.

Now Ahmed joined into the history lesson: "New York showed that the state had to make a regulatory commitment, because it was the state apparatus that controlled the utilities commission. That was true in New England, too. But New England shared the ISO — the outfit that controlled the grid for New England. That was the beginning of New New England, twenty years ago. Like I said, everyone realized the Federal cavalry wasn't riding in to save us. And New England states already had a compact to work on transportation issues. That had to happen as a region, too, because folks were commuting into Boston from New Hampshire and Rhode Island. And the trains that everyone wanted went from Massachusetts to Connecticut, and from Massachusetts to New Hampshire and Maine. Emergency preparations, roads, regional buses — it was all regional."

"So, anyway, looking at the map" — Cody gestured at the TV screen — "you can see where they were successful with microgrids, and where they haven't gotten on board."

There were pockets of dots and lines in and around New York City, Long Island, even Staten Island, and lonely stretches of blackness in New Jersey. And zooming out, since all New England states had signed on to new utility regulations, following the lead of New York, there were numerous lighted spots all over the region.

"I can't believe how much difference it made," said Cody.

Ahmed agreed. "Once the big utilities realized that it was in their financial interest to cooperate, it became a lot easier to move these microgrid projects forward. The university and the major utility started the first demonstration project more than twenty years ago.

"So, by the time the legislation was passed, we were ready to go," added Ahmed. "When Dover and Durham started to cooperate, the rest was easy — well, not easy, but just a matter of lining up the technology and the contracts," he added.

"Yeah," said Cody. "By the time we got going, the technology was advancing pretty quickly, too. We didn't really have to invent anything."

Cody remembered when he was a kid and his dad was in the

legislature, fighting for adoption of the housing, transportation, and energy innovations. Chip had been gone for hours at meetings and public hearings. Cody even remembered going to a lot of the meetings, sitting in the audience, listening to the seemingly endless pageant of consumers — citizens — going up to the microphone for their three minutes of public testimony. He remembered how the new focus built from the sum of collective testimony, until it became almost impossible for the councils to ignore.

30 | CODY

Tuesday, September 18, 11:45 PM:
Hurricane Mitch has slowed to fifteen miles
per hour and is off Long Island

Much as Cody loved these conversations, it was getting late, and he had Ethan with him. They made their exit and walked the few blocks to the station to catch the DART back to their neighborhood on The Corridor. No matter the time, there were always people on the DART, coming or going between Durham and Dover.

"So, Dad," asked Ethan, "how bad do *you* think the storm will be?"

"I don't know, Ethan; it looks like it could be the big one, but you probably know better than me. You're the one the one who has been looking at all the storm tracks and statistics; you thinking about becoming a meteorologist or something?" Cody looked at Ethan quizzically.

"Maybe," said Ethan. "It's funny that, with all of these statistics, they still can't really predict how bad the storm will be in New Hampshire."

"Yeah, they can predict a lot now, like the track of the storm, but they still don't really know how big it will blow up to — or, especially, where those rain bands will hit, or the winds. Gusts can't be predicted," he said, thinking. "And it's the gusts that take down the power lines."

Cody was impressed with Ethan's analytical thinking. He and Ethan were a lot alike. In the beginning, Cody and Alyssa had both agreed that they wanted a sustainable, renewable lifestyle. They were living at Everlee, where Chip and Katrina ran Solar NH, and Katrina, in addition, managed the extensive organic farm with a CSA. And Katrina continued her years-long commitment to helping finance and develop new sustainable business. This was definitely the sustainable, renewable life that Alyssa always wanted.

But Cody had never chosen this life. He just grew up with it. By the time The Connector was operational, and the first of the privately developed condo projects in The Corridor, Cody and Alyssa had realized that "sustainable" did not always mean the same thing to each of them. Alyssa was a back-to-the-earth woman; sustainable and renewable to her meant growing food, composting, living close to the land. Their younger son Jody was just like her — loved animals, loved running in the woods. But Cody had a much more cerebral picture of what renewable and sustainable meant. For him, it was a structural issue: living close to work, in multifamily housing, was inherently more energy-efficient. Whether he was working in a lab on campus, or in the office of the engineering company, or on one of his building projects, everything was just a few blocks away.

And Ethan took after Cody. Almost thirteen, he and Cody sometimes lived in the condo almost like two bachelors. He could be a truly independent kid. He could get to school, the library, the grocery store, and friends' houses by himself. He loved to have his dad come to his hockey games, but he could get to practice by himself.

After their five-minute trip on the DART, Ethan and Cody got off at Easton, their neighborhood square, marked by its own colorful purple-and-yellow designators to reduce confusion. It was already raining hard as they ran through the square and up Easton Street to their building

As Ethan and Cody walked in, some of their neighbors were still sitting around in one of the lounges that also served as part of the co-working space, and some sat in the pub area where someone was playing a guitar. Ethan and Cody joined the group in lounge chairs in front of the TV, watching the Climate Channel.

"Ethan, my man, what's the word?" asked their neighbor Greg. Ethan and his dad looked at each other.

"Everyone thinks this is going to be the big one. We've been watching Maya and Richard too," Ethan replied, nodding in the direction of the TV. "And I've been doing some calculations."

"Let's see," he recited from some charts on his tablet, "high tide in Montauk on Long Island is at 8:00 AM. Actually, the highest tide was earlier tonight at 7:47 PM. The storm slowed to twelve to fifteen miles per hour for six to seven hours; the eye will be close to Montauk at 5:00 to 6:00 AM, so the brunt of storm and surge will hit Montauk at nearly high tide. Storm surge comes up before high tide, and never goes down over the entire south shore of Long Island." No one was really following him.

"Fifty miles from Montauk to Cape Cod, gets to Cape Cod tomorrow at noon, traveling at twelve miles per hour, four hours, but it's widening; it's more than 250 miles across. So the leading edge of the rain and wind should arrive on the Cape in the morning."

"It looks like it's going hit Cape Cod tomorrow around noon," clarified Cody. "After that, it's going to hit the New Hampshire coast sometime in the afternoon. But you heard Eric say that waves were already picking up, right?"

"High tide at Hampton Beach is tomorrow morning at 10:45 AM," said Ethan. "It's going to be underwater. How bad it will be here depends on the rain bands and the winds."

"Well, we should go upstairs," said Cody, still looking worried. "There's not much more to see now, Ethan. It's dark, and they won't be able to really show us anything until morning. At least we don't have to worry about getting stuck in the elevators, or the electric locks not working. With our microgrid, the electricity will never go out."

WEDNESDAY

31 | KISALA AND JAZZ

Wednesday, September 19, 12:30 AM:
Hurricane Mitch is off the coast of Long Island

It was after midnight by the time Kisala and Jazz walked over to Jazz's place at Station Square. Now it was raining hard. Even with full rain gear, they were getting wet as a rain band lashed the town. They could see the water rising in the Cocheco River as they crossed the bridge in the middle of town.

"At least we're relatively safe here in Dover; we're not on the coast," said Jazz, a thought that had been going through her mind as they walked in silence.

"You know there is actually a tide station in the river, right Jazz?"

Kisala had spent hours, days even, studying tidal and sea-level rise maps in her work as a developer of projects on the coasts and rivers.

"The Cocheco River here runs into the Piscataqua River, then Little Bay, which goes into Great Bay, and then to the ocean at Portsmouth," Kisala explained. "There's actually an ocean tide here; that's why there's a tidal station. The tide probably won't be the problem here, though; the problem will be if it rains enough upstream to raise the river here. THEN, if there's a high tide, it will keep the water backed up in the river and the bay. Honestly, only Ethan could do the calcs to figure out when that might be."

By the light of the streetlight, where you could see the rain coming down. Jazz could see that Kisala was worried — worried and thoughtful. As they crossed the bridge over the river, she wondered if the water level had really risen, or was that her imagination? It wasn't a night to hope that anything might happen between them, thought Jazz — too much anxiety — but at least they could share the comfort of her bed. They made their way to Jazz's flat in the terrace of apartments and townhouses close to the river. When they got inside, they went straight to the windows overlooking the river. All they could see was waves of rain coming down, rain and more rain.

But Jazz wasn't thinking about tide tables and geography; she was thinking about Kisala — Kisala, with whom she'd hardly spent any time alone for the last ten years. Kisala who was going to spend the night. Memories of nights spent together squished into a single dorm bed their freshman year flooded her mind. Waves of memory and anxiety rose up from her diaphragm to her chest. She was both eager and anxious, but this wasn't a night for offering Kisala the couch. No, it was a night to at least sleep in the same bed and cozy up together. Jazz was too anxious to talk to Kisala about it, so she changed the subject.

"Have you heard from Dan?"

"Yeah, so far so good; he can still text. He says winds are coming up. He went out on the roof, and he could see the waves — big, big waves. The next high tide isn't till around 3:00AM. He expects the tide to break over the road and the water to come up from the bay."

"Remember that day we went to the Lobster Pound and watched the tide creep up over the parking lot?" Jazz asked. "You could calibrate the rising tide by the lines on the parking lot. It was so clear."

"Yeah, back when everyone still drove," Kisala added. "I think we had a day-car from the university, right?"

"Yeah, it's hard to imagine actually owning a car now."

"Dan says the water from the marsh hasn't reached the house yet," said Kisala. "He has a pole out in the marsh, and he drew lines on it that he can see from the back deck to measure the rise.

"I don't know what will happen if the cell phone towers go out—

well, really *when* the cell towers go out," Kisala continued with a faraway look. "Probably won't happen till tomorrow morning unless the wind picks up sooner. But, I mean, can you believe that, back in the California blackouts in 2019, cell phone towers didn't have backup power? And that the cell companies argued against passing a law requiring it? That's how fucked up things were."

"But let's hope the cell towers don't go down," Jazz offered hopefully. "I mean, they're supposed to have backup power; New New England made that a requirement. But if they're actually knocked over, all bets are off. And I think the backup power for some of them is only for the minimum of eight hours. So if the power goes out at, say, 2:00 AM, and the storm is still going tomorrow… we're all screwed."

"Right. Right. And now all we have is cell phones," said Kisala. "I mean, Dan has a satellite phone; he's always up on the latest technology. So at least he would be able to call the emergency services or anyone with a landline."

"But only if he is outside," interjected Jazz. "They only work outside, and probably not in the middle of a hurricane either."

"And anyway, still, no one will be able to get to him," Kisala put in glumly.

Finally, defeated by worry and unanswerable questions, they fell into Jazz's bed, exhausted. It was comforting for Kisala to snuggle into bed with Jazz, wondering what the morning would bring.

32 | HAMPTON BEACH AND EVERLEE

Wednesday, September 19, 5:00 AM:
low tide at Hampton Beach; Mitch has glanced off
Long Island and is traveling east-northeast parallel
to the Connecticut and Rhode Island coast,
and has slowed to 14 mph

Predicted Tides, Hampton Harbor

Wed	10:43 AM	8.98ft	H
Wed	11:01 PM	10 ft	H
Thu	11:34 AM	9.39 ft	H
Thu	11:54 PM	10.05 ft	H

By Wednesday morning, intense rain was falling as the rain bands moved in. The rain pounded on the sidewalks and streets and ran down the streets into the river. Out in back of Barney's, the river was clearly rising up to the dock. Several members of the staff had stayed overnight in the apartments above Barney's and were up by 5:00 AM for the morning shift. They came downstairs and sprinted the five feet from the apartment-building doorway to the front door of Barney's, holding their jackets over their heads in a futile attempt to stay dry.

Prepping for breakfast made it seem almost like a normal day, except for all the extra folks. Employees Jeffrey, Ashley, and Kirk, all young, single, and living closer to the Seacoast, had volunteered to stay on site, to run early-morning shift in the brewery, and to be on hand in case of emergencies. The brewing business could never actually be shut down; temps in the tanks had to be kept regulated and, of course, the product was in demand. Evacuees Hakeem and Kenton from Dorchester had bunked on the couches in one of the back rooms at Barney's that folks used as a co-working or meeting space. Randy, Phil, Owen, and the guys who'd evacuated from Boston had stayed upstairs at Barney's apartment.

They all gathered for breakfast, along with Liam, the morning shift supervisor. Barney came down from his upstairs apartment at 6:00 AM, as usual, to preside behind the coffee bar. And Grayson was manning the grill. When he came in on Tuesday, Barney had restocked with dozens of flats of eggs from the farm, as well as sacks of potatoes that Grayson was making into his famous hash-browns. Kenton was happy to step in as sous-chef just to feel like a part of things and have something to do. There was plenty of Tom's custom brewpub sausage and apple-smoked bacon — and, of course, fresh bread from the bakery up the street. And oatmeal for those who preferred it, not to mention the fresh local peaches, apples and pears, and fresh yoghurt and cheeses.

The breakfast regulars were beginning to drift in, and Barney had already turned on the TV behind the bar. With the morning light returning, the Climate Channel was already cutting to live pictures of devastation. Very little was yet known about Virginia and areas north of there; everyone on the coast had evacuated, and no one had been able to get back. So the meteorologist reviewed, again, the destruction in South and North Carolina.

"Maybe we're getting jaded," said Liam. "All these photos of beaches washed out, boardwalks that will have to be rebuilt, the oversized beach houses destroyed."

At 6:00 AM, Eric came on the TV from the local forecast center in Maine.

"Boy, he sure doesn't look good," said Hakeem. "He really looks worried. You can tell he hasn't had much sleep."

"Good morning, New England," Eric said. "As you have probably heard, Mitch is expected to make landfall on Cape Cod around noon. Right now, the eye of the hurricane is just about twenty-five miles east of Long Island, seven hours from expected landfall on Cape Cod, and moving east-northeast at fifteen miles an hour."

By this time, Harrison had arrived for his morning coffee and breakfast. With his decades of experience as a New England lineman, he had been all up and down the New England coast repairing downed lines after storms.

"You know," said Harrison, "right here is where Mitch is different from the storm of '38. Most people imagine the coast of Long Island, Connecticut, and Rhode Island runs north-south. Actually, it runs almost east-west. And the storm of '38 crashed into it nearly perpendicularly — a direct hit. That storm actually crossed Long Island and smashed right into the Connecticut shore. Then it tracked inland. And on that track, it pushed storm surge directly into Narragansett Bay and right into Providence. Mitch, here, is running parallel to that southern New England coast."

Two minutes later, Eric said almost exactly the same thing: "The eye is right off the coast of Montauk right now. They were lucky that those northeast winds peaked a few hours ago at their low tide, which was at 2:29 AM. But with high tide at 8:00 AM, they're still getting slammed. And, of course, we pulled our correspondents out last night, so we will have to wait a few hours to find out exactly what happened.

"Those early northeast winds at the leading edge of the hurricane really battered the North Shore of Long Island all night," Eric continued, "pushing the tidal surges up onto the Connecticut coast and into Narragansett Bay and Providence.

"Now, I am afraid, and I hate to say this, but the storm center is headed directly for Martha's Vineyard and the waters between Martha's Vineyard and Nantucket. Hunker down, folks! Don't be stupid and try to ride this out anywhere but in a designated storm shelter."

Barney switched back to the Climate Channel, where Maya was

checking in on New England.

"Now let's check with our correspondents. Cape Cod, Hyannis? Marie, are you there in Hyannis?"

"Yes, good morning, Maya, this is Marie. We are here at our storm headquarters by the airport in Hyannis. As you know, the eye is expected to pass over the mid-Cape this morning. We are not sending anyone out there right now. The wind is already picking up. They have registered a steady 45 mph, with gusts of 75 and 80 already.

"No one knows what is really happening on Martha's Vineyard or Nantucket," Marie continued. "Frankly, Maya, we are very worried about folks there. As you know, the radar shows that they have been under sustained winds already for hours. And they have only sporadic radio-phone communications."

"OK, Marie," said Maya, "stay safe."

Even the Climate Channel had not left reporters in Chatham or out in Provincetown. So, with no news from the Cape or Islands, the Climate Channel folks again reviewed the damage reports from farther south.

By now, half the emergency management team had come into Barney's, where everyone was waiting for something to happen. Much better to take a break and wait at Barney's over Grayson's hash browns, eggs, and fresh coffee than to sit around an office watching emergencies unfold in Boston on the scanner while waiting for local emergency calls.

Ethan and Cody turned up around 8:00 for breakfast. Not that they ate there every day, but for sure today everyone wanted to be with the crowd, to have people to experience the horror with. And Ethan turned up with a paper mock-up of the hurricane. He'd found an old drafting set in the attic at Everlee, with T-square, triangles, protractors, and two scales — engineering and architectural — and been intrigued. He was putting the drafting tools to use now to map out the hurricane. He had printed out a map of the New England coast, to scale, and then cut out a series of roughly circular hurricanes to scale: one 500 miles across, one 750, and one 1,000 miles across. He plotted the path on his map, using tracing paper to update it. Then he could move the hurricane cutouts along the plot on the map. He had the whole drawing set with him, so he could fool around with it all day.

"Why did you go to paper and pencil, Ethan?" Barney asked, coming over to the table to sit down with them and admiring Ethan's handiwork.

"It just seems so much more real," answered Ethan.

Now Kisala and Jazz drifted back in, too, sitting down at the bar, and ordering breakfast. Kisala went over to look at Ethan's handiwork, too. "Wow, Ethan. That's really cool," Kisala said, as she put her finger on the 750 mile wide storm and moved it around. Moved to the north and west, the fringes of the storm stretched all the way into Vermont and northern Maine, giving them all a sense of foreboding.

For her various jobs, Kisala had spent hours, days even, studying the sea-level rise and storm surge maps for all of Boston and the New Hampshire coast. Everything they had built in the last fifteen years had needed to meet strict standards if it was anywhere near a potential flood zone.

"All of the new construction will be ok," she said, "It all had to meet the new standards, but, too much of the existing housing will be flooded."

She traced her finger over the map of the coast of Massachusetts which she knew could be flooded. "Most of South Boston, parts of Roxbury and Dorchester, and of course low-lying Alston. North of the Cape, south of Boston, Cohasset, Scituate, and Plymouth are always hit hard in storms."

Cody chimed in, "North of Boston, here, the low-lying parts of Everett, Revere, and the old port of Salem likely to get hit bad. And Essex and Ipswich are almost in the estuaries to start with, part of the Great Marsh."

"Route 1A in Massachusetts goes right through those marshes. It will be impassable for sure," added Barney. "They'll be lucky to keep

Route 1 open. I don't know what the emergency crews are going to do down there."

"I can only imagine what Salisbury Beach will look like the next time we see it," Kisala said. And then her finger traced the New Hampshire coast, nearing Rye. "Hampton Beach, Rye…." Her voice trailed off; she couldn't find words.

Now the TV was back on the local channel, with Penny anchoring the 24/7 storm coverage. "OK," she said, "let's go to Hampton Beach now, where they're waiting for the storm to really hit later this afternoon. High tide is going to be at 10:43 AM, and it was already going to be a record high tide — at almost ten feet, one of the highest tides of the year.

"So, let's go to Jim at Hampton Beach.

"Jim, how are things there?"

"Good morning, Penny. It's the wind. Those northeast winds on the leading edge of the storm are really pummeling us. The wind has been howling all night. We have a lot of damage. Waves broke over the sea wall here last night at high tide, just about 10:00 PM. Now, everyone who has been here for a number of years has seen waves break over the sea wall at every set of King Tides in past years, and at every storm. But this appears to have been even more extreme. We're seeing damage to storefronts on Ocean Boulevard. We're seeing lots of seaweed and trash here, and we're expecting even worse at high tide later this afternoon.

"Penny, the storm surge last night reached three feet above high tide, but the storm is still pushing water into the coast, and we are just waiting for that next high tide here in just a few hours."

"Ok, so what are you seeing back on the bay side?"

"Now, back on the bay side, the water pushed up by the storm surge at high tide last night has lingered and is expected to come up another two feet. I think everyone has cleared out of the small bayside houses. You know, over ten years ago the state bought out the mobile home park on the bayside. Good thing, too, as that area is under two feet of water right now, and the water will come up higher."

"So, Jim, has anyone stayed?"

"Well, Penny, let me talk with this gentleman. Sir, you've made the decision to ride out the storm here? May I ask you why?"

"Well, I'm one of the managers of these condos here right on Route 1. My partners and I decided that someone should try to be here. I guess I drew the short straw."

"So, where are you staying?"

"I've got a third-floor condo, facing the beach. It's been quite a ride already. Of course, I have the stairway as a safe space if it gets really bad — and, believe me, the wind was bad all night. Our condos here are above a restaurant and some shops on the ground floor. We boarded all those up, put out sandbags, but we expect a lot of damage.

"Now, we went ahead and put up some solar collectors, a battery storage unit, and an inverter that can isolate us from the grid," the condo manager continued, "so we'll be able to continue using pumps and emergency lighting. In fact, you are more than welcome to come on up and have a cup of coffee if you need to dry out, Jim."

"Thanks, and good luck," said Jim. "Well, back to you, Penny."

"Wow," said Meighan, an emergency management tech, to the crowd at Barney's. "That guy is either stupid or crazy or both." She and all her cohorts were thinking dark thoughts about idiots who stayed, and then later called for help after it was too late. "I can't believe anyone thinks they are going to ride out this storm."

"Yeah, and those weather guys are crazy, too," Caleb said, agreeing with her. "Looks like they're between storm bands right now, but the wind is blowing; looks like some good gusts."

The mood around the breakfast bar was glum. There was nothing to say. Nothing really to do.

* * * *

Later that morning, out at Everlee, Holly and Lianna were keeping the IT systems running as a backup to the county emergency computers. Like the folks at the Emergency Center, they were looking at the maps of the power outages, and the lists of shelters.

Only Katrina seemed to be able to focus, as usual. Reviewing the books and financials, and the numbers on long term plans seemed to have a calming effect on her. "When this is over, more people than ever will want to install solar-energy systems," she said, as she went back to her planning.

Holly and Lianna went back to monitoring the emergency calls on the computers. It was almost lunch time. Ellie and the farm crew came in; they had been out all morning harvesting vegetables from soggy fields in the rain.

"It's going to be tough to get all the vegetables were harvesting cleaned up and ready for the markets," Ellie said to Katrina.

"Well, let's eat lunch, and then you can get some of the guests to help this afternoon." Drew, Val, and Sylvia were making themselves useful cooking lunch, cleaning the kitchen, trying to organize the profusion of groceries that Kara had managed to pick up on Tuesday.

Drew and Val had dug through the groceries and made a huge pot of chili and some cornbread — hopefully enough for all. So far, it was a pretty jolly scene. Everyone was paying little attention to the storm, other than watching the wind tossing the trees outside the windows and the rain coming down in sheets. Occasionally, someone would look out at the road to see how deep the puddles were, or whether the runoff from the fields was getting deeper. But there were hardly any cars on the road.

Adam, Drew, Sylvia, Val, Holly, Ellie, and Katrina were joined by farm workers David, Joe, and Brooklyn. It was a big crowd, but not the biggest Katrina had ever had. Back when the farm was going at a more rapid pace, it had been even more crowded during the harvest. Just as well, thought Katrina.

After lunch, Adam, Drew, Sylvia, and Val joined the farmworker crew in the barn, washing the vegetables and packing them in boxes, then washing and bundling greens. If the storm abated, they would try to deliver the vegetables to the CSA customers. All in all, the afternoon at Everlee was quiet and slow.

33 | MITCH HITS THE CAPE

Wednesday, September 19, Noon:
Mitch is crossing Cape Cod, traveling 20 mph and
turning further west

The mood at Barney's was glum. The morning news had been all reruns of damage in North Carolina, Virginia, Delaware, and New Jersey, places the storm had grazed on its move north, mostly parallel to the coast. The northeast winds had devastated the beaches, stripping them of sand, and devastating the sand dunes. Trees were down everywhere. Neither the emergency workers not the Climate Channel reporters had been able to make it to the Long Island Coast. Millions of homes had lost electricity. Everyone was nervous about what would happen closer to home when Mitch got to New England. In the corner, Ethan was still fooling around with his paper hurricane tracker and analyzing the stats.

On the local news, Penny was talking to Jim, now on the screen reporting from Hampton Beach.

"Well, Jim, the storm center is just crossing the Cape, and its northeast winds are hammering Boston Harbor and the North Shore," she said. "What is happening there?"

"I'm standing here again on the walk by the concrete sea wall, Penny," said Jim. The wind was almost blowing him over, and the rain was coming down in sheets. "The water is still up to my knees.

Earlier, at high tide, it would have been impossible to even stand here.

"You know, we always thought the storm surge danger was from the bay," Jim continued, "and, yes, the water has come up from the bay. That's the storm surge. But we never imagined the waves from a storm like this, Penny. It has been horrendous — waves actually breaking into the storefronts here on Ocean Boulevard. The first time we have ever seen that. And the winds really whipped these buildings last night."

"Thanks, Jim. Now let's go to Eric at the Weather Service. What are you seeing on radar, Eric?"

"Well, Penny, Jim, we're waiting to see if Mitch will turn into an extratropical storm after it crosses Cape Cod. That would mean that the storm is becoming more spread out, rather than being consolidated around a tight eyewall. That would be the good news. But along with that, we still have high winds, and the driving rain bands."

"If you remember Hurricane Sandy, that was more than 1,000 miles across," Eric continued. "So here we have... let's look at the radar; Hurricane Mitch is about five hundred miles across. We can see it turning a bit to the west, so it will be roughly centered just twenty-five miles off the coast as it passes Boston Harbor. We are definitely seeing rain and wind more than fifty miles inland, and we will continue to see rain.

"And, Penny, this storm has picked up some moisture coming from the south, from the tropics, that is being channeled in here. If you remember, that is what happened just a few years ago, with Hurricane Jamie, but we're going to see extreme rain here, probably well inland, so we'll likely see some extreme inland flooding as well."

"Wow," said Liam, the morning manager at Barney's. "This could be real trouble. Worst-case scenario for our area, I'd guess." Out the back windows in the kitchen, Liam had a good view of the river, which so far was still calm, despite the local rain.

Eric followed up with the official statement from the National

Weather Service: "OK, folks, we now have another warning: Extreme flood risk. This is for northeastern New Hampshire and southeastern Maine. Some of this moisture will get over into the valleys west and north of the highest peaks in the Appalachian Mountains here, the Presidentials. And you know where it is going to go, it's going to go down all of those rivers. As a result, we're expecting water beyond flood stages for all the rivers in southeastern New Hampshire and Maine."

This was tough news to hear, even though they'd all been expecting it.

Kisala was still watching the news as she nervously doodled on plans for some new projects, and she was still worried about Dan. Most of the cell towers on the coast were down. Dan had a satellite phone, he could only send messages if he went outside and the last time he'd reported had been about 2:00 AM, with the winds howling. He was holed up in the bathroom they'd designed as the safe space, so all he knew was what he heard on the Climate Channel on his broadband radio. Ironic that the oldest communication technology, radio, was now his lifeline. There was no longer any way for him to check the winds and waves outside his front door. He said that if there seemed to be a letup he would try to go out, but the rain was still too intense. Kisala kept up a steady stream of messages:

"Hampton Beach is flooded."

"No one can get to Rye Beach at all."

"Lots of flooding outside Portsmouth."

"All of the causeways to New Castle and Great Island are underwater."

"I really don't think anyone is going to Rye to rescue anyone tonight."

Barney also had his Emergency Services Radio, and they suddenly heard a call for help from a road leading out of Rye, between Rt. 1 and the Seacoast.

"Are they going to respond?" Meighan asked Barney. "It's pretty tough out there." The tension around the bar was mounting as they waited to hear an update.

Barney had to translate the scratchy coded radio. "OK, wait, looks like they are going out," he said after a few minutes.

"An older man having some kind of attack.

"Heavy, heavy rain they are saying, and the road is swamped in a few places. They are lucky they can get through at all," Barney added.

"They are saying a culvert was just about washed out."

It was difficult to get back to the chit-chat in the bar. "Why didn't they evacuate?" Meighan asked the question on everyone's mind. But they'd all heard the answers given in past storms — they didn't think it would be as bad as it was, or they thought their house would be safe.

Barney and the crew listened to the report from the Rye EMTs as they made their way out into the storm. The neighborhood was mostly deserted.

"Ok, they arrived."

Barney added in the latest: "EMT's are reporting the electricity was cut off, and the man was in pain."

"He was lucky he still had a working line to call out on," said Meighan. "What about people who didn't?"

Luckily, they hit a break in the storm and made it safely to the hospital in Portsmouth.

Jazz was listening in with the others. She knew that Kisala would want to mount a search for Dan, even without Kisala saying it. But Dan wasn't an emergency, at least as far as they knew. For the moment he could still send messages to Kisala's cell phone, but he could report nothing but the howling of the wind and the pounding of the waves.

Jazz made her way to the bar area. "I think the search will have to wait for Thursday," she said gently to Kisala.

Kisala said nothing, just nodded.

"Did you hear they're preparing for a flood in downtown Dover?" Jazz asked, trying to make conversation. But, again, Kisala said nothing.

While they were all hanging around the bar, Barney put in a call to one of his buddies in Portsmouth, a guy with a restaurant right on the water.

"How's things going?" Barney asked. "How is the storm now? The last high tide? What are they predicting?

"So, you're boarded up? … You think that's going to help? … Yeah, I know, you gotta do whatever you can.

"For god's sake, man, don't stay there. Promise me you won't stay there. Go on up to Steve's house; he's pretty much at the highest point in town. Hunker down in a safe space, OK?

"The church basement? They've got that set up as a shelter? … Yeah, that will be a good place. I guess it will be good to be with other people, and they'll have an emergency two-way radio. And food, you got food you're going to bring over from the restaurant? … OK, good. Good luck, man."

* * * *

As the afternoon wore on, so did the storm. For everyone sitting around at Barney's, the litany of destruction was now mixed with the bated-breath combination of tension, waiting, and boredom. Barney stayed because it was his place, his position behind the bar. Cody and Ethan stayed because who wanted to watch TV at home by themselves? Chip stayed because Barney's had become the de facto emergency operations center. They had a direct connection to the official center, but the storm was still raging outside and they weren't mounting any rescues yet. The emergency crews had broken out cards and chess boards. A few people were reading books.

Barney's front door opened, and everyone looked up as Jason

walked in, bringing a gust of moist wind.

"Hey Jason, you said your folks are still living on The Cape?" Barney asked.

"Yeah, I couldn't sit in my apartment and watch by myself. It was just too much."

"So, did they go to a shelter?"

"Well, I think so. I got a text yesterday afternoon, and they said they were leaving. But then the text and cell traffic on The Cape overwhelmed the systems. On the news, they told people in the shelters not to use the system and to keep it open for emergency services and for folks who were still trying to evacuate. So I haven't heard from them since they left."

"Oh, man, where do they live?" asked Barney.

"They live in the interior of The Cape, in Yarmouth," said Jason. "But I guess, really, it's almost flat. I mean, the elevation where they live is maybe fifty feet? And they're like two-and-a-half miles from the coast. So the problem there isn't really the storm surge, the water, it's really going to be the wind. So hopefully they got to the high school, with their dog."

All they could do was wait and watch the Climate Channel with a kind of morbid fascination. Hurricane porn.

34 | STORM DAMAGE

Wednesday, September 19, 3:00 PM:
High Tide Hampton Beach: 10:43 AM, 8.98 ft.
one of the highest of the year
Cape Cod to Boston Harbor: 50 miles in — 3 hours
Boston Harbor to Rye — 40 miles,
Mitch expected to hit Rye Beach directly at 6:00 PM

Richard and Maya were back at the Climate Channel desk for the afternoon, beginning with re-broadcasts of the storm damage in North Carolina, Virginia, and now Washington, DC. Even though the storm had been offshore, tremendous winds and rain had caused havoc. Virginia Beach and the naval station had been hard hit at their high tides, with large areas under water. While Virginia Beach residents had grown accustomed to King Tides bringing sunny-day flooding, the storm surges overwhelmed the new seawalls they had built. Their efforts to protect the coast had largely failed in the face of the destructive waves coming in with the hurricane on the high tides.

"You just cannot underestimate the power of water," said Richard. "We have a lot of destruction on the length of Virginia Beach, and now they're assessing the damage in Virginia from the inland rains."

"Now let's go to Washington, DC. We have Carmen on the spot there. Carmen?"

"Richard, Maya, water from record rainfall upstream on the Potomac is beginning to raise water levels heading to Washington, DC. This is exacerbated by the high tides and winds, which will keep the rising waters from flowing out into Chesapeake Bay. And the next high tide is expected at 7:50 PM. I guess, by now, everyone knows that there are tides in Washington, DC, and some of you know that whenever there are King Tides, they close a number of streets— including, ironically, Constitution Avenue. This has been going on for twenty years, and Congress has never been able to agree on protective measures for the tidal basin, near the Jefferson Memorial, so that is just the way it is.

"We're seeing the Tidal Basin filling right now," Carmen continued, "so many of the roads around the Jefferson Memorial are closed. But, as I said, that is pretty much a regular monthly occurrence now. And upstream, I hate to say that they've had upwards of eight inches of rain in the upper Potomac basin. That will bring another foot or even two to the flood levels here. Back to you, Richard, Maya."

"Ok," said Richard, looking worried. "I was going to bring in reports from the DelMarVa Peninsula: Delaware, the Eastern Shore of Maryland, and a small part of Virginia. It's a bit worrisome that we haven't heard from our reporters there. But we'll get back and update you when we get some news.

"Moving up to New Jersey," Richard continued, "as some of you may remember, many of the New Jersey towns fought the construction of dunes on the shore after Hurricane Sandy, arguing that they would obstruct the view. I guess they got their wish. Unfortunately, many of these towns are seeing a lot of damage."

"You're right," added Maya. "Sadly, as we've been saying, very few properties in these towns are still middle-class family homes. Middle-class families were priced out long ago by the cost of flood insurance. Almost all the property is owned by wealthy families or investors."

"Yeah," said Harrison, continuing the thought. "After all, the original families on Staten Island and Long Island, chased out by Sandy, are long gone. The property now all belongs to people wealthy enough to just rebuild every time their house is destroyed. It's just a bet, like a poker hand in Las Vegas."

Barney agreed: "If they lose a multi-million-dollar house... whatever."

And Kisala thought about Dan, and the house she was helping him build on the Seacoast, called *Seabourne*. Yup. She was officially part of the problem. But was it a problem? Dan had gotten millions from his company's buyout — millions that he didn't really have anything else he wanted to do with. What was wrong with him building a house, and then rebuilding it if he wanted to?

Then she thought about Jonetta and her family. They were lucky that they got apartments in the new affordable housing in Boston. But to build a million-dollar house that might be destroyed? They couldn't even imagine doing such a thing. Kisala herself felt lucky to have a nice apartment in Boston.

By now, Avery, the Dover town planner, and Spencer, who was on the Dover City Council, had joined in the vigil. "Yeah, if you go through the titles," said Avery, "most are in the name of LLCs, limited liability corporations. Might be a family, might be something else. It's completely opaque."

Spencer, who had grown up in New Hampshire, agreed. "I think they see it as an opportunity to rebuild bigger. A few million dollars for a replacement is just not an impediment for these people."

Now attention at Barney's focused on the TV again, as Richard finally had some news: "OK, we're going to move now to Staten Island, where we have Cynthia, who has been there all day."

"Yes, Richard, the storm has absolutely battered the shoreline here." Behind her, you could see and hear waves crashing, and it was still raining hard. "There was a proposal to build a multi-billion-dollar harbor protection wall, but it never happened. It was not that the technology was unproven, but successive Congresses and presidents refused to allocate money; it was just seen as too expensive. That left it up to the State of New York. New York has invested in armoring the shore of the Battery, down at the tip of Manhattan — really, to protect Wall Street. But they never did anything about Staten Island, or about those vulnerable parts of Long Island. Here is a case where inaction is a default decision. The State did buy out some property owners after Sandy, but initial funds ran out. People who were waiting for flood insurance, or private insurance? They ended up either rebuilding with their own money, or just abandoning their properties, giving the keys back to the bank if they still had a mortgage."

"Yes, Cynthia," Maya said, "unfortunately many folks ended up losing their homes."

"So now, here on Staten Island," Cynthia continued, "the houses closest to the water have been mostly gone for years. Other properties, a few blocks back, have been bought up by investors backed by hedge funds, and they have now built luxury waterfront condos. Their advantage was that they could invest in solid foundations for buildings raised ten or twelve feet above the tidal surge marks. But the old Staten Island communities, the folks who were here on family properties during Sandy, those folks are gone."

"OK, thanks, Cynthia. That's right, and we've seen that change as we have continued to report storms here on the East Coast," said Richard.

"And now, moving on up to Connecticut. As you know, 100 years ago, the Hurricane of 1938 crossed the North Shore of Long Island and slammed directly into Connecticut, then moved inland, full force, bringing tremendous rain and floods.

"Mitch has taken a different course, by and large skirting the coast, moving east, to make landfall on Cape Cod. This has saved a lot of Connecticut from the worst of the damage. However, the winds and storm surge have pushed water ashore in Rhode Island, and deep into Narraganset Bay."

There was still a large contingent at Barney's all afternoon and evening. What else was there to do? Kisala had spent an anxious afternoon doodling floor plans, sketching facades.

Ethan and Cody were still doing hurricane math.

35 | REPORTS FROM BOSTON AND HAMPTON BEACH

Wednesday, September 19, 5:30 PM:
Storm center directly on New Hampshire coast;
Mitch hits somewhere between Hampton and Rye

The crowd at Barney's was waiting for the 6:00 PM update, with the local news from the New Hampshire Seacoast and the damage at Hampton Beach. Even as the winds continued to howl, and after the surge receded after high tide, they waited together for the next high tide: 11:00 PM that night, at Hampton Beach.

But for now, reports were coming in from Boston.

"Chris, you're down there at the Seaport?" Richard asked.

"Good evening, Richard. Yes, we had a high tide here overnight— actually, about 4:00 AM—and it did come in with those strong northeast winds, a worst-case scenario. The tides came up all the way over the seawalls here.

"Now, over the last ten years," said Chris, "all of these buildings here at the Seaport were mandated to elevate their electrical and HVAC equipment, which they have done. So, although water has entered many of the buildings, they are still operational. Some of the new buildings even have elevators that serve the upper floors and terminate on the second floor, maybe at a mezzanine. Those continue to be operational, on backup power or the microgrid, so people are not stuck up there on the upper floors with no elevator.

"We have a lot of people living in these waterfront view condos," Chris continued, "and they seem to mostly have decided to shelter in place, feeling that their relatively new buildings will be strong enough to withstand the storm. But they are getting buffeted by high winds— gusts as high as eighty miles an hour. Now authorities have announced that, whatever they do, they should stay away from those windows. So far, we have not seen any broken windows. But we are hearing from you, Richard, that there could even be localized cyclones. Is that right?"

"Right, Chris. We'll be keeping an eye on that situation and reporting any developments. You stay safe. Now we're going to move over to the Boston Airport. Natalie, you're at the airport?"

"Right, Richard. I'm here at the Boston Logan Airport. As you know, this is usually a very busy airport. But all flights on the East Coast have been cancelled since yesterday.

"The issue here in Boston is the flooding of the runways. Over twenty years ago, Boston Logan began what they called their sustainability and resilience planning. Of course, when they were planning, they were just guessing as to what the real challenges would be. Furthermore, their planning was for sea-level rise; no one could really plan for the kind of storm surge we will see today and tomorrow. There was definitely water on the runways last night, from what we can see, but we aren't sure whether this was within the parameters expected.

"In fact, Richard, when they looked at the costs of actually keeping storm surge from overtopping the runways, it was just too expensive. When the New New England Regional Compact began to look at emergency response regionally, they determined that it was better to make a plan for the whole region. For critical deliveries during the emergency, the emergency services will be operating out of the designated regional airports, including Worchester, Manchester, and Pease International up in Portsmouth, New Hampshire. And Boston Logan relocated their critical infrastructure so that operations can resume when runways are clear."

"OK, Natalie, thank you," said Richard. "We are going to go now to a statement from the emergency services department in Boston. Here is Morty Levinson, Emergency Services Director, appearing at the emergency operations room in Boston."

Appearing in front of a projected map, showing areas of Boston that were underwater, Levinson said, "You know that we are experiencing an extraordinary storm. As we announced yesterday, the airport is closed. All of the tunnels in and out of Boston are closed. The lower areas of the Mass Pike are flooded, so the Mass Pike into Boston is closed. Now, you can see that a lot of our waterfront areas are underwater, as are many areas near the Charles River right in town, and of course the Fenway. Now we did implement our evacuation plan, beginning on Tuesday, as you know."

Visuals of tail-lights leaving Boston appeared as Levinson added, "And I am happy to report that we evacuated over 20,000 people on buses from low-lying areas of the city. That represents over 400 bus trips. Many of those folks were homebound, or disabled in some way, or dependent on electricity-based technology. So, our evacuation plan was very successful. Of course, we still have many thousands of residents sheltered in place. We are hopeful that city services will resume by Friday, and that people who are still here will be able to get out to the grocery store and so on. Schools in Boston are closed through Friday and will be reopening Monday."

A question came from the audience: "So, where were people evacuated to?"

"Well," said Levinson, "we have over fifty shelters that have opened in surrounding towns north and west of Boston. Altogether they are already ninety percent at capacity. We are very glad so many people took the offer to evacuate and stay safe."

As the storm vigil at Barney's continued, bands of wind and rain continued to whip the trees in the park across the street and pound the sidewalks outside. By this time, the vigil was well-lubricated, as Barney took out his special reserves from his beer cellar.

Barney's evening chef, Patrick, served fish and chips — local fish, local potatoes — along with a salad made with the greens, tomatoes, and cucumbers that Barney had brought back from his farm. No time to get involved with the full menu. Jazz and Kisala were still there, along with Chip, Cody, and Ethan. And Harrison who had just about moved in. Avery and Spencer stayed, too, along with Owen, Harry, and Phil, the Boston refugees. Fiona and Paul had recruited their college-student babysitter to stay with the kids so they could come over to Barney's for dinner. And Hakeem and Kenton were there, as well as Ahmed. The atmosphere was decidedly festive, maybe a little too giddy in the face of the catastrophic storm.

"When I started Solar NH with Katrina, back in 2006," Chip reflected, "the whole focus was on renewable energy. No one thought about the larger context of planning and housing so much. We were just putting solar collectors on individual roofs. And the big selling point was that you could reduce your electricity costs. 'Think about your dryer, your water heater; you could be running them off the power from your roof.'"

"Yeah," Cody broke in, "even though, if customers were connected to the grid, that was not strictly true. Actually, the electricity to power the house came from the grid, and the electricity produced by the collectors went to the grid. The customer saved money and contributed to the general renewables percentage."

"But that wasn't as good a selling point," responded Chip, who was the consummate salesman. "Not as enticing as producing your own electricity to power the house."

"It wasn't until people began talking about the climate crisis for serious, and then the Green New Deal, that we began really thinking about cars, about transportation, about housing, and how it all fit together."

"That's funny," said Fiona, "I was working in Mimi's transportation lab at MIT in Boston. I just wasn't thinking about solar energy then. And, in fact, we weren't even really thinking about minimizing carbon impacts until the mid-twenty-teens. We were thinking about how to prevent Boston from hitting gridlock. We

uld see that, year after year, there wasn't going to be new money
r public transportation, so we were focused on algorithms—
rmulas to make existing buses and trains somehow carry more
ople."

"Guess you failed at that," said Paul dryly.

"But, in the end, #Gridlock'23 really propelled the projects
rward," Fiona responded. "In retrospect, there was really no way
at the project of chipping away at efficiencies around the edges
uld have succeeded. Gridlock really opened the spigot for money
flow to transportation."

"Growing up as a solar panel installer," Cody interjected "I was
ways thinking about electricity. But even before I was even in
llege, it was clear that the grid itself was part of the problem. By
e time I started college, the technology for microgrids and battery
orage was already affordable and practical.

"But there were two problems," he went on. "Folks who were
mphasizing offshore wind and large-scale solar installations as the
pproach to renewable energy continued to support a robust grid for
istribution. As long as renewable energy continued to include all of
e above, the problem was shoved to the background, while
pporters of decentralized energy production continued to devise
rge-scale solutions for controlling microgrids and efficiently
tegrating renewables. That's what Ahmed was working on."

By this time, the Climate Channel was getting boring and
epetitive; it was growing dark all along the East Coast. Downed trees
nd wires prevented reporting and camera from getting out to the
oast, it was still too windy for drones, and there was no new news.
hey were rerunning photos of New York City and Long Island, and
ere was no news at all from Cape Cod. While many of the crowd
ill sat around the bar watching the TV, Kisala and Jazz sat in the
orner and schemed. They were trying figure out how to get to Dan
nd rescue him.

They would plan to go first thing Thursday morning. They were
retty sure that the last half mile of the road was washed out, so the

basis of their plan was to get a boat. They knew that Chip and Coc had a boat. Or maybe they could talk the rescue squad into a expedition. They could borrow a Solar NH truck to tow the boat t Rye, then take the back channel to Dan's. Kisala had been plannir it all day, and Jazz had to talk her out of leaving tonight; the wind wa still too strong, and the waves and storm tides would be tc dangerous. It would be dark, very dark — a long night to spend Kisala thought, in a dark house at the end of the road, with water a around.

Around 11:00 PM, Jazz and Kisala finally retreated again to Jazz place, far more comfortable than sitting up at Barney's. They share the bed again, but Kisala spent a sleepless and restless night, listenin to the wind howling around the building and dreaming of wave buffeting a perfect house, of winds tearing buildings apart, of roof flying through the air. Of being in a boat, calling and calling an calling into the wind.

THURSDAY

36 | RESCUING DAN

Thursday, September 20, 6:00 AM

Tides: Hampton Harbor

Thu	5:38 AM	-0.86 ft. L
Thu	11:34 AM	9.39 ft. H
Thu	5:56 PM	-0.62 ft. L
Thu	11:54 PM	10.05 ft. H

Thursday dawned, but barely — still cloudy and stormy. Rain continued, but winds had abated, and it was obvious that the intense part of the storm had passed. Kisala was beside herself with anxiety. The next high tide would be at 11:34 AM. Jazz and Kisala talked Cody into driving them to Rye in a Solar NH truck, trailering one of their fishing skiffs, leaving as early in the morning as possible to avoid high tide. They did not even think about the possibility that the main Rt. 16 bridge over the Piscataqua and Great Bay Inlet might be closed off — but it was. Floodwaters still expected from upstream compounded the danger from the high tides of the previous days. In fact, every road around Great Bay was compromised and potentially closed.

Their best alternative was a circuitous route south through the town of Newmarket and then east through Stratham, but when they got to the bridge over the Swampscott River on Rt. 108, where the river became an estuary of the bay, the bridge was closed and nearly underwater. Yellow highway barriers were placed prominently across the road, and a state trooper was stationed there to make sure no one tried to cross. The water came up over the top of the marsh grass, completely covering the boat ramp and nearly covering the parking lot.

"Damn," said Kisala, "I've been over this bridge a million times. We should have known." They ended up having to go south all the way to Rt. 101 — the divided highway, the only route that was not closed — then to Rt. 1, which Emergency Services had been keeping open, cutting fallen trees and clearing branches all night. They all knew these town roads, but it was hard to foresee how difficult it would be, how many roads would be closed by fallen trees and fallen wires.

The closer they got to the coast, the more destruction they saw. In an area that looked like a flat coastal plain, there were actually high and low spots — places that were just high enough for a house to still be a foot above the water, and places close by that were inundated.

Adams Road ran along an esker to the beach, an ancient gravel ridge just five feet above the coastal marshes. But that five feet was enough to be able to drive to within a half a mile of Dan's house—except that they had to get out and clear the road of debris.

Luckily, Cody had brought a chainsaw to cut through fallen trees. They only came across one fallen power line, but Jazz had thought to bring some of her lineman's tools lines, being extra careful, since she should never have attempted to clear them by herself.

Three hours later, on what should have been a thirty-minute trip, they reached the point where Adams Road met Ocean Boulevard—and found Ocean Boulevard washed out. Most of the beach beyond the road was completely gone.

They had hoped to reach the coast before high tide, when the rising water would disguise hazards and they might be fighting rip tides and currents. If they timed their trip for low tide, it might be so low that they would run into hazards. But, with a three-hour delay due to closed roads, all their planning went out the window. Now the tide was coming in fast. Their best hope was to put the boat in on the marsh side of the road and hope they didn't get stuck on debris.

There was, of course, no boat ramp; they had to back the boat down the washed-out end of the road itself. They struggled to slide the boat off the trailer, making sure the boat motor didn't hit the pavement or the trailer get stuck in the mud. They knew Dan was at the house: if he had somehow left, he would have contacted them. But was he OK? What would it look like? Kisala was tight-lipped and saying nothing.

Finally, they got the boat in the water and made their way through what was normally a non-navigable marsh, thick with marsh grasses, with just six inches of water. Dodging debris, they had to lift the motor and use the oars as poles to push the boat through water two or three feet deep — they looked down at fish swimming through the tops of the grasses that had previously risen above the water. Jazz stood up in the front to watch for floating logs, roofing shingles, window shutters, pieces of fencing. Their progress was slow. But if they'd gone in on the ocean side, they would have been sucked out in rip currents.

As they rounded the bend, Kisala's heart was in her throat; she felt nauseous. Suddenly they saw the house. At least it was still standing. They pulled up behind the house and tied up the boat to the rear steps from the deck — which would normally have been more than twenty feet from the edge of the marsh and at least ten feet above the water. Rain still sputtered out of low clouds. Would Dan hear the boat? Would he be on the roof waving? Or would he still be barricaded in the bathroom, the one room with no windows, that they'd built as a safe room?

Had he been defiant — or petrified?

37 | DAN

Thursday, September 20, 12:00 noon:
Slack tide, the calm when the tides are changing
subtly from high to low

When Dan appeared on the deck as they pulled up in the boat Kisala put her face in her hands and cried. It was then, despite the days of anxiety, of messaging, of reassuring, of trying to build up hope, that Jazz realized how deep Kisala's feelings were for Dan. Surely she would have stayed there, with him, if not for her own fears. Kisala was so relieved to just see him alive, yet she felt guilty that she hadn't stayed with him.

But Dan, unshaven, looked haggard and worn. It had only been two days, but it looked like he had aged. He and Kisala hugged — a long, relieved embrace. She cried some more. When she cried, he cried. It had truly been an ordeal.

"You can't imagine," he said. "I am so glad you didn't stay. I'm not sure I'm glad I stayed.

"The wind," he said. "The wind howled; it was fierce. I was really, really, worried that the wind would rip away the shutters, or destroy the windows, or the whole house. By the middle of the night, cooped up, I was picturing banshees. I couldn't sleep. I had electricity from my battery system, so I had lights, thank god. I had a little TV, so I could get the Climate Channel until about midnight. And until about

3:00 AM yesterday I could text you. But then the cell tower went down. I guess it was the cell tower. I still had power for the lights. I had the satellite phone, but it doesn't work inside, or in a hurricane.

"So, Wednesday. Yesterday. Wednesday was bad. The worst of the wind. That leading edge of the northeast winds picked up before noon, just as the tide was rising and I knew it was the King Tide. With the wind pushing the waves up the beach, I could hear the waves pounding, and the rain. And then the debris, I could hear debris banging on the shutters. But I really couldn't see out. I had all the window shutters closed. And the wind was driving the rain. I didn't want to try to open a door; it wouldn't have been safe. Every now and then the wind would let up a bit, but I never knew if it was just a break."

"Yeah," said Jazz. "It broke up from a hurricane into an extratropical storm after it went over Cape Cod. Did you know that?"

"I heard that, but I was still afraid that the center was going to be right over the house."

"Yeah, I guess the center went over Rye about 6:00 last night," said Cody. "That's what Eric said."

"And also what Ethan said," Jazz added. "He's our junior meteorologist; he's almost better than Eric."

"Yeah, the wind and rain kept up all afternoon," Dan replied, "and it did seem to get worse around 6:00 PM. But by that time, I guess there really wasn't an eye, so no eyewall, no calm center. I kept drifting off to sleep and having these intense dreams. They seemed so real.

"I could hear the waves, too," Dan continued. "I knew that high tide was around 4:00 PM. That's when the waves really picked up. Then I was afraid that they would attack the foundations of the house. At least my watch still worked, and I had a tide table. I'm glad I wasn't depending on the Internet for tide tables.

"I slept some on Tuesday night," Dan went on. "I had dragged all the bedding into the bathroom. I was watching the TV at that point, listening to the weather radio. Then I could hear high tide, Tuesday night, 10:00 PM. The waves got closer, but the leading edge northeast winds were pounding us, driving the water up. I drifted off Tuesday night. Then high tide Wednesday, 10:00 AM. I ran out on the deck just once, right at high tide. The beach was just about wiped out, and the waves were breaking right at the road.

"I still had radio, and I knew that the hurricane was crossing the Cape at 3:00 PM and I heard the reports from Boston as the hurricane passed outside the harbor. I can't believe those guys were still reporting from high-rises in Boston. That must have been scary. So, anyway, the storm was getting stronger, the winds were getting stronger, especially the gusts. Then I could hear the debris from the neighbors' houses beginning to blow around. I was waiting for the 11:00 PM high tide, ten feet. That's a high tide even without a storm, like the highest tide of the year. I was afraid the waves would come all the way over the road and up to the house. As far as I know, they didn't.

"That high tide was like the worst, the height of the winds too. From then till like early this morning. It seemed like a lifetime. That whole time, I was just hunkered down listening to the wind batter the house, debris crashing into the house. Thank god for the shutters, and all the hurricane ties in the framing."

At some point, Dan had lost the TV reception and the Wi-Fi, but he'd still been able to get radio reception, and he had power for the radio. Ironic that, with all the innovations of the 21st century, the only reliable communication was still the hundred-year-old technology of radio waves. The radio, with an emergency police scanner and a weather channel, kept him apprised of the progress of the storm.

They walked into the house, and found, thankfully, that it looked much like it had when they'd left Dan there — except for the huddle of blankets on the floor where Dan had been cocooned when he hadn't been in the bathroom. Then they peered into the bathroom. It looked like the camp of a crazed survivalist: Empty beer bottles in one trash can, empty cans in another. One pan on a hot plate. A coffee maker. He could charge his cell phone, but the cell towers went down.

He had been in the bathroom for, what, thirty-six hours?

Yes, he had been frightened — scared, but ecstatic at how well the house was performing. Exactly as they had planned. The shutters held. The wind deflected around the house. The water came up under the piers but didn't wash out the foundation. The house was like a boat, a bird.

Dan hadn't slept since his short sleep Tuesday night. He had waited up, listening to the waves, since the first surge of the high tide Tuesday night.

Dan, Kisala, Jazz, and Cody went out onto the front deck to survey the damage.

"Wednesday morning, I made one trip out onto the deck during the high tide," Dan said. "The surge came in over the road in front of the house, and then waves broke on the road, almost up to the house. I could see that some of the older, smaller houses were just gone, destroyed by the waves.

"But the folks who owned those houses," Dan continued, "most of them had been bought in the last ten or fifteen years by wealthy people from the city. So, let's not feel too sorry for them. These weren't the family home; don't think about the couple bemoaning the loss of their only home.

"The folks who bought these houses saw them as expendable. Especially after what we've been through in the last ten years, no one could have seen these houses as anything but expendable. They bought them for the property, and then paid the flood insurance. They were just waiting for the houses to come down in a storm so they could collect and then build something new. Actually, they really don't even need flood insurance. They could all easily rebuild a multi-million-dollar house — which is crazy, I should know. There is no one to feel sorry for here."

"Why don't they just build a beach shack?" asked Jazz.

"Because why should they?" asked Dan. "A multi-million-dollar house for them is like the cost of a beach shack for you. But wow, it sure was a wild ride out here. The house performed just as we planned, Kisala. It hardly even shook. The timber frame, just a bit of give. And like we learned, it isn't the structure itself; it's the way it's fastened, held together, especially the way the roof is fastened, and the way the walls are attached to the floor. When the house is up on piles, and the wind can get under it, that sets up a whole lot of new forces trying to tear the house apart. So, we did good hiring the engineering company from Florida. They really know their shit.

"And I'm glad we got the stormproof windows," Dan continued. "But it was the shutters, those steel shutters that come down over the windows — every window, totally worth it."

"So, let's go up and see how the solar array held up," said Cody. "I've always wondered if a hurricane would tear apart a solar array. I know Chip always says he's the best at constructing these."

Dan went over and manipulated the chains that opened the shutters. The chains were a backup to the electric motors that could be controlled over his phone.

"You were right, KiKi, when you said we shouldn't count on electrically operating the shutters," said Dan. "Yeah, even though theoretically they should operate on the battery storage system, you don't want that system to go down at the wrong moment."

My God, thought Jazz, *he even has a pet name for her!*

"The only problem is if you weren't here to operate the house; suppose you couldn't get here?"

"You just have to hope that either the app works, or you can get here. Nothing is completely foolproof, I guess."

Dan talked a mile a minute as they toured the house, opened all the shutters on the guest rooms, then went upstairs and opened the shutters on the rest of the rooms. Then they climbed the third flight of stairs and emerged through the bulkhead door to the roof.

There was actually debris on the roof, even seaweed that had been blown there and stuck onto the supports for the solar collectors. But otherwise, everything was in order on the roof.

Looking out over the landscape, though, it was a different story. The beach was as clean as it usually is after a storm: cleaned free of debris, pristine. But the road, Rt. 1, Ocean Boulevard, was nearly washed away. Water still lapped up onto the shoulder of the road from the bay side, even as the water in the ocean was still going out to a minus tide.

"Just before slack tide," said Kisala.

Looking out over the river mouth, they could see the Grand Hotel. It had not fared well. Standing out huge and white, larger than anything on the island, it reflected a sun that was going in and out of the clouds. The wind was still blowing, and they could see pieces of the roof still blowing and banging in the wind. Light waves crossed the patio and rolled into the dining room.

Now Dan was ready to leave. He gathered a few things, and they retreated the way they had come in: out to the back porch and down the steps to the boat. The water level in the marsh was lower now, as the tide was going out. With the motor lifted, they poled the boat the half-mile back to the road.

When they got back to their truck, the four of them — Dan, Kisala, Jazz, and Cody — stood on the edge of what remained of the road, a slight, very slight, bluff over the water. They guided the boat onto the trailer, then pulled it out of the water. Then Kisala and Jazz squeezed into the kid sized jump seats in the back of the pickup cab and they took off.

Cody had the police scanner on as they drove back on the high road to Rt. 1 and Rye, so they all heard the calls for rescues from the area around Portsmouth. They felt selfish for rescuing Dan first. They had a boat, and they were on the right side of the bridges that had held them up earlier, so they headed toward Portsmouth to see what they could do.

With the storm surge, the tides had come up much farther into town than anyone had predicted. In the eerie dusk, it was hard to tell what was water, what was land. They drove as far as they could toward the water, and then Cody and Jazz put the boat into the water again. But now the tide was at its lowest, which only increased the danger from all the detritus in the water. So many buildings destroyed, so much wreckage in the water, it was almost impossible to navigate.

38 | LITTLE RIVER

Thursday, September 20, 8:00 AM

Back at Little River Farm, they had spent a mostly sleepless night. The rain and wind were relentless, band after band. They had been able to hear the water rising in the river at the back of the farm all night long. Just before midnight Alyssa had sent Morgan and Dylan, the farmworkers, out with headlamps to walk out and see what they could see. After they came back and reported that the bank was washing out, Alyssa knew it was just too dangerous to send anyone out again in the dark.

At first light, Alyssa herself had driven up the road to the bridge, only to find a gaggle of neighbors — and the bridge gone. Instead, there was a chasm. The police were there, deploying barriers where the bridge had been.

"The bridge went out sometime last night, after midnight," the police lieutenant said. "Thankfully, no one was stupid enough to try this road last night."

The police had put up barriers, cutting off access a mile back at Sim's Road. That would be the only way out now, adding almost fifteen miles to the trip to Dover. That would certainly make things more difficult, but at least there was a way out and they weren't entirely cut off.

Luckily, with all of Barney's efforts on the micro-grid and energy storage, all systems on the farm were working and they could continue their daily routines, milking the cows and goats, chilling the milk, and making yoghurt and cheese. And Barney had insisted on maintaining a landline phone at Little River in case of emergencies. So Alyssa was able to call and tell Barney about the bridge washout and the road closure. Barney told her about the rising rivers in town, the flood threat.

"We're just carrying on with the farm work," Alyssa told him. "We're mapping out what we have to do, where we have to go over the next few weeks, and how we'll get there. I guess we'll have to go through Berwick; that's only a twenty-mile detour. Ha, ha. And there's a steady stream of neighbors coming over to charge stuff up and use the Internet, too."

Also, luckily, the DART had already begun a limited connector service on the Amtrak tracks to North Berwick, the closest town. It wouldn't be life as usual, but at least they could get into town and beyond until the bridge was rebuilt.

39 | RESCUING PORTSMOUTH

Thursday, September 20, 6:00 PM

Tides, Portsmouth:

Thu 3:31 AM	-0.04 ft. L
Thu 9:32 AM	3.52 ft. H
Thu 3:53 PM	-0.07 ft. L
Thu 9:57 PM	3.54 ft. H

Dan and Kisala watched as Jazz and Cody got into the boat, with Cody steering. Jazz aimed a flashlight ahead of them as they made their way slowly through the debris. They headed for a house where they could hear people yelling for help. In fact, as Kisala and Dan stood on the street corner, they could hear people crying out for help all through the low-lying area, where the oldest houses in town were located.

Jazz and Cody picked up the closest people, Richard and Debbie, with a four-year-old boy. They were sitting on the front stoop of their home, not exactly in danger, but certainly stranded. They loaded the family into the boat and brought them back to the where the truck was parked, where Dan and Kisala tried to warm them up around a fire they had managed to make with scrap wood and tree branches. Luckily, they had found the emergency blankets Chip kept in the truck.

"We just never ever thought we would have to be rescued," said Richard. "We were lucky the house wasn't exactly under water, but there was no way to get out. All of a sudden, the water around the house was too deep to wade through."

"And then we realized that the tide was still coming in," added Debbie.

Dan and Kisala, Richard and Debbie discussed what to do next. Best would be to ferry folks to the nearest emergency shelter, but they weren't really sure where that was. They could hear reports on the police scanner, but the cell towers were down. Cody used the truck's two-way radio to call his Dad.

"We're here in Portsmouth, Dad. We're picking up folks who are stranded, but we don't know where to take them." While they were waiting for an answer, they drove around the eerie edge of the drowned part of town.

Cody and Jazz went back out in the boat to look for more people to rescue. Everywhere they looked, there were more teams of rescuers—on fire trucks, in rescue vehicles, in front-end loaders, in kayaks and canoes and skiffs—but there were few cars or trucks: anyone who had a car had already evacuated.

People who had been rescued were standing around waiting to be transported to a shelter, so Dan and Kisala dropped their rescuees off to wait with a large group. The roof had blown off the nearest shelter, the gym at the local school, and the hospital had been evacuated. Even the senior housing that Jazz had set up with a microgrid had been evacuated; although it was on higher ground, officials feared that the residents would be unreachable in the storm. Someone had brought blankets and coffee, and the refugees were huddled around a small firepit someone had brought from a yard. They were burning debris, as they waited for the firemen and the national guard to bring a bus to take people to the Pease Airport, the last-resort shelter.

After dropping Richard and Debbie off to wait with the others, Dan and Kisala stayed around for a few minutes to warm up by the fire before driving back around to pick up more folks who'd been rescued by Cody and Jazz. Over the two-way radio from they could hear the Portsmouth firefighters calling for the National Guard.

40 | SEARCHING THE COUNTY

Thursday, September 20, 8:00 AM:

On Thursday morning, Barney and Chip set out with other emergency teams to search the back roads in the rural area beyond Dover. While the worst of the storm had passed, it was still raining upstream, and they knew that local streams and rivers would continue to rise. As volunteer emergency workers, they had two-way radios and emergency light racks on their trucks. They had access to the equipment at the E-Ops center too. First thing was to coordinate into the plan at HQ among all the area emergency workers. With cell phone service and electricity out, some people couldn't even call 911.

Barney and Chip were assigned the low-lying area on both sides of the Salmon Falls River, which formed the Maine-New Hampshire border. The area was cut through with small creeks and streams leading to the river — all of them now overflowing. They knew what they were likely to find: Half the places at the end of the road, the old trailer parks and subdivisions on low-lying land, would be underwater. But if not, the folks there were pretty self-sufficient and would undoubtedly refuse to be rescued. If they did find people in trouble, they would have to call for backup.

Maine had become more progressive in the 2020s and the state had funded solar power for every school, and every town fire department. The bigger towns were all old mill towns, and they had repurposed their old mills into housing, and renovated their old dams into low-head hydropower plants, all integrated into microgrids powering and controlling power in the towns' central areas. All the new housing had been built sustainably and included solar energy, too.

But despite all this, in the rural areas nostalgia for the mid-twentieth century reigned. The first problem was the original housing, in the low-lying areas near a creek or marsh. It was terrible housing, old places that should probably have been torn down years ago. But instead, they had been added onto multiple times.

Then there were the manufactured-home parks, first platted out back in the 1950s, then later embraced again as a solution to the affordable housing and senior housing crises in the early 2020s. But these parks totally lacked public transportation. Now the roads were cut off and people were stranded.

Most manufactured-home parks in New Hampshire had been able to transition into co-op ownership, and a small subset had embraced new energy-efficient tiny houses. Collectively they were able to finance community solar energy and microgrids. But for the most part they were still the trailer parks of old.

Barney and Chip knew where all these places were; they had been down all the dead ends. So they split up to cover more ground, each with a helper. Barney took Kisala's friend Hakeem, from Dorchester, and Chip took Meighan, the EMT. Barney and Hakeem headed east, toward the river, then turned off on every little road.

"We don't have much time," Barney said, "the rivers are rising already. I mean, look what happened out by Little River."

Down Old River Road, they came to what could only be compared to an encampment—an eighty-year-old single-wide trailer with a moldering, framed-in front porch. There were four or five junk cars, and a couple of other shacks or sheds. One shack looked like it was being lived in.

"Wow," said Hakeem, "I have never seen squalor like this." He, himself, was living in Dorchester, which had once been the ghetto in

Boston. But he lived in one of the newer affordable housing buildings, built less than fifteen years ago — a green, energy efficient building. With heat-recovery ventilation to control the growth of mold, it was clean, comfortable, and healthy.

"Hard to believe anyone lives here," said Hakeem. "What were they thinking?"

"Maybe years of exposure to mold means they can't think at all," said Barney. "I've talked to folks like these a lot. They say they like living in their own place, they don't want anyone to bother them. They don't want anyone telling them what to do or how to live. Then they have kids, and the ones who don't move away don't change at all; they just keep up the same lifestyle because that's what they're used to.

"It's not like they don't have schools," Barney continued. "Every school in this part of Maine was rebuilt in the last twenty years — all the latest in technology, all light and airy. And Maine raised teachers' salaries, too. There's no excuse for this except willful ignorance."

They waded through a foot of water, climbed up on the front porch, and knocked on the front door. Amazingly enough, a man answered. Barney recognized him from the pub. The guy, bearded, in his forties, introduced himself as Hal—Hal Logan. In the background, Barney could see a woman with two kids sitting at the table with her, coloring in coloring books.

"We're just checking on everyone, making sure you're OK," said Barney.

"Hey, Barney, thanks, man — yeah, we're fine. We get cut off electricity so often that we're used to not having it. We got a little generator for the refrigerator. And we use propane lamps. Old fashioned, right? Ha ha. Yeah, the water will probably go down in a few days. We got a truck parked out by the road if we need to get out. So, no worries. Thanks, bro."

"OK, then," Barney said, and they retreated to the truck. Barney had seen all this. It was what he was expecting, but Hakeem was dumbfounded.

"How can anyone live like that?"

"To each his own, I guess," said Barney, and they drove off to the next place.

"There are a lot of folks who just don't want to deal with the modern world," Barney added, as they navigated the roads strewn with tree branches. "In fact, more and more folks like Hal have been moving up here to the woods. They find this attractive. Some of them are libertarians, some are just paranoid and want to keep their guns. I don't know. But, you know, Alyssa is kind of like that. She's a little more ambitious, but she left Cody because he wanted to live on The Corridor, where everything was convenient and new. Alyssa says she can't stand big buildings, or committees, or rules, or hallways. She's just not cut out for it. She's lucky she found me, right? And I enable her, I guess."

"Yeah, you do, bro, but Little River is not like this."

The next driveway was a mile away. This was a different story.

"Old Mrs. Stokes has been living here for years," said Barney. "We know about her, she has grown kids, but has absolutely refused to move. The county social workers come out once a year to see if she is ready for the senior home, but nope. Won't move."

They stopped on the road and scoped out the dirt driveway, now a sea of mud interrupted by a stream that crossed just before the house. Barney grabbed two pairs of rubber overshoes from the back of the truck. Mrs. Stokes' place was also a single-wide trailer, like Hal's, with a closed-in front porch and a 250-gallon oil tank on a stand right next to the place. They could see that it leaked by the rainbow sheen on the puddles.

"It's still heated with an oil space heater," explained Barney. "They don't even make them anymore. This must be one of the few places in the country where they even have a distributor who delivers oil."

Again, they waded through eight inches of water and climbed onto the front porch. They knocked and knocked again. No answer.

"Uh oh," said Barney, "I don't think this is going to be such a happy picture."

Barney banged on the door again. "Mrs. Stokes? Mrs. Stokes?"

Then he radioed to HQ dispatch. "René, we're at Mrs. Stokes' place off Old River Road." He paused. "Yeah, no answer; we're going in." Barney signed off, then put his shoulder to the flimsy door. It gave way all too easily.

Mrs. Stokes was on the floor, and water was already seeping up through the floor around her. Was she dead?

Barney radioed HQ dispatch again.

"Send an ambulance, René. We'll feel for a pulse. Doesn't look good."

Miraculously, holding a finger to her neck, Barney discovered a pulse. She was still breathing, though it looked like she had hypothermia from lying on the cold, wet floor. Together, Barney and Hakeem lifted her onto the couch. The sickly-sweet smell of oil exhaust tainted the air in the trailer. They found a few blankets in the back room and covered her up as best they could. It seemed that the oil stove had backfired, maybe flooded. "You won't see these old pot-burner oil space heaters anywhere else but around here in rural New England," said Barney. "This is like an antique." In this case, it was lucky that the trailer had so many air leaks; it felt like there were breezes blowing through.

They sat down on the kitchen chairs to wait for the ambulance. They couldn't really leave her alone, and Barney certainly wasn't going to let Hakeem stay there by himself. Hakeem went to get their thermos of coffee, and Barney put a kettle of water on.

"Really," said Hakeem, his nose wrinkling at the combination of oil blowback, dirty dishwater, and mold. He held his head in his hands.

"No one should live like this," he said, as if he blamed Barney, or himself, personally.

"People get to have a choice, Hakeem," said Barney. "I know this doesn't look like a choice. But I've seen her before. She's old enough that she could have gone to one of the town's senior homes. But she refused to leave this." He gestured around the room: the old rocker upholstered in brown plush fabric, the braided rug, the worn-out 1960s laminate kitchen counters, ruffled curtains hanging at the window over the sink, the row of mugs hanging on hooks.

"God, I'm tired," said Barney. "Wish we could get on with it. But I can't leave you here, and I'm sure not going to leave her alone. I hope she can't hear us."

They drank the coffee from the thermos, found Mrs. Stokes' Folgers can and made more, and sat.

"I really don't understand it, Barney," said Hakeem, looking around. "I just don't understand white people. Us folks," he said, lapsing into the kind of language he hardly ever used, "we want to be with our families. My mom, brothers and sisters, aunts and uncles, we all live within a few blocks of each other. And we're always trying to do better. My mom never had anything, but the house was spotless. Always spotless. And she signed up for every affordable housing project that came along, even though they were all lotteries, back fifteen-twenty years ago. Lotteries to get a place to rent, with 500 people on a list for maybe ten apartments. But Mom kept at it, and eventually she did get a new place. And I thank god for that."

"Well, Mrs. Stokes, when she was bringing up her kids, the schools out here weren't so good, and the opioid epidemic hit hard out here," said Barney, in a futile effort to try to explain, to try to understand. "A couple of her kids died of overdoses, back in the heroin epidemic. She just couldn't move forward. Refused to be helped. The other kids moved away. Trying to save themselves. A few of them live on the road here, in the mobile home park. One lives in Berwick. But, like I said, no one could talk her into moving." Hakeem just shook his head, they both stared into their coffee, and waited.

* * * *

On the other side of the river, Chip and Meighan visited all the new subdivisions built in the past forty years, most on the better ground on high ridges, with curving roads ending in cul-de-sacs, with large pseudo-colonial houses with impressive entries on one- or two-acre lots. Chip and Meighan knocked on doors which were answered by ordinary middle-class moms and dads. No one had evacuated; no one seemed worried that the power was out. They all had two four-wheel drive vehicles in the driveway and garage shelves full of emergency food supplies, in addition to their go-kits ready to leave if needed, even though they had no intention of going. "God knows what they are going to do if they run out of diesel or propane for the generator," said Chip, "but if they want to stay, that's what they get to do."

Then, as they came down into the lowlands of a creek valley, they came to a series of trailer parks.

Kingswood was the first they came to. The homes themselves weren't under water, but the floodwaters completely covered the access road, and had probably flooded the community septic system as well. Many people had old cars, or no cars at all. They had not been able to afford shelves stocked with extra food. They had not imagined that the small creeks that flowed through a culvert under the access road would wash out.

Chip and Meighan had to park on the road and wade through the overflow to get into the park. Like most of the manufactured home parks in the area, the residents of Kingswood had been able to buy their park from the original owner and turn it into a cooperative community. As a coop, they had been able to get financing for their own solar collectors and microgrid, so they still had electricity. And, they had a community council, so they were well organized and had accounted for all residents. Many people were gathered in their community center, where they were cooking soup for everyone. Still, a few residents were running out of medications, and some were just uneasy, and were ready to be evacuated. Chip called René.

"Chip here, René, we have some folks who need to be evacuated." He explained the situation: boats needed to get people over the break in the road, or a National Guard high-wheeled rescue vehicle, and then a bus or van to transport people.

41 | BATTLE OF PORTSMOUTH

Thursday, September 20, 10:00 PM:

Portsmouth Tides

Thu 3:53 PM	-0.07 ft. L
Thu 9:57 PM	3.54 ft. H

The battle to rescue folks stranded in the low-lying areas of Portsmouth had been long and contentious. There were not enough National Guard trucks and transports, and it had been unclear where those rescued should be taken, until they decided on the airport at Pease. Jazz and Cody had stayed at their mission of picking up stranded folks in the boat, ferrying them to points where they could be transferred to land vehicles. Dan and Kisala turned to just manning the transfer point, keeping the fire going, setting up tables of donated food, making sure there were coffee and hot drinks, finding chairs, and sending folks out to scrounge blankets from neighbors.

Filling up coffee cups, adding wood to the fire, they had time to talk.

"I had a lot of time to think while I was holed up in that bathroom, Kisala. You know, for my whole life I have only focused on work. I spent my whole college career, my whole grad career, in biology and biotech labs. It's all I knew. I had no time for a girlfriend. My friends began to wonder if I was even interested in women. And the worst thing was that I didn't even have an answer for them.

"But while I was in my safe-space, for all those hours," Dan continued, "all I had was time. And I wasn't thinking about a new biotech invention. I needed some time out. The house, getting this house designed and built was my time out. There have been so many things to think about. So many puzzles. And you always had the answers, or else you were always willing to think it through with me. I can't tell you how much I admire that," he said staring off into the distance. "I can't even say when it turned into something more.

"But anyway... All I thought about was you ... no, that's not entirely true. I took to keeping my mind occupied, thinking through all the details of the house: the deck railings, the trim around the shutters, the cabinets, the countertops, and the backsplash. And every time I got to a new detail, I imagined what you would say about it. I can't thank you enough for introducing me to this world — your world. But, for me, it's not all embodied in this house. I want you to be part of it. The real you.

"You know, people think I wanted to build the house here in Rye just because I am some rich jerk from Boston who could afford it. People don't know that I grew up in the county here, and not in a wealthy household either. We moved all the time, town to town, wherever my folks could find cheap rent. But every summer I worked at Jimmy's Clam Place. That was my constant. The seacoast. And I got a surfboard. Those were my happy places. I worked at Jimmy's all though college. And surfed.

"So that's why, when all of a sudden I got money, I wanted to build a house here. I'd always had my eye on this spot. You were the one who helped me create a vision, and you were the one who helped me bring that dream to life. It's so special. Just like you."

Kisala was overwhelmed. It was more words about his feelings that Dan had ever uttered. But she was not surprised. She knew he had feelings for her, that they had feelings for each other. But she didn't know what to say; she just grabbed Dan's hand and looked at him, then stared into the fire.

That was one of the problems with Jazz, as Kisala had come to see it. Jazz just couldn't talk about her own feelings. She was almost embarrassed. And, for years, Kisala had had the same problem. But trying to be in a relationship with someone else with the same issues… it was just too much; there was no way to foster an intentional path forward.

Renewable energy, affordable housing, sustainable living. That had been Jazz's main focus for years. For a while they had seen that as their mutual future.

But, peering into the fire, she tried to see what a future with Dan would look like. Now she knew that she and Dan would always be part of each other's lives. But was she going to move out of Dorchester? Would they live together? She tried to picture them living in the house, *Seabourne*. Even Dan, of course, wouldn't really live in the house in Rye; it would always be a second home. But Kisala had an even harder time picturing herself with a vacation house. Committing to Dan would require a leap of faith in a future she couldn't really see.

Then Cody and Jazz texted. The tide was going out all the way to a minus tide at 4:00 AM, so there was less and less they could do with the boat. They needed Dan and Kisala to bring the truck over to where they could take out the boat. After getting the boat onto the trailer, Dan and Kisala brought drove Cody and Jazz back to the fire to warm up, then turned over their fire and coffee duties to new arrivals. Exhausted, they were all ready to head back to Barney's, hoping the late crew would be there with hot food. Rt. 16, the bridge over Great Bay, was still closed. They had to go around again on 101, an almost hour-long trip for what would normally take twenty minutes.

They straggled into Barney's, wet, bedraggled, dispirited, and depressed from the storm destruction, and the many people who were displaced from their homes. Needing to decompress and debrief, glad to see Barney behind the bar. Hakeem was sitting at a table by the fireplace with Kenton. Even though it was still September Barney had made a roaring fire to counteract the chill of the rain.

Jazz, Chip, Kisala, and Dan went to sit at the bar. Of course, they were relieved to have rescued Dan, and glad that he had survived the storm at the house, but the chaos in Portsmouth had been overwhelming. Barney got them hot toddies, and then his famous 12 bean soup, with sourdough biscuits, which would transport anyone away from whatever had been bothering them. Soup. Everyone at the bar listened to Dan's tale of surviving the storm in the house, and then to Cody's and Jazz's stories about rescuing folks in Portsmouth.

Hakeem had still not gotten over the trauma of seeing people stranded in awful shacks and trailers, mired in mud if not flooded out. He and Barney had spent all day checking on people they could reach and calling for 911 rescues. To make matters worse, some folks had been more grumpy than grateful, as if the whole mess were someone's fault.

And now here was Dan. Everyone knew about the house; Jazz and Kisala had been talking about it the day before, when they were planning to rescue him. *Why should one rich white guy be able to build that huge house?* Everyone knew he wasn't even going to live there; it was just a second home. Cognitive dissonance: when the world around you doesn't fit together. Some people had mansions, some people lived in shacks by the river, and some didn't have houses at all.

Hakeem looked at Kisala, and Dan. He had known Kisala most of his life, since he was in middle school, and she was the architect of the building his family had moved into and lived in ever since. She lived in the same building. She was a friend. If he had the chance to live with someone like Dan… would he? Could he? Would he want to?

But it seemed that no one really wanted to challenge Dan. Hakeem didn't feel like he should be the one to speak up.

Suddenly, Barney's night manager Lorraine piped up, saying exactly what Hakeem was thinking: "Why should one rich white guy be able to build that huge house, on the coast of all places, when so many people still don't have a place to live? It's just not right."

Lorraine was the kind of person who fades into the background, someone you don't even notice. But when she was in college, back in 2020 and 2021, she had been an organizer for a well-known and energetic climate activist group. It was exhilarating at the time. They all expected that their efforts would lead to worldwide and dramatic action on climate change, and they seemed to have some early success with the Green New Deal. But when the plan got whittled down to almost nothing, after all that work and hope, she became totally cynical.

"I mean, I'm glad the Green New Deal has resulted in lots more construction of energy-efficient housing, but, aside from the DART and The Corridor, and people driving electric cars, it doesn't seem to have made much of a difference. People were still driving on freeways, the strip malls haven't disappeared, there are still natural gas lines all over the state. And the ocean is still rising.

"And it certainly hasn't equalized the field in terms of haves and have-nots. Year after year congress brings up a sur-tax on wealth and year after year it goes nowhere. I mean I'm glad people have finally agreed that everyone should have a place to live. Thank god, there are no longer hundreds of people in tents under highway bridges. But," she continued, "some people still have too much money, everything else is just a compromise with the reactionary capitalists."

This was the first time Lorraine had spoken up in months. Everyone was stunned into silence. Hakeem was stunned, too. He had been talking with her the last few days, as they were all just about stranded at Barney's, and he was surprised to find she shared so many of his own views. Kisala stepped in to defend Dan.

"Are we going to start limiting how much money people can make? Dan should be able to build whatever he wants."

Jazz looked on, not sure what to think, what to say. Deep inside, she agreed with Lorraine. But she didn't want to condemn Dan. "Look," she said, "Dan just spent hours with us in Portsmouth helping to rescue people; now is no time to jump on him. Have this discussion another time." She wanted to say: you're just jealous. But as soon as the thought popped into her head, she realized that maybe she was the one who was jealous... of Kisala. Yes, she was still in love with Kisala, but it was a dream-state kind of love that she'd held inside all these years — a love she never expected to be actualized again in a real relationship.

42 | RIVER RISING

Thursday, September 20, 11:30 PM: Dover

Portsmouth Tides

Thu	9:51 PM	3.21	H
Fri	3:59 AM	-0.09	L
Fri	10:11 AM	3.3	H
Fri	4:29 PM	-0.06	L

No one had noticed that the water behind the mill was rising until Cody came in.

"Water is coming up fast out there," he had told Barney. "It's close to overtopping the loading dock. I would stay up if I were you; it's hard to tell how much more it might come up."

Barney himself was indeed focused on that as he kept one eye on the TV screen behind the bar, where Maya and Richard were discussing this very issue, with charts and graphs of flood stages, storm surge, and tidal range.

But on TV, the issues in in New Hampshire and Maine — the issues that mattered to the group at Barney's — were secondary to the news from Boston, Providence, and New York. In Boston, as on the whole coast, the rising tide was just one component; there was still the surge pushed into the bays and estuaries and harbors from the ferocious northeast winds. Even as it continued to rain upstream in the watersheds, water had nowhere to go, meaning continually rising sea levels.

Finally, Maya turned to the news they wanted to hear: "We're going to go to Eric, at the National Weather Service in Gray, Maine, to discuss issues in New Hampshire and Maine."

Ethan was still up, focused on his maps, and his data, despite it being almost midnight. "Yup," he said, "the high tide here was just an hour or so ago. So, on that end, things might get a little better. But, like Maya is saying about Boston, there's still high water which has been pushed by the tide into the Great Bay, leaving high water in its tributary rivers with nowhere to go. And if you look at the maps, it's still raining; some places upstream have gotten as much as six inches already. This is only the beginning. And then the tide comes up again at 10:00 tomorrow morning."

"I've got things pretty secure here," said Barney. "We moved the HVAC and control systems to the second floor years ago — and the grain storage, and the canning line."

"The production line is still in the basement," said Ashley, the brew manager, "but everything is off the ground and we moved everything moveable out of there."

"Do you think we should get sandbags?" asked Cody. "When we drove by, we noticed that they're filling and distributing them out at the dump." Cody really didn't feel like going out again in the truck. He was exhausted from the day's excursions.

"We'll take a few trucks over," Chip said. "Hakeem, want to come? It'll be back-breaking work. We can get some of the brew crew who are still here to start sandbagging the openings on the docks on the river side."

Barney figured he had two feet of elevation to spare before the water got to the lowest level in the building, the production floor. Even though he had spent years planning, Barney never imagined the water from the river would get that high.

Barney turned to Ethan. "How long is it going to rain, Ethan?"

"Hard to say, Barney," Ethan said. "When Eric came on at 11:00, he said the storm had slowed to ten or twelve miles per hour. So if the storm is really only 250 miles across, it would last at least ten hours here. But then he said that these extratropical storms spread out, so if it slows down more it might last longer. And, anyway, it's still moving northwest — right through the Upper Valley watersheds of the rivers that feed the Great Bay. So the worst of the floodwater hasn't even gotten here yet."

Now even Ethan looked dismayed, as the whole thing became more than just numbers and paper maps. Cody realized, even as Barney and his crew mobilized to get sandbags, that he needed to intervene and get Ethan home.

"Come on, big boy, this isn't going to be over any time soon. Time to go home."

Both of them were exhausted from the day, so Cody and Ethan headed for the door, the DART, and home.

Jazz, Kisala, and Dan also slipped out in the steadily falling rain, heading together to Jazz's flat on Station Square. Making their way down the main street, toward the steadily rising river, they saw that the water level had come up at least a few feet, drowning the low-lying parts of the local riverside park. Dan and Kisala hung back, holding hands.

Jazz headed over the bridge, then stopped, leaning over the railing to watch the churn of the water. She thought back to when she'd arrived back in Dover. Had she really expected to get back together with Kisala? Actually, she had to admit to herself that that a reunion with Kisala had never been her intention when she left Kirk. It wasn't really Kirk; it was her atomized life in Alaska, driving everywhere, school to house to store, everything in her life separated by car rides. And then when she talked with Kirk about moving, it was his response; she could see that none of it bothered him at all. That's when she knew she would just have to leave. Moving back to Dover and Durham was the logical step. Back to where she had felt safe and appreciated, and where she knew she could work for Chip and

Katrina. When she was thinking about moving, she remembered that when they had graduated, and Kisala got the fellowship in Boston, she had asked Jazz to move there with her. But Jazz had been in Boston a few times, and she just couldn't see living there, even with Kisala. She couldn't picture what she would do there. But had it been a mistake not to move to Boston with Kisala?

Kisala came up from behind Jazz, reached out and grabbed her hand, and pulled her into a trio.

"Come on, girl. We're not leaving you out to dry. We love you."

FRIDAY

43 | CAPE AND ISLANDS REPORTING

Friday, September 21, 8:00 AM

Portsmouth Tides

Fri	3:59 AM	-0.09	L
Fri	10:11 AM	3.3	H
Fri	4:29 PM	-0.06	L

Jazz woke up on the edge of her bed and looked at the two sleeping forms of Kisala and Dan. She had offered to sleep on the couch, but they didn't want to leave her out, and the king-sized bed she'd gotten from someone who moved out was big enough for all of them. Now, looking out the windows, up at the sky, she could see clouds skittering overhead. But it was brighter than yesterday's dark, rainy skies. Getting out of bed, she looked out the window at the river — still raging and drowning the trees on the riverbank. It looked even higher than it had the night before. She was glad the apartments were on a high enough bluff to not worry about being flooded out.

She tiptoed into the kitchen, trying not to wake the sleeping pair. She had just enough coffee to make a pot with the French press — enough to get them all up and about and on their way to Barney's for breakfast. Before long, Dan appeared from the bedroom, then Kisala.

It was still raining lightly as they left the flat and made their way down the path along the river. The water was clearly even higher than it had been the night before, creeping up the bank, almost reaching the level of the paved path and the bridge itself. The river was raging, and the water looked angry as it crossed over the old mill dam, now only two feet from the bottom of the bridge.

"Morning, folks," said Barney from the behind the bar. He was drinking an Americano and looking like his usual cheerful self, but dialed down a few notches, still worried about the river. "Sit down, what are you all having?"

"The spinach omelette with their own fresh mozz is the thing," said Jazz, mostly to Dan, who did not get to Barney's regularly.

"Ok," said Dan, "the same, I'll go for that."

"Your French toast with the bakery brioche is my comfort food," said Kisala, "and I definitely need some this morning."

It was surprising that Barney could still be so cheerful after an exhausting Thursday of damage and rescues. And then there'd been the sandbagging and watching the rising river. But so far, the water hadn't breached the building.

The day was getting a later start but many of the regulars were there, as well as the staff. Grayson was at the grill, making sure everyone was fed, and the TV was tuned to the Climate Channel.

Some news had come in Thursday about the extensive damage on Cape Cod and in Boston, but everyone had been too busy with rescues and flood preparations to absorb what little news there was.

Jazz, Kisala, and Dan had missed the 6:00 AM local report from the National Weather Service in Gray, Maine. Now Richard and Maya were back at the Climate Channel desk, and they were focusing on the damage at Cape Cod.

"Let's pick up with Cheryl in Hyannis," said Maya.

"OK, thanks, Richard, Maya. Let me just recap for you. By the time the worst of the storm passed it was later Wednesday evening, and already dark. Fortunately, most people had evacuated. Those who stayed had been told to prepare to die, from falling trees, roof collapse, or drowning. No one could get out during the storm, and rescue was impossible."

According to the recap, the emergency teams had started their surveys on Thursday morning, accompanied by a few reporters and TV crews. The teams started in the neighborhoods of smaller houses in Hyannis, Dennis, and Yarmouth, where ferocious winds had demolished roofs and blown over trees. They proceeded house-to-house with their yellow caution tape and red "unfit for habitation" stickers. There was heavy damage but, thankfully, few people had stayed. As the emergency teams were leaving, National Guard troops were arriving to provide security for the abandoned streets.

"I think you're rolling footage of the surveys and the National Guard, right, Maya?" asked Cheryl.

Indeed, on the screen, the gang at Barney's watched the images of parties in boats going door to door in neighborhoods of small cottages. By Thursday afternoon, the emergency survey teams had reached the larger homes on the coast. Now the images were of some of the large coastal mansions — images you hardly ever got to see, as the rich were typically secretive.

"Many of these larger homes, Maya, have sustained quite a bit of damage because they were right on the coast, with large windows facing the waves," said Cheryl. "You can see broken windows, roofs torn off."

The waves looked to have crested every cliff and overtopped every shore barrier. Even with windows boarded up, the waves and the wind had not spared the mansions of the wealthy.

"But note, Maya, that many areas at the end of the Cape are still inaccessible, including Chatham and, of course, Provincetown. We have heard over the radios that while most folks did evacuate, there is a lot of damage."

"OK, thanks, Cheryl. And now Marie, who is also in Hyannis, has been getting news from Martha's Vineyard and Nantucket. We have some footage here from folks on the islands. I know some of you have seen this on social media."

Richard had just shown footage of ripped-apart warehouses and pieces of metal roofing blown off.

Now Marie was on the screen, in front of the airport in Hyannis. "Richard, I should emphasize that the airport is operational. They were underwater and out of commission on Wednesday, and on part of Thursday, but they are open now."

Jason had just walked into Barney's and was sitting at the bar drinking a latte.

"Yeah," he said, "I've been to that site a million times. If they pan a little to the right, you'll probably see the airport is fine. Nothing is blown over because nothing is there. It's the biggest flat place on the Cape."

"OK," said Richard, "let's continue to Martha's Vineyard and Nantucket. We have a Ms. Lucy Stevens, Emergency Services Manager there. Ms. Stevens, thank you for agreeing to speak with us. Could you just tell us where you are, and what has happened there on the Island?"

"Well, Richard, first I would like to say that Island residents are very resilient," Lucy began. "I'm in the shelter at the high school. Most of our folks did take refuge in our shelters. Those who stayed in their homes have experienced storms before; many of them had basements to shelter in. But the folks we talked to said they have never been so scared. It was ten full hours of winds on the front side, then that eerie calm when the eye went over the Island, and then ten hours or more on the back side of the storm — listening to the wind scraping at the roof and the sounds of trees crashing. We sent survey crews out this morning. The downed trees blocked many of our roads. There's a lot of damage out there. And, as you may have heard, we also seem to have had a tornado or a microburst that ripped through the Island, reducing buildings and trees to splinters."

"Yes," interjected Richard, "for our listeners, a microburst is a small localized very intense wind event, like a small tornado."

"Many houses have been built closer and closer to the bluffs in the last twenty years," Lucy continued, "and they have sustained a lot of damage. Some are just too big and have too many windows to board up. There just isn't enough manpower on the Island to board up all the windows in that short amount of time. You know, in the past, people were more willing to build farther back from the bluff, to pick a protected location. In the last twenty years, it seems some homeowners are tearing down smaller houses and building more extravagant homes that command the bluffs. And these houses have sustained a lot of damage.

"Of course, in addition to the high winds, we also have a fair amount of water damage; water has overtopped bluffs, and we are hearing reports that storm surge has breached some protective barrier beaches."

"Thank you, Lucy," said Richard. "Now, Marie, we have been getting a lot of questions about the turbines out at Cape Wind. Do you have any reports?"

"Richard, Maya, it turns out that the wind turbines were not something to worry about," Marie replied. "I have here Donovan Showalter, who is in charge of Cape and Islands Utilities."

"Marie, the turbines have been out there almost twenty years," said Donovan. "They were engineered by Dutch manufacturers and modeled and refined on designs that have been in use for more than forty years. They were built to withstand ferocious North Sea storms. In fact, they produced more electricity as the winds increased, and much of that is stored in our Island battery array. With our central microgrids, all of the hospitals, schools, and emergency facilities are up and running. We undergrounded most of the utilities years ago because we knew we couldn't count on help from utility crews from the mainland. So, except for a few outliers, everyone is still connected. The bigger problem is in the damage to the actual houses."

"Well, best of luck to you, and to everyone out there. And now," Maya said, "let's go to Boston. In Boston itself, there were not so many rescues, very few people got caught in the storm itself. But the storm surge and high tides have been devastating. But, as you can see, the storm surge barriers along the seaport have been overtopped," Maya said as the images on the screen showed the overtopped coastal barriers. "We have with us Emergency Services Manager Mordechai

'Morty' Levinson to explain what's going on here. Morty?"

"This overtopping of the surge barriers is not really a surprise, Maya; they were never built for a massive hurricane like Mitch. We have these barriers to minimize damage from the monthly flooding we experience. But we have embraced readiness for the 500-year storms without major damage to systems. There are no more furnaces or electric panels in basements, we have the flood doors in the subways, and the new apartment and condo buildings were all built with utilities above the first floor.

"Now, it has proved much more difficult to protect the highway tunnels under Boston," Morty continued, "but, again, our planning process accepted that they would have to be sacrifice zones. Trying to make them totally stormproof was just not worth the cost. Of course, we blocked off the tunnels before the storm, so no one was stranded or drowned."

"And Morty, can you explain what is going on at the Boston Logan airport?"

"Yes, Richard, the airport is kind of the same story. The runways are technically below sea level now that climate change has raised that level. Raising the runways or trying to engineer total protections—frankly, that would have been impossible. We have barriers that protect the airport from the everyday storms, the ten-year storms. But we accept that, in a major storm like this, the runways will be underwater. That's why, in a major storm, we always planned to rely on the regional airports: Manchester, Pease, Worchester, and T.F. Green in Providence, Rhode Island. Unfortunately, in this situation, T.F. Green went under water before Boston did."

"So do we know when the airport might open?"

"Actually, Richard, we don't, since this has never happened before. We are seeing that so much water has filled the basin created by the seawalls, we just don't know how long it will take to either wait for it to go down or to pump it out."

"Well, that is certainly a situation we will be watching with you, Morty. Now let's go out to Anthony in Dorchester."

"Richard, Maya, Dorchester seems to be in pretty good shape," said Anthony. "The city of Boston was proactive and reconfigured the Dorchester neighborhood coastline and beaches so that there are parks designed to be underwater, with dikes that have functioned as outdoor recreation areas all these years; this approach has been working very effectively. With enough area for the excess water to flow into, the inundation of city streets has been minimal. Planners knew there would be flooding in big storms, so all the new affordable housing has utilities on the second floor or higher. All of the housing in newer neighborhood housing has been connected with microgrids so that they were not a risk from grid failures.

"Now there is water in some of the streets, some of the older housing in the neighborhood has been flooded. We knew it was at risk, and we urged people to evacuate, and as you know we provided buses for evacuation. We evacuated disabled folks and those whose health was threatened to facilities outside Boston."

"Well they did evacuate everyone," interjected Hakeem, "but I am hearing from folks that it was still chaos."

44 | GOING HOME

Friday, September 21, 8:00 AM:
most of the storm had passed, but it was still
raining up in the mountains

The sun was coming out at Little River Farm as Jonetta, DeShauna, and their families got ready to leave, but the Little River Bridge would be out for at least a few weeks. The word from Boston was that the seaport was still experiencing some high-tide flooding, and the airport was still closed, runways underwater. But the Dorchester neighborhood, despite some closed streets, was opening for business. Evacuees were streaming back.

Jonetta and DeShauna called for a LaMA van to transport them to the Amtrak station in North Berwick, now the closest station to the farm since they were cut off from Dover. They were glad that the southern Maine region had implemented a robust transportation network to connect to the station, and that the rail bridges had all survived the storm. Shoring up bridges and main-line mass transit infrastructure was one area that the New New England Climate Change Readiness task force had focused on.

The kids had had a great time on the farm, playing in the barn and visiting with the animals. Shauna was ready to go home, but her sister Sharice was curious about the whole farming thing. She decided to stay for the weekend and go to the farmers market with Alyssa.

Jonetta thought it had been a great vacation, but she wasn't interested in a rural lifestyle.

The idea of having guests had never appealed to Alyssa before, but the storm had inspired her to think about building some vacation cottages to enhance the income from the farm.

Jackson and Rosemary and their kids, from Hampton Beach, faced more difficult choices. Most of Hampton Beach was still inaccessible. They decided that the kids would stay, while Jackson and Rosemary drove down to see how their inn had fared. From what they could see on the maps the town had released, and from what they had heard from friends, the inn might or might not have sustained damage. They would borrow kayaks if need be, to at least assess the damage. Meanwhile, Sharice would watch the kids for the day on the farm.

Through the whole adventure, Alyssa and her team had continued to milk the cows, goats, and sheep, and continued the yoghurt and cheese production. Those could never stop. Alyssa, Morgan, Dylan, and Sharice were readying the cheese, yoghurt, milk, butter, and produce to take to Saturday's farmers markets in North Berwick and Dover.

Down at Everlee, Drew, Adam, Sylvia, and Val, who had been with Katrina for nearly a week, faced the same problems at York Beach as Jackson and Rosemary were facing at Hampton Beach. The reports coming out of York were inconsistent and confusing. They were unsure how their house and business had fared, but they decided to just pack up and go back. If they needed to return, so be it. But they were uncertain about the route to take. Bridges and culverts had been washed out. Had they been fixed? Val went over the route with Chip on the emergency ops website.

Ellie and her farmworkers were out assessing the rain damage to the vegetable beds and getting ready to put the plastic high tunnels back up. With a few more weeks of warm sunny weather, their crops would recover.

* * * *

Kisala had always been so disciplined that she thought her life plan was her destiny, and that if and when she met "the one," he or she would fit into that tidy plan. Certainly, living with someone in a multi-million-dollar house on the beach fit into no plan she'd ever imagined. It was totally outside the bounds of what she'd even considered. But the feelings she had for Dan, especially when he was in danger? Those couldn't be explained by a plan. It was beyond all considerations of what might or might not be sustainable.

That wasn't just clear to Kisala; it was clear to Jazz as well. Jazz knew that she would never compromise her own values like that. And she knew that what she wanted was community. She had found it in Dover, at Barney's, in Station Square, with Katrina and Chip, and with friends all along The Corridor, who formed a tight community—easy to get together with, to work or hang out.

Jazz accepted that she and Kisala would be forever friends. Just forever friends.

SIX MONTHS LATER

After the excitement of the storm, Jazz stepped up to help Katrina and Chip run Solar NH. Around the same time, Cody decided to step out of his parents' business, and move on more fully to designing controllers for microgrids, which were more in demand than ever. Cody and his girlfriend Charlotte were in a more permanent relationship, even though they decided for the good of the relationship not to move in together. Cody still had his spacious two-bedroom penthouse with plenty of room for the boys.

Kisala and Dan were now an item. She had given up her affordable apartment in Dorchester and had moved into Dan's apartment in Boston. Even though she would miss Dorchester and her friends, she knew that surely there was someone who needed that place more than she did. But she and Dan also had a place in Portsmouth, which she used when she was working on projects there. She and Dan were now developers together, focusing on building affordable, net-zero-energy housing in the whole region around Portsmouth.

* * * *

On an overcast evening in April, Barney and Chip drove over to the county administration building. They had to drive out there because, like much of the physical plant built in the late twentieth century, the central services building for the county was in a rural location, halfway between Dover and Somersworth, that could hardly be accessed without driving. In this case, the administration building was on what had been the county farm, dating back to the earliest settlement of the area, when the "poor farm" was the basic method of caring for citizens who couldn't care for themselves. At least they had solar power at the courthouse, now surrounded by a range of other buildings in a complex connected with a microgrid.

Spring had brought blooming apple orchards, cornfields being planted, and vegetable production in the many high tunnels. But many solar arrays had also sprouted in farm fields over the last two decades. Anyone could see that there weren't many cows left, since the advent of new fermentation processes that made non-dairy milk. Truth be told, the milk was just as good, and without the troublesome methane that the cows, their burps, and their manure produced. But no one had managed to successfully recreate cheeses, so some cows remained.

Barney and Chip were headed to a regional public hearing for Rockingham and Strafford Counties, New Hampshire, and York County, Maine. On the docket was an analysis of what had happened during the storm: what had worked, and what hadn't. In addition, there would be an attempt to chart a path for the future, to improve the emergency response — but, more important, to design a new future in which more people lived in a safe and stormproof environment, where they wouldn't have to be rescued at all. Just as New New England had formed because the states had to work with each other, the three counties realized that they would be better off if they charted their path together, even though they would continue to work independently. And the emergency service agencies from the three counties, all organized by the towns, joined in.

Bernard Brooks (Barney) and Charles Miller (Chip) were dressed up to speak at the hearing. Barney wore a suit jacket and a tie — probably the first time in years that anyone had seen him wearing anything but his overalls. Barney was paunchier than he'd been thirty years before, when he started the brewery, but he still had his now graying reddish hair pulled back in a ponytail. Chip, too, was wearing a jacket and tie, and was still the tall, charismatic salesman he had been when he first served in the legislature.

Chip began their remarks:

"As we live together, here in our corner of New Hampshire and Maine, there are three defining factors to our modern lifestyle: power and electricity, transportation, and housing. All of our developments in the last twenty years that centralized people and housing around nodes, have been entirely successful. These nodes, whether older historic villages, or our new Corridor are now thriving communities that can sustain themselves, just like the old-time New England villages. In these villages, we can efficiently provide residents with city-level services, including uninterruptible electricity with renewable energy, and battery storage with microgrids, and safe water, and district geothermal heat in some case.

"You know, our modern Western occupation of Indian lands began here because of the available power, the power from the rivers we live on: the Salmon Falls River, the Cocheco, and the Piscataqua. Indian names surround us. We fought the Indians for this land, back in King Phillip's War. We exterminated and drove out the Abenaki, and we freed up the locations for the great textile mills.

"But electricity killed the mills. Yes, the very electricity that we are so dependent on. When electric motors could power mills, the mill owners moved their businesses away from the rivers, and down south where labor was cheaper.

"For almost a century, we gave utilities a monopoly on producing and distributing electricity. That was just the way it was done. And we not only gave utility companies a monopoly; we, their customers, guaranteed them a high rate of return on their investments on our behalf: their investments in coal and nuclear plants and those high-voltage transmission lines to move power from their power plants to our homes and businesses. There was no opt-out clause, because we did not see a way to opt out of using electricity, or a way to produce t ourselves.

"The strangest part of the system was that there was no way to balance production and usage. Every electron produced was pushed out through the electrical lines. Production had to precisely meet demand at every moment. So, our utility companies built peaking plants, special generating plants that could be started up in a moment to generate additional electricity on demand on a cold winter night, or a hot summer afternoon, mostly burning coal. And they had to keep this energy flowing, or the whole system crashed.

"While we liked to tout our modern industrial system, it was amazing how often the system actually did crash: power lines down in storms, explosions, fires. And instead of looking for another way, we simply accepted it, letting the utilities repair and rebuild, and paying them to do so — until the system really began to fail us. Was it the massive power outages? Or was it the fires started by PG&E in California? Or was it PG&Es forced power outages when they cut off power to millions of people for three or four days at a time?

"For our neighboring state of New York, the light bulb came on, so to speak, when Hurricane Sandy wiped out the power to so many millions of people, back in 2012. That's when they had their 'aha' moment and realized that their own public utility policies had driven the utilities in a direction that did not well serve their residents, their citizens.

"For California, the 'aha' moment came in 2019, when PG&E cut the power to its customers. Upon investigation, the state realized that the private company had been cutting maintenance, while paying outsized salaries to their executives and outsized dividends to their shareholders. Everyone began to question for whose benefit the utilities were operating.

"New York rewrote their utility policies, and California bought out the bankrupt PG&E and turned it into a state-operated utility. But this revolution would not have been possible without the emergence of new technologies — specifically, reliable wind energy and solar photovoltaic energy, and especially affordable battery storage of electric power. The third technology that's made the energy revolution possible has been the development of new types of controls for these technologies, which allow for sharing of different energy sources and for balancing of energy sources so that peaking plants are no longer necessary. In other words, we need no longer be dependent on just-in-time systems. In our travels through the region after Hurricane Mitch, and the tremendous rains and floods it brought, we found that the communities that had adopted and embraced these new technologies came through the storms with little damage to their utility systems, and almost no disruption to service.

"These new technologies are not affordable for a single-family dwelling. They are only feasible when people agree to work together, and live closer together. We are talking here not just about our wonderful towns of Durham, Dover, Somersworth, Rochester, Rollinsford, Berwick, York, and others. Folks who looked to the future realized that rural living would not be really economical and feasible unless they developed community energy systems. These include Agrihoods, cohousing communities, even small rural subdivisions and cooperatively owned manufactured-home parks.

"However, as you all know, there are still many communities that have not adopted these new systems and are still dependent on overhead electrical lines. And we all know how that turned out during Hurricane Mitch: we saw some areas, some families without electricity for weeks. The people who have suffered are those who continue to live outside our denser communities, whether by choice of for economic reasons. But there are also municipalities that have not mandated energy upgrades, allowing some rural landlords to continue to operate unsafe and unstainable housing. We also have municipalities that have continued to let developers set the parameters for development, and not taken the reins to be proactive.

"The second major factor in creating sustainable and resilient communities for our region is housing. There are two aspects to housing. First, as has already been demonstrated, we must continue to transition existing housing by making energy-efficiency improvements, and by replacing all fossil-fuel heating systems. We have made great progress, but there is a long way to go. We must also work to make sure that all new housing in our communities is built to net-zero standards. That is, the housing projects as a whole must generate more energy than they use, and from renewable sources. And we have seen over the last decade or more that this is entirely feasible. Where municipalities have mandated it, the new housing we have built has all been net-zero and sustainable. But municipalities must set and enforce these higher standards.

"The second aspect of housing is building in the right places. Housing must be concentrated along corridors with accessible public transportation. Our own Corridor is a great example of how successful this can be. Almost 8,000 people live and work on The Corridor with access to grocery and drug stores, cafés, co-working spaces, and community services. The totally independent rural lifestyle is just not sustainable unless people are fantastically wealthy, or unless they are part of a collective settlement pattern. And it's long past time to decide that we have enough suburban housing. We understand that some people in New Hampshire and Maine will always want to live in a rural or suburban setting, and the subdivisions we have are not going away. But let's resolve that we have enough of this type of housing already. Let's resolve that all new housing will be on corridors with easy access to transportation. And rural residents must embrace collective solutions for housing, energy, and transportation.

"Transportation is the third leg of this sustainable-community stool. We have certainly made progress over the last twenty years, in that 90% of vehicles on the road today are electric vehicles. Twenty years ago, EV owners had trouble finding charging stations; today, people who drive traditional gas-powered vehicles may have trouble finding legacy gas stations.

"That is great progress and furthermore, our electric light rail — our DART Connector between Dover and Durham, and now North Berwick — has been a huge success. More than one third of the population of the county now lives within a ten minute walking distance to the Dart. And everyone benefits from the Freeway Flyers, the autonomous electric trams that run up and down I-93 and I-95 to Boston, and on all our major state routes to 101, and Rt. 16 between our towns, and Portsmouth and Manchester. People who use the new mass transit alternatives certainly benefit, but everyone benefits from the reduction of traffic, which was reaching the point where we would have had to widen all our roads. And we have seen the electrification of the Amtrak line to and from Boston, with increased service just ten years ago. Finally, we benefit from the commitment of our regional governments to the last mile LaMAs, without which the light rail and the Amtrack would not be the viable solution that they are today. We now have EVs for transportation, for delivery trucks, for buses, and for nearly all forms of transportation. Which brings us back around to housing and energy. We must continue our commitment to 100% renewable energy and transportation in our region in the next ten years."

At this point, Barney took over:

"Now, energy, housing, and transportation are not what you invited us here to talk about. You invited us here to talk about our recent hurricane and flood emergency. We are here to tell you that individuals and communities that have refused to adopt change saw devasting disruption and lives lost. This was not just about power systems. Housing and zoning were the most important factors.

"We know that some people want to continue their traditional lifestyles, on their own properties at the end of the road. But some of those people are dead now. Their homes were in the flood zone, and their heating, cooling and energy systems failed during the storms. After everyone dropped their landline phones, cell towers proved to be vulnerable; they had no way to call 911 — and even if they had, we would have had no way to rescue them in a timely manner. Many properties were inaccessible due to flooding, washouts, and downed trees and wires. It's time to face up to the fact that, due to our planet-wide lack of action for so long, climate change has produced stronger and wetter storms, storms that produce the kind of rainfall we saw with Mitch. In some places, we saw fifteen inches of rain or more in just two days.

"It was while we were driving out on back roads and came to older farmhouses and mobile homes on private properties that we found the real problems. Isolated and dependent on power lines, some people did not even have a generator or battery storage. But meanwhile, the working farms that have expanded into Agrihoods have added cottages, and have value-added businesses such as a farm store, cheesemaking, growing poinsettias, or selling Christmas wreaths — these people could afford to set up a micro-grid with renewable energy. When we stopped by after the storm, they had hot coffee, they were still working.

"When we stopped in some towns, even small towns, those that made use of Green New Deal grants and loans and used town land for affordable housing or a senior home, near their fire stations, schools, emergency services, town halls, and consolidated these services geographically then developed renewable energy sources and connected them all to a microgrid have avoided power outages. They had their emergency shelters up and running and all services going smoothly.

"On the other hand, towns that had ignored the advice, the grants, and the directives, and towns that refused to spend money on upgrades, refused to set up affordable housing, and chose to go it on their own terms — they were in bad shape. The power was down, even in some of the emergency services buildings. Their emergency vehicles still run on gas, their generators use gas or diesel. Yes, they did have a big fuel tank out back, but how long could they stay up and running before the gas runs out?

"Now, the new village nodes — like the ones that Alfred's has been building around their old strip malls locations — these are also a great success. They have been able to deploy plenty of rooftop solar arrays, lots of battery storage, and some of the latest innovative solid-to-liquid batteries. These solutions are just not affordable for one house or one farm, except for those who are wealthy enough to go i alone. So we have a situation of 'haves and have-nots.' The wealthier folks have their own systems, the poorer folks have been left behind.

"One of the major decisions made here in New Hampshire and New England was to finally declare that all new buildings are energy-efficient. Weatherization and energy efficiency were proven invaluable more than fifty years ago, but it took a renewed political will to actually mandate and enforce new building codes. It was an especially important step since at the same time, there was an extreme housing shortage; the region needed over 100,000 housing units. And in the course of building new housing, and other facilities, I am pleased to say that 90% of this construction has been within the guidelines of green building. This has drastically reduced energy use in the entire region. All it took was political will.

"By accepting the mandate to reform our planning and zoning, to finally put an end to the dominance of the private automobile when designing transportation systems, we have also not only curbed the use of fossil-fuel-powered vehicles, reduced miles driven, and reduced our regional production of greenhouse gases, we have also created more livable towns and cities. At the same time, we have respected the rural areas of New England — the towns and landscapes that New Englanders prize.

"We have the technology, we have the design expertise, we know what we love and respect; we need to get on with it."

REFLECTIONS

I started this book in early 2019 as a utopian book. I was seeing too many dystopias. I thought, the world needs a vision of a positive future. I had in mind the book Ecotopia, which I had read many years before. But then, searching for a plot, it started to morph into a disaster book, featuring a hurricane. I am a big follower of the weather channel. And King Tides. The idea came to me of what a major hurricane would do to New England if it arrived with a huge storm surge at the King Tides. Of course, most of the book was written while I was at home during the pandemic.

I started with the characters of Chip and Katrina, and Cody. I immediately had to think about how the progress and development of sustainable and renewable ideas would affect different generations. And of course, how quickly electric vehicles would arrive, and how quickly would the northeast replace fossil fuels? And of course, even as I was in the process of writing, the world was changing, renewables were advancing.

I am actually a historian, so even though this a novel, I did a lot of research; I wanted it to be realistic. (Yes, I have footnotes, but I left them out for readability. I am going to put them on the web page.) I have been very committed to energy efficient housing and to renewable energy, so those were areas of intensive research, in addition to rising seas, storm surge, and the history of hurricanes in

New England

Dover and Durham caught my interest because they are only six miles apart and connected by the Amtrak line which is now used by the Portland to Boston Downeaster. What would happen if it were a light rail line that really connected the two towns with every ten-minute service? And if there were autonomous electric vehicles and people did not have to get in their cars at all? I spent a long time looking at the geography of Dover Durham. I imagined a new corridor of buildings along the new light rail line. I imagined UNH building all of their new dorms and labs on the Corridor.

Then it occurred to me that UNH is doing a lot of research already, and will continue to do a lot of research, and it would logically be a center of innovation. I found out that UNH is already using nearly 100% renewable energy.

Almost all of the trends and technology are happening already, including microgrids, battery storage for energy, malls being repurposed to housing and village centers. I am not making anything up out of whole cloth, I am just putting it all together, trying to see beyond. In fact, in January 2021, Saudi Arabia announced a linear city. "NEOM, a futuristic $500-billion, clean-energy powered city of the future that consists of several 'city modules' arranged along one single 106-mile long road in the middle of the desert." Far larger and more elaborate than my six-mile-long corridor between Dover and Durham. Where my corridor centers around a modest six-mile DART connector, "the Saudis have an underground Hyperloop train that will cover the 100-mile journey from one end of the city the other in just 20 minutes." They also seem to have well paid publicists.

What has not happened, yet, is the transportation revolution. Ten years ago, people said that Uber and Lyft were the disruption, but Uber and Lyft have really only brought increased traffic and congestion. Sometime, experiments go wrong, the supposed solution is not the real solution. So, Uber and Lyft have pointed to a solution, but they are not the solution. They are a wrong turn.

While I was planning, California was burning, and PG&E was

preemptively cutting off power to hundreds of thousands of people. And finally, even PG&E was thinking about microgrids, so there was more in the news.

Then I got seriously into the weeds on the path and timing of the devastating 1938 hurricane; I decided that Hurricane Mitch would roughly follow the same path and timing, on a week in September or October of 2040, a week that featured a king tide, for maximum impact.

The longer I work on this book, the more I look objectively at what is around me. The triad of housing/energy/transportation is definitely the focus. We are so damned car dependent. And the way we have configured our built environment ensures that that continues. At the same time, we configure the space this way because we are so enamored of cars. And cars use energy. Specifically, gasoline. This has to come to an end. People just have a total lack of imagination when it comes to what the future will have to look like. It is just so wasteful to have a pickup truck to drive to Hannaford's a mile away.

As far as housing, it seems pretty clear that the free market is not going to provide enough housing. And it is not just a matter of clearing the obstacles of zoning in a few towns outside of Boston. The obstacle is cost and profit. There just is not enough profit in affordable housing, and Section 8 is a clumsy and inefficient provider of housing.

When I look around, I see cars, cars, cars. Overcrowded interstates on the brink of complete standstill, and parking lots and more parking lots. People are underestimating the dramatic change that is going to happen. And how fast. And the market forces are just not going to supply it.

And of course, names.

The names of the characters, the minor characters, the roads, streets, and names of the farms. Believably local, but not something that exists now.

I am really obsessed with making this book and its disaster plausible, as if it could really happen. That is why I am getting into a real week in 2040, with actual tide tables, although from the point of view of a disaster movie, it is probably not strictly necessary.

NOTES

The Hurricane of 1938
(before hurricanes were given names)

Jennifer Compton, "Experts warn: Hurricane like 1938's could happen again," WMUR News, Sept 8, 2013 https://www.wmur.com/article/experts-warn-hurricane-like-1938-s-could-happen-again/5184644

Emily Lord, "Remembering the Hurricane of 1938, and Forecasting in the Future: A harrowing tale from the worst hurricane in New England history," *Forest Journal*, Society for the Protection of New Hampshire Forests, September 30, 2018. https://forestsociety.org/forest-journal-column/remembering-hurricane-1938-and-forecasting-future

"The Great New England Hurricane of 1938: 82nd Anniversary - September 21, 1938," National Weather Service. https://www.weather.gov/okx/1938HurricaneHome

Patricia Grossi, "The 1938 Great New England Hurricane: Looking to the Past to Understand Today's Risk," Risk Management Services, 2008. https://forms2.rms.com/rs/729-DJX-565/images/tc_1938_great_new_england_hurricane.pdf

"Hercules Had It Easy Compared to the Great 1938 Hurricane Tree Cleanup," New England Historical Society, 2019 http://www.newenglandhistoricalsociety.com/hercules-had-it-easy-compared-to-the-great-1938-hurricane-tree-cleanup/

Barney's Brews

The carbon dioxide (CO2) reclamation system was developed by the Alaskan Brewing Company, Juneau, Alaska. https://alaskanbeer.com/beerpoweredbeer/

See also, Eric P. Fisher, *Mighty Storms of New England: The Hurricanes, Tornadoes, Blizzards, and Floods That Shaped the Region,* Rowman & Littlefield, *2021*

Mass Timber Sidewalk Toronto: https://www.sidewalktoronto.ca/plans/quayside

"What is Mass timber?" What Is Mass Timber? - Design + Construction | naturally:wood (naturallywood.com)

Autonomous Electric Vehicles

Tony Seba makes the case that batteries, electric vehicles, ride-sharing, autonomous vehicles and solar energy are on a path to converge in the 2020s — making it the most disruptive decade in history — and totally remaking energy and transportation infrastructure. "And by 2030, it will be done." "Transportation" RethinkX

https://www.rethinkx.com/transportation-executive-summary"

ISO- the language of the grid

ISO New England: 2019 Final PV Forecast, April 29, 2019 https://www.iso-ne.com/static-assets/documents/2019/04/final-2019-pv-forecast.pdf

Bangladesh Plan

Amy Yee, "In Bangladesh, More Shelter From the Storms," New

York Times, July 24, 2013.
https://opinionator.blogs.nytimes.com/2013/07/24/in-bangladesh-more-shelter-from-the-storms/

Like that famous billionaire on Martha's Vineyard

Olivia Hull, "One year later Schifter House Settles In," Vineyard Gazette, July 3, 2014
He built in a bad spot, then he badgered the Island government until they let him move his, get this, 8,000 square foot house back from the bluff
https://vineyardgazette.com/news/2014/07/03/one-year-later-schifter-house-settles

In the winter of 2018, a Nor'easter wiped out power for more than 2 million people on the East Coast.
"Monster nor'easter pummels East Coast; at least 7 dead." ABC News, March 3, 2018. https://abcnews.go.com/US/massive-bomb-cyclone-pounds-northeast-bringing-strong-winds/story?id=53459604
"List of Major power outages," Wikipedia. https://en.wikipedia.org/wiki/List_of_major_power_outages#cite_note-233

Emanuella Grinberg, Jon Ostrower, Madison Park and Christina Zdanowicz, "Atlanta's Hartsfield-Jackson airport restores power after crippling outage," CNN News, Dec. 18, 2017. https://www.cnn.com/2017/12/17/us/atlanta-airport-power-outage/index.html

PG&E Rolling Blackouts in California
Debra Kahn and Colby Bermel, "California has first rolling blackouts in 19 years — and everyone faces blame," Policito, August 18, 2020.

https://www.politico.com/states/california/story/2020/08/18/calif
ornia-has-first-rolling-blackouts-in-19-years-and-everyone-faces-
blame-1309757

UNH Microgrid

Staff, "Eversource, UNH, Durham plan community microgrid:
Goal to enhance resiliency, advance solar and battery storage clean
energy technologies, " Foster's Daily Democrat, May 23, 2019 .
https://www.fosters.com/news/20190523/eversource-unh-
durham-plan-community-microgrid

Malaya Careta "Landline phones, assuming they are not wireless,
generally work during a power outage," Off the Grid News.
https://www.offthegridnews.com/how-to-2/landlines-the-dinosaur-
phone-technology-that-could-save-you-in-a-crisis/

Rent seeking

I researched rent seeking in connection with political corruption in
Denver in the 1880s and 1890s. A tsunami of election corruption was
overwhelming the state. Powerful interests blamed it on a ring of
bunco men, or con men. However, I show that the powerful interests
themselves representing both the trolly system and electrical utilities
were seeking to control the state legislature and the Denver municipal
council in order to gain monopoly franchises. These franchises would
obligate every citizen to pay the utilities for services ie — rents.

Sebastián L. Mazzuca, "Rentiers" in Encyclopedia of Governance
ed. Mark Bevir (Newbury Park, CA, Sage Publication, 2007). In the
nineteenth century sense a rentier was a land or asset owning
capitalist whose income derived mainly from rents on land or, more
broadly, from assets rather than labor. Orthodox economist Gordon
Tullock first re-defined the concept of rent-seeking in 1967 and
coined the term "rent-seeking" in 1974. Rent-seeking is the
competition for politically protected transfers of wealth.
"Governments are more likely to create political prizes, and induce

rent-seeking, when such prizes involve (1) large benefits for a small well-organized interest group, and (2) small costs for a large number of consumers or taxpayers in the unorganized public. A further insight is that the very decision to establish the political prize — not just the competition for it — is a rent-seeking activity, thus including politicians as rent-seekers." While this is a modern definition, it applies to the creation of, and competition for, utility franchises in the late nineteenth century.

Jane G. Haigh, "Political power, patronage, and protection rackets: Con men and political corruption in Denver 1889-1894," University of Arizona, 2009. P. 261, see note 438.

https://repository.arizona.edu/bitstream/handle/10150/195958/az u_etd_10740_sip1_m.pdf?sequence=1&isAllowed=y

ACKNOWLEDGEMENTS

I want to thank my family for putting up with me while I spent so much time writing this book. I want to think the members of my book club for their first reading, and other friends too numerous to mention who also read and commented on various versions.

Thanks to my longtime friend Carol Venolia for patiently editing and Tom Holbrook for the final edit and production

ABOUT THE AUTHOR

Jane Haigh lived in Alaska for almost forty years and is an award winning author of books about the Alaska Goldrush including *Gold Rush Women*, *Children of the Gold Rush*, *King Con: the Story of Soapy Smith*, and *Searching for Fannie Quigley*. She has been interested in renewable energy, energy conservation, and urban planning since attending architecture school, and designed and built a superinsulated passive solar house with solar collectors in Fairbanks in 1986. If the world had adopted these strategies, starting thirty years ago we wouldn't be where we are now.

Tired of dystopian futures, I decided the world needed a new vision of a positive future and I thought a novel would be fun way to explore the possibilities. My experiences as a homesteading Alaskan-turned green architect drove the vision and now, as a resident of New Hampshire for almost seven years, I am enchanted with its rural towns and eighteen miles of fabled coastline. But I needed a plot. I remembered my grandmother talking about the Hurricane of 1938 in Providence, and I began to wonder if New England was ready for another one.

I got very excited about the Green New Deal, and its very vagueness led me to imagine all of the wonderful opportunities. Then when political realities tanked it, I got very discouraged.

If we can't imagine the future we want, we won't get there.

Made in the USA
Middletown, DE
26 April 2023

29220173R00175